Scottish
Ghost
Stories

This edition is first published in 2022 by Flame Tree 451

FLAME TREE 451
6 Melbray Mews,
Fulham, London SW3 3NS
United Kingdom
www.flametree451.com

Flame Tree 451 is an imprint of Flame Tree Publishing Ltd
www.flametreepublishing.com

A CIP record for this book is available from the British Library

Print ISBN 978-1-80417-237-7
ePub ISBN 978-1-80417-253-7

22 24 26 27 25 23
1 3 5 7 8 6 4 2

Printed and bound in Great Britain by Clays Ltd, Elcograf S.p.A.

Scottish Ghost Stories

With an introduction by
Helen McClory

451
FLAME TREE

Contents

A Taste for the Fantastic

From mystery to crime, the supernatural and fantasy to science fiction, the terrific range of paperbacks and ebooks from Flame Tree 451 offers a healthy diet of werewolves and mechanicals, vampires and villains, mad scientists, secret worlds, lost civilizations, escapist fantasies and dystopian visions. Discover a storehouse of tales gathered specifically for the reader of the fantastic.

Great works by H.G. Wells and Bram Stoker stand shoulder to shoulder with gripping reads by titans of the gothic novel (Charles Brockden Brown, Nathaniel Hawthorne), and individual novels by literary giants (Jane Austen, Charles Dickens, Emily Brontë) mingle with the intensity of H.P. Lovecraft and the psychological magic of Edgar Allan Poe.

Of course there are classic Conan Doyle adventures, Wilkie Collins mysteries and the pioneering fantasies of Mary Shelley, but there are so many other tales to tell: *The White Worm, Black Magic, The Murder Monster, The Awakening, Darkwater* and more.

Check our website for regular updates and new additions to our curated range of speculative fiction at *flametreepublishing.com*

Introduction

So you're here, at last. You've stepped into this book through the great creaking doors of the cover, and you find yourself in this antechamber. As you move forward into the stories, it might do to pause and orient yourself a moment – though perhaps you have already read the collection, and have come back to the introduction to see what it might offer you, now that spoilers are no risk. Either way, you can ask yourself, what was the country you came through, can you recall? It might have been the wild moorland of the Borders where the ling bells toss in the unfettered winds, or else a ride through a grand estate, tree-lined and shady, or perhaps the treachery of a rocky strand, lapped by those eerily calm waters that mark riptides, just awaiting some young soul full of hubris to drag them out to sea. In all lands are to be found corners of strangeness and abandonment, but it does seem that Scotland in particular has a good share of ruin and lonely shoreline, and that even the gentlest of haughs and glens can turn hostile at a moment's notice, or at the settling in of night.

The landscape and culture in which a writer is immersed inevitably find their way under the skin of the writing, forming some of the hard surface beneath. It would be difficult to write ghost stories in a country like Scotland without a hint at least of rock and water, old stone upon old stone and brambles peeking through glassless windows, the whisper of the old ways and fireside murmurings – and historical wickedness. And that is what you will find in the stories that follow. In Allan Cunningham's 'The Haunted Ships' as in 'The Sin Eater' by Fiona MacLeod (pen name of William Sharp) there's the cold spray and frightening isolation of the coast, though one is on the Solway firth and the other near and on Iona. The sea and its shoreline is a place between, meant for fated destinies and ritual, and those who ignore either or both are in for much trouble.

Other landscapes seem easier to traverse, but hide hidden pains, and bring them up when conditions are right. Margaret Oliphant's lengthy and entrancing tale 'The Open Door' is set in Brentwood, a refined country estate the protagonist is renting with his family after a troubled stay in India. They seek the calm greenness of the Scottish lowlands after living for many years in a place they were ill suited to – that ruined their health but evidently filled their coffers, only to find the fabric of reality draws back over the ruins on their doorstep. British colonization, to which many Scots applied themselves heartily and which was still in active process when these stories were written, creates layers to both this story and 'The Ghost of the Hindu Child' by Elliott O'Donnell. In the latter, a vengeful ghost claims more of our sympathy as modern readers – though O'Donnell lightly gestures towards a singular act of cruelty, the broader, numberless atrocities of empire we can infer. Ghost stories, by their universal shared element, that of the return of the dead to trouble the living, are good at allowing room for this: saying that there is more standing in the shadows in front and behind us than we allow ourselves to believe on our splendid sunlit days. That what we imagine immutable, almost without thinking – our health, our families, our names – might just be crumbling beneath us.

Sometimes a ghost or supernatural creature functions as a force of rebalancing, the idea of the long arc of divine justice – even if it is a justice with collateral damage. Many of these stories tell of people who are secure, moneyed, being almost undone by a personal or familial legacy of evil ways, as in 'The Old Nurse's Story' by George MacDonald, or simply, like in 'The Open Door', by a history the new family is not privy to, and only the servants and locals can ken. In others, desperation, as much as entitlement and greed, can open the door to the supernatural – like the long-suffering shepherding parents of Mary Burnet in James Hogg's eponymous tale, or Neil Ross, driven to eating sins for his coin.

The outsider, the loathed scapegoat, the singular figure who can bear a burden or message in their very bodies is seen too in 'Thrawn Janet' – there's much to be discussed regarding Robert Louis Stevenson's racist choice to depict a black man as the figure that bedevils Soulis alongside witchy Janet. There is detail to notice and interpret, as you read on your way: scary tales of morality and immorality, tempered here by the complexities and nuances of tellings, and, too, of unexpected levity. A devil of a very different sort lands Buchan's Duncan Stewart on 'A Journey of Little Profit', when he stumbles into a fine and welcoming house, out on those Borders moors, while driving his ill-gotten sheep too late from the nearest tavern. And the ghosts of Glamis Castle, in Elliott O'Donnell's second story, are more a cavalcade of bogies than a tide of dread.

Amidst this chatter of themes and imagery, the talking around the stories, there is something I've neglected – the moments within many which are genuinely frightening, in sometimes a quiet and other times oppressively sudden way. Darkness moves, and forms within it shift and come slowly, slowly, nearer. A body buckles in a way a living body should not. A blank stare denotes a battle inside with terrible, unknowable forces. Will it come back to you again as it has to me, the peculiarly Scottish strangeness of a ghost of a juniper tree, or the placing of bread upon the chest of a corpse? The sense of loss and the sense of inescapable return? What lies ahead of you, or behind you, is this: what you allow yourself to attend to might come creeping inside, to make of *you*, if even for a moment, a haunted landscape.

Helen McClory

FANTASTIC TALES

Scottish
Ghost
Stories

A Journey of Little Profit

John Buchan

The Devil he sang, the Devil he played
High and fast and free.
And this was ever the song he made
As it was told to me.
"Oh, I am the king of the air and the ground,
And lord of the seasons' roll,
And I will give you a hundred pound,
If you will give me your soul."
The Ballad of Grey Weather

The cattle market of Inverforth is, as all men know north of the Tweed, the greatest market of the kind in the land. For days in the late Autumn there is the lowing of oxen and the bleating of sheep among its high wooden pens, and in the rickety sale-rings the loud clamour of auctioneers and the talk of farmers. In the open yard where are the drovers and the butchers, a race always ungodly and law-despising, there is such a Babel of cries and curses as might wake the Seven Sleepers. From twenty different adjacent eating-houses comes the clatter of knives, where the country folk eat their dinner of beef and potatoes, with beer for sauce, and the collies grovel on the ground for stray morsels. Hither come a hundred types of men, from the Highland cateran, with scarce a word of English, and the gentleman-farmer of Inverness and Ross, to lowland graziers and city tradesmen, not to speak of blackguards of many nationalities and more professions.

It was there I first met Duncan Stewart of Clachamharstan, in the Moor of Rannoch, and there I heard this story. He was an old man when I knew him, grizzled and wind-beaten; a prosperous man, too, with many herds like Jacob and much pasture. He had come down from the North with kyloes, and as he waited on the Englishmen with whom he had trysted, he sat with me through the long day and beguiled the time with many stories. He had been a drover in his youth, and had travelled on foot the length and breadth of Scotland; and his memory went back hale and vigorous to times which are now all but historical. This tale I heard among many others as we sat on a pen amid the smell of beasts and the jabber of Gaelic: –

"When I was just turned of twenty-five I was a wild young lad as ever was heard of. I had taken to the droving for the love of a wild life, and a wild life I led. My father's heart would be broken long syne with my doings, and well for my mother that she was in her grave since I was six years old. I paid no heed to the ministrations of godly Mr. Macdougall of the Isles, who bade me turn from the error of my ways, but went on my own evil course, making siller, for I was a braw lad at the work and a trusted, and knowing the inside of every public from the pier of Cromarty to the streets of York. I was a wild drinker, caring in my cups for neither God nor man, a great hand with the cards, and fond of the lasses past all telling. It makes me shameful to this day to think on my evil life when I was twenty-five.

"Well, it chanced that in the back of the month of September I found myself in the city of Edinburgh with a flock of fifty sheep which I had bought as a venture from a drunken bonnet-laird and was thinking of selling somewhere wast the country. They were braw beasts, Leicester every one of them, well-fed and dirt-cheap at the price I gave. So it was with a light heart that I drove them out of the town by the Merchiston Road along by the face of the Pentlands. Two or three friends came with me, all like myself for folly, but maybe a little bit poorer. Indeed, I cared little for them, and they valued me only for the whisky which I gave them to drink my health in at the parting. They left me on the near side of Colinton, and I went on my way alone.

"Now, if you'll be remembering the road, you will mind that at the place called Kirk Newton, just afore the road begins to twine over the Big Muir and almost at the head of the Water o' Leith, there is a verra fine public. Indeed, it would be no lee to call it the pest public between Embro' and Glesca. The good wife, Lucky Craik by name, was an old friend of mine, for many a good gill of her brandy have I bought; so what would I be doing but just turning aside for refreshment? She met me at the door verra pleased-like to see me, and soon I had my legs aneath her table and a basin of toddy on the board before me. And whom did I find in the same place but my old comrade Toshie Maclean from the backside of Glen-Lyon. Toshie and I were acquaintances so old that it did not behove us to be parting quick. Forbye the day was chill without; and within the fire was grand and the crack of the best.

"Then Toshie and I got on quarrelling about the price of Lachlan Farawa's beasts that he sold at Falkirk; and, the drink having aye a bad effect on my temper, I was for giving him the lie and coming off in a great rage. It was about six o'clock in the evening and an hour to nightfall, so Mistress Craik comes in to try and keep me. 'Losh, Duncan,' says she, 'ye'll never try and win ower the muir the nicht. It's mae than ten mile to Carnwath, and there's nocht atween it and this but whaups and heathery braes.' But when I am roused I will be more obstinate than ten mules, so I would be going, though I knew not under Heaven where I was going till. I was too full of good liquor and good meat to be much worth at thinking, so I got my sheep on the road an' a big bottle in my pouch, and set off into the heather. I knew not what my purpose was, whether I thought to reach the shieling of Carnwath, or whether I expected some house of entertainment to spring up by the wayside. But my fool's mind was set on my purpose of getting some miles further in my journey ere the coming of darkness.

"For some time I jogged happily on, with my sheep running well before me and my dogs trotting at my heels. We left the trees behind and struck out on the broad grassy path which bands the moor like the waist-strap of a sword. It was most dreary and lonesome with never a house in view, only bogs and grey hillsides, and ill-looking waters. It was stony, too, and this more than aught else caused my Dutch courage to fail me, for I soon fell wearied, since much whisky is bad travelling fare, and began to curse my folly. Had my pride no kept me back, I would have returned to Lucky Craik's; but I was like the devil for stiffneckedness, and thought of nothing but to push on.

"I own that I was verra well tired and quite spiritless when I first saw the House. I had scarce been an hour on the way, and the light was not quite gone; but still it was geyan dark, and the place sprang somewhat suddenly on my sight. For, looking a little to the left, I saw over a little strip of grass a big square dwelling with many outhouses, half farm and half pleasure-house. This, I thought, is the verra place I have been seeking and made sure of finding, so whistling a gay tune, I drove my flock toward it.

"When I came to the gate of the court, I saw better of what sort was the building I had arrived at. There was a square yard with monstrous high walls, at the left of which was the main block of the house, and on the right what I took to be the byres and stables. The place looked ancient, and the stone in many places was crumbling away; but the style was of yesterday, and in no way differing from that of a hundred steadings in the land. There were some kind of arms above the gateway, and a bit of an iron stanchion; and when I had my sheep inside of it, I saw that the court was all grown up with green grass. And what seemed queer in that dusky half-light was the want of sound. There was no neichering of horses, nor routing of kye, nor clack of hens, but all as still as the top of Ben Cruachan. It was warm and pleasant, too, though the night was chill without.

"I had no sooner entered the place than a row of sheep-pens caught my eye, fixed against the wall in front. This I thought mighty convenient, so I made all haste to put my beasts into them; and finding that there was a good supply of hay within, I left them easy in my mind, and turned about to look for the door of the House.

"To my wonder, when I found it, it was open wide to the wall; so, being confident with much whisky, I never took thought to knock, but walked boldly in. There's some careless folk here, thinks I to myself, and I much misdoubt if the man knows aught about farming. He'll maybe just be a town's body taking the air on the muirs.

"The place I entered upon was a hall, not like a muirland farmhouse, but more fine than I had ever seen. It was laid with a verra fine carpet, all red and blue and gay colours, and in the corner in a fireplace a great fire crackled. There were chairs, too, and a walth of old rusty arms on the walls, and all manner of whigmaleeries that folk think ornamental. But nobody was there, so I made for the staircase which was at the further side, and went up it stoutly. I made scarce any noise, so thickly was it carpeted, and I will own it kind of terrified me to be walking in such a place. But when a man has drunk well he is troubled not overmuckle with modesty or fear, so I e'en stepped out and soon came to a landing where was a door.

"Now, thinks I, at last I have won to the habitable parts of the house; so laying my finger on the sneck I lifted it and entered, and there before me was the finest room in all the world; indeed I abate not a jot of the phrase, for I cannot think of anything finer. It was hung with braw pictures and lined with big bookcases of oak well-filled with books in fine bindings. The furnishing seemed carved by a skilled hand, and the cushions and curtains were soft velvet. But the best thing was the table, which was covered with a clean white cloth and set with all kind of good meat and drink. The dishes were of silver, and as bright as Loch Awe water in an April sun. Eh, but it was a braw, braw sight for a drover! And there at the far end, with a great bottle of wine before him, sat the master.

"He rose as I entered, and I saw him to be dressed in the best of town fashion, a man of maybe fifty years, but hale and well-looking, with a peaked beard and trimmed moustache and thick eyebrows. His eyes were slanted a thought, which is a thing I hate in any man, but his whole appearance was pleasing.

"'Mr. Stewart?' says he courteously, looking at me. 'Is it Mr. Duncan Stewart that I will be indebted to for the honour of this visit?'

"I stared at him blankly, for how did he ken my name?

"'That is my name,' I said, 'but who the devil tell't you about it?'

"'Oh, my name is Stewart myself,' says he, 'and all Stewarts should be well acquaint.'

"'True,' said I, 'though I don't mind your face before. But now I am here, I think you have a most gallant place, Mr. Stewart.'

"'Well enough. But how have you come to't? We've few visitors.'

"So I told him where I had come from, and where I was going, and why I was forewandered at this time of night among the muirs. He listened keenly, and when I had finished, he says verra friendly-like, 'Then you'll bide all night and take supper with me. It would never be doing to let one of the clan go away without breaking bread. Sit ye down, Mr. Duncan.'

"I sat down gladly enough, though I own that at first I did not half like the whole business. There was something unchristian about the place, and for certain it was not seemly that the man's name should be the same as my own, and that he should be so well posted in my doings. But he seemed so well-disposed that my misgivings soon vanished.

"So I seated myself at the table opposite my entertainer. There was a place laid ready for me, and beside the knife and fork a long horn-handled spoon. I had never seen a spoon so long and queer, and I asked the man what it meant. 'Oh,' says he, 'the broth in this house is very often hot, so we need a long spoon to sup it. It is a common enough thing, is it not?'

"I could answer nothing to this, though it did not seem to me sense, and I had an inkling of something I had heard about long spoons which I thought was not good; but my wits were not clear, as I have told you already. A serving man brought me a great bowl of soup and set it before me. I had hardly plunged spoon intil it, when Mr. Stewart cries out from the other end: 'Now, Mr. Duncan, I call you to witness that you sit down to supper of your own accord. I've an ill name in these parts for compelling folk to take meat with me when they dinna want it. But you'll bear me witness that you're willing.'

"'Yes, by God, I am that,' I said, for the savoury smell of the broth was rising to my nostrils. The other smiled at this as if well-pleased.

"I have tasted many soups, but I swear there never was one like that. It was as if all the good things in the world were mixed thegether – whisky and kale and shortbread and cockyleeky and honey and salmon. The taste of it was enough to make a body's heart loup with fair gratitude. The smell of it was like the spicy winds of Arabia, that you read about in the Bible, and when you had taken a spoonful you felt as happy as if you had sellt a hundred yowes at twice their reasonable worth. Oh, it was grand soup!

"'What Stewarts did you say you corned from?' I asked my entertainer.

"'Oh,' he says, 'I'm connected with them all, Athole Stewarts, Appin Stewarts, Rannoch Stewarts, and a'. I've a heap o' land thereaways.'

"'Whereabouts?' says I, wondering. 'Is't at the Blair o' Athole, or along by Tummel side, or wast the Loch o' Rannoch, or on the Muir, or in Benderloch?'

"'In all the places you name,' says he.

"'Got damn,' says I, 'then what for do you not bide there instead of in these stinking lawlands?'

"At this he laughed softly to himself. 'Why, for maybe the same reason as yoursel, Mr. Duncan. You know the proverb, "A' Stewarts are sib to the Deil."'

"I laughed loudly, 'Oh, you've been a wild one, too, have you? Then you 're not worse than mysel. I ken the inside of every public in the Cowgate and Cannongate, and there's no another drover on the road my match at fechting and drinking and dicing.' And I started on a long shameless catalogue of my misdeeds. Mr. Stewart meantime listened with a satisfied smirk on his face.

"'Yes, I've heard tell of you, Mr. Duncan,' he says. 'But here's something more, and you 'll doubtless be hungry.'

"And now there was set on the table a round of beef garnished with pot-herbs, all most delicately fine to the taste. From a great cupboard were brought many bottles of wine, and in a massive silver bowl at the table's head were put whisky and lemons and sugar. I do not know well what I drank, but whatever it might be it was the best ever brewed. It made you scarce feel the earth round about you, and you were so happy you could scarce keep from singing. I wad give much siller to this day for the receipt.

"Now, the wine made me talk, and I began to boast of my own great qualities, the things I had done and the things I was going to do. I was a drover just now, but it was not long that I would be being a drover. I had bought a flock of my own, and would sell it for a hundred pounds, no less; with that I would buy a bigger one till I had made money enough to stock a farm; and then I would leave the road and spend my days in peace, seeing to my land and living in good company. Was not my father, I cried, own cousin, thrice removed, to Maclean o' Duart, and my mother's uncle's wife a Rory of Balnacrory? And I am a scholar too, said I, for I was a matter of two years at Embro' College, and might have been roaring in the pulpit, if I hadna liked the drink and the lasses too well.

"'See,' said I, 'I will prove it to you;' and I rose from the table and went to one of the bookcases. There were all manner of books, Latin and Greek, poets and philosophers, but in the main, divinity. For there I saw Richard Baxter's 'Call to the Unconverted,' and Thomas Boston of Ettrick's 'Fourfold State,' not to speak of the *Sermons* of half a hundred auld ministers, and the 'Hind let Loose,' and many books of the covenanting folk.

"'Faith,' I says, 'you've a fine collection, Mr. What's-your-name,' for the wine had made me free in my talk. 'There is many a minister and professor in the Kirk, I'll warrant, who has a less godly library. I begin to suspect you of piety, sir.'

"'Does it not behove us,' he answered in an unctuous voice, 'to mind the words of Holy Writ that evil communications corrupt good manners, and have an eye to our company? These are all the company I have, except when some stranger such as you honours me with a visit.'

"I had meantime been opening a book of plays, I think by the famous William Shakespeare, and I here broke into a loud laugh. 'Ha, ha, Mr. Stewart,' I says, 'here's a sentence I've lighted on which is hard on you. Listen!' The Devil can quote Scripture to advantage.'

"The other laughed long. 'He who wrote that was a shrewd man,' he said,' but I'll warrant if you'll open another volume, you'll find some quip on yourself.'

"I did as I was bidden, and picked up a white-backed book, and opening it at random, read: 'There be many who spend their days in evil and wine-bibbing, in lusting and cheating, who think to mend while yet there is time; but the opportunity is to them for ever awanting, and they go down open-mouthed to the great fire.'

"'Psa,' I cried, 'some wretched preaching book, I will have none of them. Good wine will be better than bad theology.' So I sat down once more at the table.

"'You're a clever man, Mr. Duncan,' he says, 'and a well-read one. I commend your spirit in breaking away from the bands of the kirk and the college, though your father was so thrawn against you.'

"'Enough of that,' I said, 'though I don't know who told you.' I was angry to hear my father spoken of, as though the grieving him was a thing to be proud of.

"'Oh, as you please,' he says; 'I was just going to say that I commended your spirit in sticking the knife into the man in the Pleasaunce, the time you had to hide for a month about the backs o' Leith.'

"'How do you ken that?' I asked hotly. 'You've heard more about me than ought to be repeated, let me tell you.'

"'Don't be angry,' he said sweetly; 'I like you well for these things, and you mind the lassie in Athole that was so fond of you. You treated her well, did you not?'

"I made no answer, being too much surprised at his knowledge of things which I thought none knew but myself.

"'Oh, yes, Mr. Duncan. I could tell you what you were doing today, how you cheated Jock Gallowa out of six pounds, and sold a horse to the farmer of Hay path that was scarce fit to carry him home. And I know what you are meaning to do the morn at Glesca, and I wish you well of it.'

"'I think you must be the Devil,' I said blankly.

"'The same, at your service,' said he, still smiling.

"I looked at him in terror, and even as I looked I kenned by something in his eyes and the twitch of his lips that he was speaking the truth.

"'And what place is this, you...' I stammered.

"'Call me Mr. S.,' he says gently, 'and enjoy your stay while you are here and don't concern yourself about the lawing.'

"'The lawing!' I cried in astonishment,'and is this a house of public entertainment?'

"'To be sure, else how is a poor man to live?'

"'Name it,' said I, 'and I will pay and be gone.'

"'Well,' said he,' I make it a habit to give a man his choice. In your case it will be your wealth or your chances hereafter, in plain English your flock or your—'

"'My immortal soul,' I gasped.

"'Your soul,' said Mr. S., bowing, 'though I think you call it by too flattering an adjective.'

"'You damned thief,' I roared, 'you would entice a man into your accursed house and then strip him bare!'

"'Hold hard,' said he, 'don't let us spoil our good fellowship by incivilities. And, mind you, I took you to witness to begin with that you sat down of your own accord.'

"'So you did,' said I, and could say no more.

"'Come, come,' he says, 'don't take it so bad. You may keep all your gear and yet part from here in safety. You've but to sign your name, which is no hard task to a college-bred man, and go on living as you live just now to the end. And let me tell you, Mr. Duncan Stewart, that you should take it as a great obligement that I am willing to take your bit soul instead of fifty sheep. There's no many would value it so high.'

"'Maybe no, maybe no,' I said sadly, 'but it's all I have. D'ye no see that if I gave it up, there would be no chance left of mending? And I'm sure I do not want your company to all eternity.'

"'Faith, that's uncivil,' he says; 'I was just about to say that we had had a very pleasant evening.'

"I sat back in my chair very down-hearted; I must leave this place as poor as a kirk-mouse, and begin again with little but the clothes on my back. I was strongly tempted to sign the bit paper thing and have done with it all, but somehow I could not bring myself to do it. So at last I says to him: 'Well, I've made up my mind. I'll give you my sheep, sorry though I be to lose them, and I hope I may never come near this place again as long as I live.'

"'On the contrary,' he said, 'I hope often to have the pleasure of your company. And seeing that you've paid well for your lodging, I hope you'll make the best of them. Don't be sparing on the drink.'

"I looked hard at him for a second. 'You've an ill name, and an ill trade, but you're no a bad sort yoursel, and, do you ken, I like you.'

"'I'm much obliged to you for the character,' says he, 'and I'll take your hand on't.'

"So I filled up my glass and we set to, and such an evening I never mind of. We never got fou, but just in a fine good temper and very entertaining. The stories we telled and the jokes we cracked are still a kind of memory with me, though I could not come over one of them. And then, when I got sleepy, I was shown to the brawest bedroom, all hung with pictures and looking-glasses, and with bedclothes of the finest linen and a coverlet of silk. I bade Mr. S. good- night, and my head was scarce on the pillow ere I was sound asleep.

"When I awoke the sun was just newly risen, and the frost of a September morning was on my clothes. I was lying among green braes with nothing near me but crying whaups and heathery hills, and my two dogs running round about and howling as they were mad."

The Haunted Ships
Allan Cunningham

Along the sea of Solway, romantic on the Scottish side, with its woodlands, its bays, its cliffs, and headlands, – and interesting on the English side, with its many beautiful towns with their shadows on the water, rich pastures, safe harbors, and numerous ships, – there still linger many traditional stories of a maritime nature, most of them connected with superstitions singularly wild and unusual. To the curious these tales afford a rich fund of entertainment, from the many diversities of the same story; some dry and barren, and stripped of all the embellishments of poetry; others dressed out in all the riches of a superstitious belief and haunted imagination. In this they resemble the inland traditions of the peasants; but many of the oral treasures of the Galwegian or the Cumbrian coast have the stamp of the Dane and the Norseman upon them, and claim but a remote or faint affinity with the legitimate legends of Caledonia. Something like a rude prosaic outline of several of the most noted of the Northern ballads, the adventures and depredations of the old ocean kings, still lends life to the evening tale; and among others, the story of the Haunted Ships is still popular among the maritime peasantry.

One fine harvest evening I went on board the shallop of Richard Faulder, of Allanbay; and, committing ourselves to the waters, we allowed a gentle wind from the east to waft us at its pleasure toward the Scottish coast. We passed the sharp promontory of Siddick; and skirting the land within a stone-cast, glided along the shore till we came within sight of the ruined Abbey of Sweetheart. The green mountain of Criffell ascended beside us; and the bleat of the flocks from its summit, together with the winding of the evening horn of the reapers, came softened into something like music over land and sea. We pushed our shallop into a deep and wooded bay, and sat silently looking on the serene beauty of the place. The moon glimmered in her rising through the tall shafts of the pines of Caerlaverock; and the sky, with scarce a cloud, showered down on wood, and headland, and bay, the twinkling beams of a thousand stars, rendering every object visible. The tide, too, was coming with that swift and silent swell observable when the wind is gentle; the woody curves along the land were filling with the flood, till it touched the green branches of the drooping trees; while in the centre current the roll and the plunge of a thousand pellocks told to the experienced fisherman that salmon were abundant.

As we looked, we saw an old man emerging from a path that winded to the shore through a grove of doddered hazel; he carried a halve-net on his back, while behind him came a girl, bearing a small harpoon with which the fishers are remarkably dexterous in striking their prey. The senior seated himself on a large gray stone, which overlooked the bay, laid aside his bonnet, and submitted his bosom and neck to the refreshing sea-breeze; and taking his harpoon from his attendant, sat with the gravity and composure of a spirit of the flood, with his ministering nymph behind him. We pushed our shallop to the shore, and soon stood at their side.

"This is old Mark Macmoran, the mariner, with his grand-daughter Barbara," said Richard Faulder, in a whisper that had something of fear in it; "he knows every creek and cavern and quicksand in Solway, – has seen the Spectre Hound that haunts the Isle of Man; has heard him bark, and at every bark has seen a ship sink; and he has seen, too, the Haunted Ships in full sail; and, if all tales be true, he has sailed in them himself: he's an awful person."

Though I perceived in the communication of my friend something of the superstition of the sailor, I could not help thinking that common rumour had made a happy choice in singling out old Mark to maintain her intercourse with the invisible world. His hair, which seemed to have refused all intercourse with the comb, hung matted upon his shoulders; a kind of mantle, or rather blanket, pinned with a wooden skewer round his neck, fell mid-leg down, concealing all his nether garments as far as a pair of hose, darned with yarn of all conceivable colours, and a pair of shoes, patched and repaired till nothing of the original structure remained, and clasped on his feet with two massy silver buckles. If the dress of the old man was rude and sordid, that of his grand-daughter was gay, and even rich. She wore a bodice of fine wool, wrought round the bosom with alternate leaf and lily, and a kirtle of the same fabric, which, almost touching her white and delicate ankle, showed her snowy feet, so fairy-light and round that they scarcely seemed to touch the grass where she stood. Her hair, a natural ornament which woman seeks much to improve, was of bright glossy brown, and encumbered rather than adorned with a snood, set thick with marine productions, among which the small clear pearl found in the Solway was conspicuous. Nature had not trusted to a handsome shape, and a sylph-like air, for young Barbara's influence over the heart of man; but had bestowed a pair of large bright blue eyes, swimming in liquid light, so full of love and gentleness and joy, that all the sailors from Annanwater to far Saint Bees acknowledged their power, and sung songs about the bonnie lass of Mark Macmoran. She stood holding a small gaff-hook of polished steel in her hand, and seemed not dissatisfied with the glances I bestowed on her from time to time, and which I held more than requited by a single glance of those eyes which retained so many capricious hearts in subjection.

The tide, though rapidly augmenting, had not yet filled the bay at our feet. The moon now streamed fairly over the tops of Caerlaverock pines, and showed the expanse of ocean dimpling and swelling, on which sloops and shallops came dancing, and displaying at every turn their extent of white sail against the beam of the moon. I looked on old Mark the Mariner, who, seated motionless on his gray stone, kept his eye fixed on the increasing waters with a look of seriousness and sorrow in which I saw little of the calculating spirit of a mere fisherman. Though he looked on the coming tide, his eyes seemed to dwell particularly on the black and decayed hulls of two vessels, which, half immersed in the quicksand, still addressed to every heart a tale of shipwreck and desolation. The tide wheeled and foamed around them; and creeping inch by inch up the side, at last fairly threw its waters over the top, and a long and hollow eddy showed the resistance which the liquid element received.

The moment they were fairly buried in the water, the old man clasped his hands together, and said, "Blessed be the tide that will break over and bury ye forever! Sad to mariners, and sorrowful to maids and mothers, has the time been you have choked up this deep and bonnie bay. For evil were you sent, and for evil have you continued. Every season finds from you its song of sorrow and wail, its funeral processions, and its shrouded corses. Woe to the land where the wood grew that made ye! Cursed be the axe that hewed ye on the mountains, the hands that joined ye together, the bay that ye first swam in, and the wind that wafted ye here! Seven times have ye put my life in peril, three fair sons have you swept from my side, and two bonnie grand-bairns; and now, even now, your waters foam and flash for my destruction, did I venture my infirm limbs in quest of food in your deadly bay. I see by that ripple and that foam, and hear by the sound and singing of your surge, that ye yearn for another victim; but it shall not be me nor mine."

Even as the old mariner addressed himself to the wrecked ships, a young man appeared at the southern extremity of the bay, holding his halve-net in his hand, and hastening into the current. Mark rose, and shouted, and waved him back from a place which, to a person unacquainted with the dangers of the bay, real and superstitious, seemed sufficiently perilous: his grand-daughter, too, added her voice to his, and waved her white hands; but the more they strove, the faster advanced the peasant, till he stood to his middle in the water, while the tide increased every moment in depth and strength. "Andrew, Andrew," cried the young woman, in a voice quavering with emotion, "turn, turn, I tell you: O the ships, the Haunted Ships!" But the appearance of a fine run of fish had more influence with the peasant than the voice of bonnie Barbara, and forward he dashed, net in hand. In a moment he was borne off his feet, and mingled like foam with the water, and hurried toward the fatal eddies which whirled and roared round the sunken ships. But he was a powerful young man, and an expert swimmer: he seized on one of the projecting ribs of the nearest hulk, and clinging to it with the grasp of despair, uttered yell after yell, sustaining himself against the prodigious rush of the current.

From a shealing of turf and straw, within the pitch of a bar from the spot where we stood, came out an old woman bent with age, and leaning on a crutch. "I heard the voice of that lad Andrew Lammie; can the chield be drowning, that he skirls sae uncannilie?" said the old woman, seating herself on the ground, and looking earnestly at the water. "Ou aye," she continued, "he's doomed, he's doomed; heart and hand can never save him; boats, ropes, and man's strength, and wit, all vain! vain! he's doomed, he's doomed!"

By this time I had thrown myself into the shallop, followed reluctantly by Richard Faulder, over whose courage and kindness of heart superstition had great power; and with one push from the shore, and some exertion in sculling, we came within a quoitcast of the unfortunate fisherman. He stayed not to profit by our aid; for when he perceived us near, he uttered a piercing shriek of joy, and bounded toward us through the agitated element the full length of an oar. I saw him for a second on the surface of the water; but the eddying current sucked him down; and all I ever beheld of him again was his hand held above the flood, and clutching in agony at some imaginary aid. I sat gazing in horror on the vacant sea before us: but a breathing time before, a human being, full of youth and strength and hope, was there: his cries were still ringing in my ears and echoing in the woods; and now nothing was seen or heard save the turbulent expanse of water, and the sound of its chafing on the shores. We pushed back our shallop, and resumed our station on the cliff beside the old mariner and his descendant.

"Wherefore sought ye to peril your own lives fruitlessly," said Mark, "in attempting to save the doomed? Whoso touches those infernal ships, never survives to tell the tale. Woe to the man who is found nigh them at midnight when the tide has subsided, and they arise in their former beauty, with forecastle, and deck, and sail, and pennon, and shroud! Then is seen the streaming of lights along the water from their cabin windows, and then is heard the sound of mirth and the clamour of tongues, and the infernal whoop and halloo, and song, ringing far and wide. Woe to the man who comes nigh them!"

To all this my Allanbay companion listened with a breathless attention. I felt something touched with a superstition to which I partly believed I had seen one victim offered up; and I inquired of the old mariner, "How and when came these haunted ships there? To me they seem but the melancholy relics of some unhappy voyagers, and much more likely to warn people to shun destruction, than entice and delude them to it."

"And so," said the old man with a smile, which had more of sorrow in it than of mirth, "and so, young man, these black and shattered hulks seem to the eye of the multitude. But things are not what they seem: that water, a kind and convenient servant to the wants of man, which seems so smooth, and so dimpling, and so gentle, has swallowed up a human soul even now; and the place which it covers, so fair and so level, is a faithless quicksand, out of which none escape. Things are otherwise than they seem. Had you lived as long as I have had the sorrow to live; had you seen the storms, and braved the perils, and endured the distresses which have befallen me; had you sat gazing out on the dreary ocean at midnight on a haunted coast; had you seen comrade after comrade, brother after brother, and son after son, swept away by the merciless ocean from your very side; had you seen the shapes of friends, doomed to the wave and the quicksand, appearing to you in the dreams and visions of the night, – then would your mind have been prepared for crediting the maritime legends of mariners; and the two haunted Danish ships would have had their terrors for you, as they have for all who sojourn on this coast.

"Of the time and the cause of their destruction," continued the old man, "I know nothing certain: they have stood as you have seen them for uncounted time; and while all other ships wrecked on this unhappy coast have gone to pieces, and rotted, and sunk away in a few years, these two haunted hulks have neither sunk in the quicksand, nor has a single spar or board been displaced. Maritime legend says, that two ships of Denmark having had permission, for a time, to work deeds of darkness and dolor on the deep, were at last condemned to the whirlpool and the sunken rock, and were wrecked in this bonnie bay, as a sign to seamen to be gentle and devout. The night when they were lost was a harvest evening of uncommon mildness and beauty: the sun had newly set; the moon came brighter and brighter out; and the reapers, laying their sickles at the root of the standing corn, stood on rock and bank, looking at the increasing magnitude of the waters, for sea and land were visible from Saint Bees to Barnhourie. The sails of two vessels were soon seen bent for the Scottish coast; and with a speed outrunning the swiftest ship, they approached the dangerous quicksands and headland of Borranpoint. On the deck of the foremost ship not a living soul was seen, or shape, unless something in darkness and form resembling a human shadow could be called a shape, which flitted from extremity to extremity of the ship, with the appearance of trimming the sails, and directing the vessel's course. But the decks of its companion were crowded with human shapes: the captain, and mate, and sailor, and cabin-boy, all seemed there; and from them the sound of mirth and minstrelsy echoed over land and water. The coast which they skirted along was one of extreme danger; and the reapers shouted to warn them to beware of sandbank and rock; but of this friendly counsel no notice was taken, except that a large and famished dog, which sat on the prow, answered every shout with a long, loud, and melancholy howl. The deep sandbank of Carsethorn was expected to arrest the career of these desperate navigators; but they passed, with the celerity of waterfowl, over an obstruction which had wrecked many pretty ships.

"Old men shook their heads and departed, saying, 'We have seen the fiend sailing in a bottomless ship; let us go home and pray': but one young and wilful man said, 'Fiend! I'll warrant it's nae fiend, but douce Janet Withershins, the witch, holding a carouse with some of her Cumberland cummers, and mickle red wine will be spilt atween them. Dod I would gladly have a toothfu'! I'll warrant it's nane o' your cauld, sour slae-water, like a bottle of Bailie Skrinkie's port, but right drap-o'-my-heart's-blood stuff, that would waken a body out of their last linen. I wonder where the cummers will anchor their craft?' – 'And I'll vow,' said another rustic, 'the wine they quaff is none of your visionary drink, such as a drouthie body has dished out to his lips in a dream; nor is it shadowy and unsubstantial, like the vessels they sail in, which are made out of a cockleshell or a cast-off slipper, or the paring of a seaman's right thumb-nail. I once got a hansel out of a witch's quaigh myself, – auld Marion Mathers, of Dustiefoot, whom they tried to bury in the old kirkyard of Dunscore, but the cummer raise as fast as they laid her down, and naewhere else would she lie but in the bonnie green kirkyard of Kier, among douce and sponsible fowk. So I'll vow that the wine of a witch's cup is as fell liquor as ever did a kindly turn to a poor man's heart; and be they fiends, or be they witches, if they have red wine asteer, I'll risk a drouket sark for ae glorious tout on't.' – 'Silence, ye sinners,' said the minister's son of a neighbouring parish, who united in his own person his father's lack of devotion with his mother's love of liquor. 'Whisht! – speak as if ye had the fear of something holy before ye. Let the vessels run their own way to destruction: who can stay the eastern wind, and the current of the Solway sea? I can find ye Scripture warrant for that: so let them try their strength on Blawhooly rocks, and their might on the broad quicksand. There's a surf running there would knock the ribs together of a galley built by the imps of the pit, and commanded by the Prince of Darkness. Bonnilie and bravely they sail away there; but before the blast blows by they'll be wrecked: and red wine and strong brandy will be as rife as dyke-water, and we'll drink the health of bonnie Bell Blackness out of her left-foot slipper.'

"The speech of the young profligate was applauded by several of his companions, and away they flew to the bay of Blawhooly, from whence they never returned. The two vessels were observed all at once to stop in the bosom of the bay on the spot where their hulls now appear: the mirth and the minstrelsy waxed louder than ever; and the forms of maidens, with instruments of music, and wine-cups in their hands, thronged the decks. A boat was lowered; and the same shadowy pilot who conducted the ships made it start toward the shore with the rapidity of lightning, and its head knocked against the bank where the four young men stood, who longed for the unblest drink. They leaped in with a laugh, and with a laugh were they welcomed on deck; wine-cups were given to each, and as they raised them to their lips the vessels melted away beneath their feet; and one loud shriek, mingled with laughter still louder, was heard over land and water for many miles. Nothing more was heard or seen till the morning, when the crowd who came to the beach saw with fear and wonder the two Haunted Ships, such as they now seem, masts and tackle gone; nor mark, nor sign, by which their name, country, or destination could be known, was left remaining. Such is the tradition of the mariners; and its truth has been attested by many families whose sons and whose fathers have been drowned in the haunted bay of Blawhooly."

"And trow ye," said the old woman, who, attracted from her hut by the drowning cries of the young fisherman, had remained an auditor of the mariner's legend, – "and trow ye, Mark Macmoran, that the tale of the Haunted Ships is done? I can say no to that. Mickle have mine ears heard; but more mine eyes have witnessed since I came to dwell in this humble home by the side of the deep sea. I mind the night weel: it was on Hallowmass eve: the nuts were cracked, and the apples were eaten, and spell and charm were tried at my fireside; till, wearied with diving into the dark waves of futurity, the lads and lasses fairly took to the more visible blessings of kind words, tender clasps, and gentle courtship. Soft words in a maiden's ear, and a kindly kiss o' her lip, were old-world matters to me, Mark Macmoran; though I mean not to say that I have been free of the folly of daunering and daffin with a youth in my day, and keeping tryste with him in dark and lonely places. However, as I say, these times of enjoyment were passed and gone with me; the mair's the pity that pleasure should fly sae fast away, – and as I could nae make sport I thought I should not mar any; so out I sauntered into the fresh cold air, and sat down behind that old oak, and looked abroad on the wide sea. I had my ain sad thoughts, ye may think, at the time: it was in that very bay my blythe goodman perished, with seven more in his company, and on that very bank where ye see the waves leaping and foaming, I saw seven stately corses streeked, but the dearest was the eighth. It was a woful sight to me, a widow, with four bonnie boys, with nought to support them but these twa hands, and God's blessing, and a cow's grass. I have never liked to live out of sight of this bay since that time; and mony's the moonlight night I sit looking on these watery mountains, and these waste shores; it does my heart good, whatever it may do to my head. So ye see it was Hallowmass night; and looking on sea and land sat I; and my heart wandering to other thoughts soon made me forget my youthful company at hame. It might be near the howe hour of the night; the tide was making, and its singing brought strange old-world stories with it; and I thought on the dangers that sailors endure, the fates they meet with, and the fearful forms they see. My own blythe goodman had seen sights that made him grave enough at times, though he aye tried to laugh them away.

"Aweel, atween that very rock aneath us and the coming tide, I saw, or thought I saw, for the tale is so dream-like, that the whole might pass for a vision of the night, I saw the form of a man: his plaid was gray; his face was gray; and his hair, which hung low down till it nearly came to the middle of his back, was as white as the white sea-foam. He began to howk and dig under the bank; an' God be near me, thought I, this maun be the unblessed spirit of Auld Adam Gowdgowpin, the miser, who is doomed to dig for shipwrecked treasure, and count how many millions are hidden forever from man's enjoyment. The Form found something which in shape and hue seemed a left-foot slipper of brass; so down to the tide he marched, and placing it on the water, whirled it thrice round; and the infernal slipper dilated at every turn, till it became a bonnie barge with its sails bent, and on board leaped the form, and scudded swiftly away. He came to one of the Haunted Ships; and striking it with his oar, a fair ship, with mast, and canvas, and mariners, started up: he touched the other Haunted Ship, and produced the like transformation; and away the three spectre ships bounded, leaving a track of fire behind them on the billows which was long unextinguished. Now was nae that a bonnie and a fearful sight to see beneath the light of the Hallowmass moon? But the tale is far frae finished; for mariners say that once a year, on a certain night, if ye stand on the Borranpoint, ye will see the infernal shallops coming snoring through the Solway; ye will hear the same laugh, and song, and mirth, and minstrelsy, which our ancestors heard; see them bound over the sandbanks and sunken rocks like sea-gulls, cast their anchor in Blawhooly Bay, while the shadowy figure lowers down the boat, and augments their numbers with the four unhappy mortals, to whose memory a stone stands in the kirkyard, with a sinking ship and a shoreless sea cut upon it. Then the spectre ships vanish, and the drowning shriek of mortals and the rejoicing laugh of fiends are heard, and the old hulls are left as a memorial that the old spiritual kingdom has not departed from the earth. But I maun away, and trim my little cottage fire, and make it burn and blaze up bonnie, to warm the crickets, and my cold and crazy bones, that maun soon be laid aneath the green sod in the eerie kirkyard." And away the old dame tottered to her cottage, secured the door on the inside, and soon the hearth-flame was seen to glimmer and gleam through the key-hole and window.

"I'll tell ye what," said the old mariner, in a subdued tone, and with a shrewd and suspicious glance of his eye after the old sibyl, "it's a word that may not very well be uttered, but there are many mistakes made in evening stories if old Moll Moray there, where she lives, knows not mickle more than she is willing to tell of the Haunted Ships and their unhallowed mariners. She lives cannilie and quietly; no one knows how she is fed or supported; but her dress is aye whole, her cottage ever smokes, and her table lacks neither of wine, white and red, nor of fowl and fish, and white bread and brown. It was a dear scoff to Jock Matheson, when he called old Moll the uncannie carline of Blawhooly: his boat ran round and round in the centre of the Solway, – everybody said it was enchanted, – and down it went head foremost: and had nae Jock been a swimmer equal to a sheldrake, he would have fed the fish; but I'll warrant it sobered the lad's speech; and he never reckoned himself safe till he made auld Moll the present of a new kirtle and a stone of cheese."

"O father," said his grand-daughter Barbara, "ye surely wrong poor old Mary Moray; what use could it be to an old woman like her, who has no wrongs to redress, no malice to work out against mankind, and nothing to seek of enjoyment save a cannie hour and a quiet grave, – what use could the fellowship of fiends, and the communion of evil spirits, be to her? I know Jenny Primrose puts rowan-tree above the door-head when she sees old Mary coming; I know the good wife of Kittlenaket wears rowan-berry leaves in the headband of her blue kirtle, and all for the sake of averting the unsonsie glance of Mary's right ee; and I know that the auld laird of Burntroutwater drives his seven cows to their pasture with a wand of witch-tree, to keep Mary from milking them. But what has all that to do with haunted shallops, visionary mariners, and bottomless boats? I have heard myself as pleasant a tale about the Haunted Ships and their unworldly crews, as any one would wish to hear in a winter evening. It was told me by young Benjie Macharg, one summer night, sitting on Arbiglandbank: the lad intended a sort of love meeting; but all that he could talk of was about smearing sheep and shearing sheep, and of the wife which the Norway elves of the Haunted Ships made for his uncle Sandie Macharg. And I shall tell ye the tale as the honest lad told it to me.

"Alexander Macharg, besides being the laird of three acres of peatmoss, two kale gardens, and the owner of seven good milch cows, a pair of horses, and six pet sheep, was the husband of one of the handsomest women in seven parishes. Many a lad sighed the day he was brided; and a Nithsdale laird and two Annandale moorland farmers drank themselves to their last linen, as well as their last shilling, through sorrow for her loss. But married was the dame; and home she was carried, to bear rule over her home and her husband, as an honest woman should. Now ye maun ken that though the flesh and blood lovers of Alexander's bonnie wife all ceased to love and to sue her after she became another's, there were certain admirers who did not consider their claim at all abated, or their hopes lessened, by the kirk's famous obstacle of matrimony. Ye have heard how the devout minister of Tinwald had a fair son carried away, and bedded against his liking to an unchristened bride, whom the elves and the fairies provided; ye have heard how the bonnie bride of the drunken laird of Soukitup was stolen by the fairies out at the back-window of the bridal chamber, the time the bridegroom was groping his way to the chamber-door; and ye have heard – But why need I multiply cases? such things in the ancient days were as common as candle-light. So ye'll no hinder certain water-elves and sea-fairies, who sometimes keep festival and summer mirth in these old haunted hulks, from falling in love with the weel-faured wife of Laird Macharg; and to their plots and contrivances they went how they might accomplish to sunder man and wife; and sundering such a man and such a wife was like sundering the green leaf from the summer, or the fragrance from the flower.

"So it fell on a time that Laird Macharg took his halve-net on his back, and his steel spear in his hand, and down to Blawhooly Bay gaed he, and into the water he went right between the two haunted hulks, and placing his net awaited the coming of the tide. The night, ye maun ken, was mirk, and the wind lowne, and the singing of the increasing waters among the shells and the pebbles was heard for sundry miles. All at once lights began to glance and twinkle on board the two Haunted Ships from every hole and seam, and presently the sound as of a hatchet employed in squaring timber echoed far and wide. But if the toil of these unearthly workmen amazed the Laird, how much more was his amazement increased when a sharp shrill voice called out, 'Ho! brother, what are you doing now?' A voice still shriller responded from the other haunted ship, 'I'm making a wife to Sandie Macharg!' and a loud quavering laugh running from ship to ship, and from bank to bank, told the joy they expected from their labour.

"Now the Laird, besides being a devout and a God-fearing man, was shrewd and bold; and in plot, and contrivance, and skill in conducting his designs, was fairly an overmatch for any dozen land-elves; but the water-elves are far more subtle; besides, their haunts and their dwellings being in the great deep, pursuit and detection is hopeless if they succeed in carrying their prey to the waves. But ye shall hear. Home flew the Laird, collected his family around the hearth, spoke of the signs and the sins of the times, and talked of mortification and prayer for averting calamity; and finally, taking his father's Bible, brass clasps, black print, and covered with calf-skin, from the shelf, he proceeded without let or stint to perform domestic worship. I should have told ye that he bolted and locked the door, shut up all inlet to the house, threw salt into the fire, and proceeded in every way like a man skilful in guarding against the plots of fairies and fiends. His wife looked on all this with wonder; but she saw something in her husband's looks that hindered her from intruding either question or advice, and a wise woman was she.

"Near the mid-hour of the night the rush of a horse's feet was heard, and the sound of a rider leaping from its back, and a heavy knock came to the door, accompanied by a voice saying, 'The cummer drink's hot, and the knave bairn is expected at Laird Laurie's to-night; sae mount, goodwife, and come.'

"'Preserve me!' said the wife of Sandie Macharg; 'that's news indeed! who could have thought it? the Laird has been heirless for seventeen years! Now, Sandie, my man, fetch me my skirt and hood.'

"But he laid his arm round his wife's neck, and said, 'If all the lairds in Galloway go heirless, over this door threshold shall you not stir to-night; and I have said, and I have sworn it: seek not to know why or wherefore; but, Lord, send us thy blessed mornlight.' The wife looked for a moment in her husband's eyes, and desisted from further entreaty.

"'But let us send a civil message to the gossips, Sandie; and hadnae ye better say I am sair laid with a sudden sickness? though it's sinful-like to send the poor messenger a mile agate with a lie in his mouth without a glass of brandy.'

"'To such a messenger, and to those who sent him, no apology is needed,' said the austere Laird, 'so let him depart.' And the clatter of a horse's hoofs was heard, and the muttered imprecations of its rider on the churlish treatment he had experienced.

"'Now, Sandie, my lad,' said his wife, laying an arm particularly white and round about his neck as she spoke, 'are you not a queer man and a stern? I have been your wedded wife now these three years; and, beside my dower, have brought you three as bonnie bairns as ever smiled aneath a summer sun. O man, you a douce man, and fitter to be an elder than even Willie Greer himself, I have the minister's ain word for't, to put on these hard-hearted looks, and gang waving your arms that way, as if ye said, "I winna take the counsel of sic a hempie as you"; I'm your ain leal wife, and will and maun have an explanation.'

"To all this Sandie Macharg replied, 'It is written, "Wives, obey your husbands"; but we have been stayed in our devotion, so let us pray.' And down he knelt: his wife knelt also, for she was as devout as bonnie; and beside them knelt their household, and all lights were extinguished.

"'Now this beats a',' muttered his wife to herself; 'however, I shall be obedient for a time; but if I dinna ken what all this is for before the morn by sunket-time, my tongue is nae langer a tongue, nor my hands worth wearing.'

"The voice of her husband in prayer interrupted this mental soliloquy; and ardently did he beseech to be preserved from the wiles of the fiends, and the snares of Satan; 'from witches, ghosts, goblins, elves, fairies, spunkies, and water-kelpies; from the spectre shallop of Solway; from spirits visible and invisible; from the Haunted Ships and their unearthly tenants; from maritime spirits that plotted against godly men, and fell in love with their wives – '

"'Nay, but His presence be near us!' said his wife in a low tone of dismay. 'God guide my gudeman's wits: I never heard such a prayer from human lips before. But, Sandie, my man, Lord's sake, rise: what fearful light is this? – barn and byre and stable maun be in a blaze; and Hawkie and Hurley, – Doddie, and Cherrie, and Damson-plum, will be smoored with reek and scorched with flame.'

"And a flood of light, but not so gross as a common fire, which ascended to heaven and filled all the court before the house, amply justified the good wife's suspicions. But to the terrors of fire, Sandie was as immovable as he was to the imaginary groans of the barren wife of Laird Laurie; and he held his wife, and threatened the weight of his right hand – and it was a heavy one – to all who ventured abroad, or even unbolted the door. The neighing and prancing of horses, and the bellowing of cows, augmented the horrors of the night; and to any one who only heard the din, it seemed that the whole onstead was in a blaze, and horses and cattle perishing in the flame. All wiles, common or extraordinary, were put in practice to entice or force the honest farmer and his wife to open the door; and when the like success attended every new stratagem, silence for a little while ensued, and a long, loud, and shrilling laugh wound up the dramatic efforts of the night. In the morning, when Laird Macharg went to the door, he found standing against one of the pilasters a piece of black ship oak, rudely fashioned into something like human form, and which skilful people declared would have been clothed with seeming flesh and blood, and palmed upon him by elfin adroitness for his wife, had he admitted his visitants. A synod of wise men and women sat upon the woman of timber, and she was finally ordered to be devoured by fire, and that in the open air. A fire was soon made, and into it the elfin sculpture was tossed from the prongs of two pairs of pitchforks. The blaze that arose was awful to behold; and hissings, and burstings, and loud cracklings, and strange noises, were heard in the midst of the flame; and when the whole sank into ashes, a drinking-cup of some precious metal was found; and this cup, fashioned no doubt by elfin skill, but rendered harmless by the purification with fire, the sons and daughters of Sandie Macharg and his wife drink out of to this very day. Bless all bold men, say I, and obedient wives!"

Mary Burnet

James Hogg

The following incidents are related as having occurred at a shepherd's house, not a hundred miles from St. Mary's Loch; but, as the descendants of one of the families still reside in the vicinity, I deem it requisite to use names which cannot be recognised, save by those who have heard the story.

John Allanson, the farmer's son of Inverlawn, was a handsome, roving, and incautious young man, enthusiastic, amorous, and fond of adventure, and one who could hardly be said to fear the face of either man, woman, or spirit. Among other love adventures, he fell a-courting Mary Burnet, of Kirkstyle, a most beautiful and innocent maiden, and one who had been bred up in rural simplicity. She loved him, but yet she was afraid of him; and though she had no objection to meeting with him among others, yet she carefully avoided meeting him alone, though often and earnestly urged to it. One day, the young man, finding an opportunity, at Our Lady's Chapel, after mass, urged his suit for a private meeting so ardently, and with so many vows of love and sacred esteem, that Mary was so far won as to promise, that perhaps she would come and meet him.

The trysting place was a little green sequestered spot, on the very verge of the lake, well known to many an angler, and to none better than the writer of this old tale; and the hour appointed, the time when the King's Elwand (now foolishly termed the Belt of Orion) set his first golden knob above the hill. Allanson came too early; and he watched the sky with such eagerness and devotion, that he thought every little star that arose in the south-east the top knob of the King's Elwand. At last the Elwand did arise in good earnest, and then the youth, with a heart palpitating with agitation, had nothing for it but to watch the heathery brow by which bonny Mary Burnet was to descend. No Mary Burnet made her appearance, even although the King's Elwand had now measured its own equivocal length five or six times up the lift.

Young Allanson now felt all the most poignant miseries of disappointment; and, as the story goes, uttered in his heart an unhallowed wish – he wished that some witch or fairy would influence his Mary to come to him in spite of her maidenly scruples. This wish was thrice repeated with all the energy of disappointed love. It was thrice repeated, and no more, when, behold, Mary appeared on the brae, with wild and eccentric motions, speeding to the appointed place. Allanson's excitement seems to have been more than he was able to bear, as he instantly became delirious with joy, and always professed that he could remember nothing of their first meeting, save that Mary remained silent, and spoke not a word, either good or bad. In a short time she fell a-sobbing and weeping, refusing to be comforted, and then, uttering a piercing shriek, sprung up, and ran from him with amazing speed.

At this part of the loch, which, as I said, is well known to many, the shore is overhung by a precipitous cliff, of no great height, but still inaccessible, either from above or below. Save in a great drought, the water comes to within a yard of the bottom of this cliff, and the intermediate space is filled with rough unshapely pieces of rock fallen from above. Along this narrow and rude space, hardly passable by the angler at noon, did Mary bound with the swiftness of a kid, although surrounded with darkness. Her lover, pursuing with all his energy, called out, "Mary! Mary! my dear Mary, stop and speak with me. I'll conduct you home, or anywhere you please, but do not run from me. Stop, my dearest Mary – stop!"

Mary would not stop; but ran on, till, coming to a little cliff that jutted into the lake, round which there was no passage, and, perceiving that her lover would there overtake her, she uttered another shriek, and plunged into the lake. The loud sound of her fall into the still water rung in the young man's ears like the knell of death and if before he was crazed with love, he was now as much so with despair. He saw her floating lightly away from the shore towards the deepest part of the loch but, in a short time, she began to sink, and gradually disappeared, without uttering a throb or a cry. A good while previous to this, Allanson had flung off his bonnet, shoes, and coat, and plunged in. He swam to the place where Mary disappeared but there was neither boil nor gurgle on the water, nor even a bell of departing breath, to mark the place where his beloved had sunk. Being strangely impressed, at that trying moment, with a determination to live or die with her, he tried to dive, in hopes either to bring her up or to die in her arms; and he thought of their being so found on the shore of the lake, with a melancholy satisfaction; but by no effort of his could he reach the bottom, nor knew he what distance he was still from it. With an exhausted frame, and a despairing heart, he was obliged again to seek the shore, and, dripping wet as he was, and half-naked, he ran to her father's house with the woeful tidings. Everything there was quiet. The old shepherd's family, of whom Mary was the youngest, and sole daughter, were all sunk in silent repose; and oh, how the distracted lover wept at the thoughts of wakening them to hear the doleful tidings! But waken them he must; so, going to the little window close by the goodman's bed, he called, in a melancholy tone, "Andrew! Andrew Burnet, are you waking?"

"Troth, man, I think I be; or, at least, I'm half-and-half. What hast thou to say to auld Andrew Burnet at this time o' night?"

"Are you waking, I say?"

"Gudewife, am I waking? Because if I be, tell that stravaiger sae. He'll maybe tak your word for it, for mine he winna tak."

"O Andrew, none of your humour to-night; I bring you tidings the most woeful, the most dismal, the most heart-rending, that ever were brought to an honest man's door."

"To his window, you mean," cried Andrew, bolting out of bed, and proceeding to the door. "Gude sauff us, man, come in, whaever you be, and tell us your tidings face to face; and then we'll can better judge of the truth of them. If they be in concord Wi' your voice, they are melancholy indeed. Have the reavers come, and are our kye driven?"

"Oh, alas! waur than that – a thousand times waur than that! Your daughter – your dear beloved and only daughter, Mary—"

"What of Mary?" cried the good-man. "What of Mary?" cried her mother, shuddering and groaning with terror; and at the same time she kindled a light.

The sight of their neighbour, half-naked, and dripping with wet, and madness and despair in his looks, sent a chillness to their hearts, that held them in silence, and they were unable to utter a word, till he went on thus "Mary is gone; your darling and mine is lost, and sleeps this night in a watery grave – and I have been her destroyer!"

"Thou art mad, John Allanson," said the old man, vehemently, "raving mad; at least I hope so. Wicked as thou art, thou hadst not the heart to kill my dear child. O yes, you are mad – God be thankful, you are mad. I see it in your looks and demeanour. Heaven be praised, you are mad You are mad; but you'll get better again. But what do I say?" continued he, as recollecting himself – "We can soon convince our own senses. Wife, lead the way to our daughter's bed."

With a heart throbbing with terror and dismay, old Jean Linton led the way to Mary's chamber, followed by the two men, who were eagerly gazing, one over each of her shoulders. Mary's little apartment was in the farther end of the long narrow cottage; and as soon as they entered it, they perceived a form lying on the bed, with the bedclothes drawn over its head; and on the lid of Mary's little chest, that stood at the bedside, her clothes were lying neatly folded, as they wont to be. Hope seemed to dawn on the faces of the two old people when they beheld this, but the lover's heart sunk still deeper in despair. The father called her name, but the form on the bed returned no answer; however, they all heard distinctly sobs, as of one weeping. The old man then ventured to pull down the clothes from her face; and, strange to say, there indeed lay Mary Burnet, drowned in tears, yet apparently nowise surprised at the ghastly appearance of the three naked figures. Allanson gasped for breath, for he remained still incredulous. He touched her clothes – he lifted her robes one by one – and all of them were dry, neat, and clean, and had no appearance of having sunk in the lake.

There can be no doubt that Allanson was confounded by the strange event that had befallen him, and felt like one struggling with a frightful vision, or some energy beyond the power of man to comprehend. Nevertheless the assurance that Mary was there in life, weeping although she was, put him once more beside himself with joy; and he kneeled at her bedside, beseeching permission but to kiss her hand. She, however, repulsed him with disdain, saying with great emphasis "You are a bad man, John Allanson, and I entreat you to go out of my sight. The sufferings that I have undergone this night have been beyond the power of flesh and blood to endure; and by some cursed agency of yours have these sufferings been brought about. I therefore pray you, in His name, whose law you have transgressed, to depart out of my sight."

Wholly overcome by conflicting passions, by circumstances so contrary to one another, and so discordant with everything either in the works of Nature or Providence, the young man could do nothing but stand like a rigid statue, with his hands lifted up, and his visage like that of a corpse, until led away by the two old people from their daughter's apartment. Then they lighted up a fire to dry him, and began to question him with the most intense curiosity; but they could elicit nothing from him, but the most disjointed exclamations – such as, "Lord in Heaven, what can be the meaning of this?" And at other times: "It is all the enchantment of the devil; the evil spirits have got dominion over me!"

Finding they could make nothing or him, they began to form conjectures of their own. Jean affirmed that it had been the Mermaid of the loch that had come to him in Mary's shape, to allure him to his destruction; but Andrew Burnet, setting his bonnet to one side, and raising his left hand to a level with it, so that he might have full scope to motion and flourish, suiting his action to his words, thus began, with a face of sapience never to be excelled:

"Gudewife, it doth strike me that thou art very wide of the mark. It must have been a spirit of a great deal higher quality than a meer-maiden, who played this extraordinary prank. The meer-maiden is not a spirit, but a beastly sensitive creature, with a malicious spirit within it. Now, what influence could a cauld clatch of a creature like that, wi' a tail like a great saumont-fish, hae ower our bairn, either to make her happy or unhappy? Or where could it borrow her claes, Jean? Tell me that. Na, na, Jean Linton, depend on it, the spirit that courtit wi' poor sinfu' Jock there, has been a fairy; but whether a good ane or an ill ane, it is hard to determine."

Andrew's disquisition was interrupted by the young man falling into a fit of trembling that was fearful to look at, and threatened soon to terminate his existence. Jean ran for the family cordial, observing by the way, that "though he was a wicked person, he was still a fellow-creature, and might live to repent;" and influenced by this spark of genuine humanity, she made him swallow two horn-spoonfuls of strong aquavite. Andrew then put a piece of scarlet thread round each wrist, and taking a strong rowan-tree staff in his hand, he conveyed his trembling and astonished guest home, giving him at parting this sage advice:

"I'll tell you what it is, Jock Allanson – ye hae run a near risk o' perdition, and, escaping that for the present, o' losing your right reason. But take an auld man's advice – never gang again out by night to beguile ony honest man's daughter, lest a worse thing befall thee."

Next morning Mary dressed herself more neatly than usual, but there was manifestly a deep melancholy settled on her lovely face, and at times the unbidden tear would start into her eye. She spoke no word, either good or bad, that ever her mother could recollect, that whole morning; but she once or twice observed her daughter gazing at her, as with an intense and melancholy interest. About nine o'clock in the morning, she took a hay-raik over her shoulder, and went down to a meadow at the east end of the loch, to coil a part of her father's hay, her father and brother engaging to join her about noon, when they came from the sheepfold. As soon as old Andrew came home, his wife and he, as was natural, instantly began to converse on the events of the preceding night; and in the course of their conversation Andrew said, "Gudeness be about us' Jean, was not yon an awfu' speech o' our bairn's to young Jock Allanson last night?"

"Ay, it was a downsetter, gudeman, and spoken like a good Christian lass."

"I'm no sae sure o' that, Jean Linton. My good woman, Jean Linton, I'm no sae sure o' that. Yon speech has gi'en me a great deal o' trouble o' heart; for d'ye ken, an' take my life – ay, an' take your life, Jean – nane o' us can tell whether it was in the Almighty's name or the devil's that she discharged her lover."

"O fy, Andrew, how can ye say sae? How can ye doubt that it was in the Almighty's name?"

"Couldna she have said sae then, and that wad hae put it beyond a' doubt? And that wad hae been the natural way too; but instead of that she says, 'I pray you, in the name of him whose law you have transgressed, to depart out o' my sight.' I confess I'm terrified when I think about yon speech, Jean Linton. Didna she say too that 'her sufferings had been beyond what flesh and blood could have endured?' What was she but flesh and blood. Didna that remark infer that she was something mair than a mortal creature? Jean Linton, Jean Linton! what will you say if it should turn out that our daughter is drowned, and that yon was the fairy we had in the house a' the night and this morning?"

"O haud your tongue, Andrew Burnet, and dinna make my heart cauld within me. We hae aye trusted in the Lord yet, and he has never forsaken us, nor will he yet gie the Wicked One power ower us or ours."

"Ye say very well, Jean, and we maun e'en hope for the best," quoth old Andrew; and away he went, accompanied by his son Alexander, to assist their beloved Mary on the meadow.

No sooner had Andrew set his head over the bents, and come in view of the meadow, than he said to his son, "I wish Jock Allanson maunna hae been east-the-loch fishing for geds the day, for I think my Mary has made very little progress in the meadow."

"She's ower muckle ta'en up about other things this while to mind her wark," said Alexander; "I wadna wonder, father, if that lassie gangs a black gate yet."

Andrew uttered a long and a deep sigh, that seemed to ruffle the very fountains of life, and, without speaking another word, walked on to the hayfield. It was three hours since Mary had left home, and she ought at least to have put up a dozen coils of hay each hour. But, in place of that, she had put up only seven altogether, and the last was unfinished. Her own hay-raik, that had an M and a B neatly cut on the head of it, was leaning on the unfinished coil, and Mary was wanting. Her brother, thinking she had hid herself from them in sport, ran from one coil to another, calling her many bad names, playfully; but after he had turned them all up, and several deep swathes besides, she was not to be found. This young man, who slept in the byre, knew nothing of the events of the foregoing night, the old people and Allanson having mutually engaged to keep them a profound secret, and he had therefore less reason than his father to be seriously alarmed. When they began to work at the hay Andrew could work none; he looked this way and that way, but in no way could he see Mary approaching; so he put on his coat and went away home, to pour his sorrows into the bosom of his wife; and, in the meantime, he desired his son to run to all the neighbouring farming-houses and cots, every one, and make inquiries if anybody had seen Mary.

When Andrew went home and informed his wife that their darling was missing, the grief and astonishment of the aged couple knew no bounds. They sat down and wept together, and declared over and over that this act of Providence was too strong for them, and too high to be understood. Jean besought her husband to kneel instantly, and pray urgently to God to restore their child to them; but he declined it, on account of the wrong frame of his mind, for he declared, that his rage against John Allanson was so extreme as to unfit him for approaching the throne of his Maker. "But if the profligate refuses to listen to the entreaties of an injured parent," added he, "he shall feel the weight of an injured father's arm."

Andrew went straight away to Inverlawn, though without he least hope of finding young Allanson at home; but, on reaching the place, to his amazement, he found the young man lying ill of a burning fever, raving incessantly of witches, spirits, and Mary Burnet. To such a height had his frenzy arrived, that when Andrew went there, it required three men to hold him in the bed. Both his parents testified their opinions openly, that their son was bewitched, or possessed of a demon, and the whole family was thrown into the greatest consternation. The good old shepherd, finding enough of grief there already, was obliged to confine his to his own bosom, and return disconsolate to his little family circle, in which there was a woeful blank that night.

His son returned also from a fruitless search. No one had seen any traces of his sister, but an old crazy woman, at a place called Oxcleuch, said that she had seen her go by in a grand chariot with young Jock Allanson, toward the Birkhill Path, and by that time they were at the Cross of Dumgree. The young man said he asked her what sort of a chariot it was, as there was never such a thing in that country as a chariot, nor yet a road for one. But she replied that he was widely mistaken, for that a great number of chariots sometimes passed that way, though never any of them returned. Those words appearing to be merely the ravings of superannuation, they were not regarded; but when no other traces of Mary could be found, old Andrew went up to consult this crazy dame once more, but he was not able to bring any such thing to her recollection. She spoke only in parables, which to him were incomprehensible.

Bonny Mary Burnet was lost. She left her father's house at nine o'clock on a Wednesday morning, 17th of September, neatly dressed in a white jerkin and green bonnet, with her hay-raik over her shoulder; and that was the last sight she was doomed ever to see of her native cottage. She seemed to have had some presentiment of this, as appeared from her demeanour that morning before she left it. Mary Burnet of Kirkstyle was lost, and great was the sensation produced over the whole country by the mysterious event. There was a long ballad extant at one period on the melancholy catastrophe, which was supposed to have been composed by the chaplain of St. Mary's; but I have only heard tell of it, without ever hearing it sung or recited. Many of the verses concluded thus:

> *"But Bonny Mary Burnet*
> *We will never see again."*

The story soon got abroad, with all its horrid circumstances (and there is little doubt that it was grievously exaggerated), and there was no obloquy that was not thrown on the survivor, who certainly in some degree deserved it, for, instead of growing better, he grew ten times more wicked than he was before. In one thing the whole country agreed, that it had been the real Mary Burnet who was drowned in the loch, and that the being which was found in her bed, lying weeping and complaining of suffering, and which vanished the next day, had been a fairy, an evil spirit, or a changeling of some sort, for that it never spoke save once, and that in a mysterious manner; nor did it partake of any food with the rest of the family. Her father and mother knew not what to say or what to think, but they wandered through this weary world like people wandering in a dream. Everything that belonged to Mary Burnet was kept by her parents as the most sacred relics, and many a tear did her aged mother shed over them. Every article of her dress brought the once comely wearer to mind. Andrew often said, "That to have lost the darling child of their old age in any way would have been a great trial, but to lose her in the way that they had done, was really mair than human frailty could endure."

Many a weary day did he walk by the shores of the loch, looking eagerly for some vestige of her garments, and though he trembled at every appearance, yet did he continue to search on. He had a number of small bones collected, that had belonged to lambs and other minor animals, and, haply, some of them to fishes, from a fond supposition that they might once have formed joints of her toes or fingers. These he kept concealed in a little bag, in order, as he said, "to let the doctors see them." But no relic, besides these, could he ever discover of Mary's body.

Young Allanson recovered from his raging fever scarcely in the manner of other men, for he recovered all at once, after a few days' raving and madness. Mary Burnet, it appeared, was by him no more remembered. He grew ten times more wicked than before, and hesitated at no means of accomplishing his unhallowed purposes. The devout shepherds and cottages around detested him; and, both in their families and in the wild, when there was no ear to hear but that of Heaven, they prayed protection from his devices, as if he had been the Wicked One; and they all prophesied that he would make a bad end.

One fine day about the middle of October, when the days begin to get very short, and the nights long and dark, on a Friday morning, the next year but one after Mary Burnet was lost, a memorable day in the fairy annals, John Allanson, younger of Inverlawn, went to a great hiring fair at a village called Moffat in Annandale, in order to hire a housemaid. His character was so notorious, that not one young woman in the district would serve in his father's house; so away he went to the fair at Moffat, to hire the prettiest and loveliest girl he could there find, with the intention of ruining her as soon as she came home, This is no supposititious accusation, for he acknowledged his plan to Mr. David Welch of Cariferan, who rode down to the market with him, and seemed to boast of it, and dwell on it with delight. But the maidens of Annandale had a guardian angel in the fair that day, of which neither he nor they were aware.

Allanson looked through the hiring-market, and through the hiring-market, and at length fixed on one young woman, which indeed was not difficult to do, for there was no such form there for elegance and beauty. Mr. Welch stood still and eyed him. He took the beauty aside. She was clothed in green, and as lovely as a new-blown rose.

"Are you to hire, pretty maiden?"

"Yes, sir."

"Will you hire with me?"

"I care not though I do. But if I hire with you, it must be for a long term."

"Certainly. The longer the better. What are your wages to be?"

"You know, if I hire, I must be paid in kind. I must have the first living creature that I see about Inverlawn to myself."

"I wish it may be me, then. But what do you know about Inverlawn?"

"I think I should know about it."

"Bless me! I know the face as well as I know my own, and better. But the name has somehow escaped me. Pray, may I I ask your name?"

"Hush! hush!" said she solemnly, and holding up her hand at the same time. "Hush, hush, you had better say nothing about that here."

"I am in utter amazement," he exclaimed. "What is the meaning of this? I conjure you to tell me your name!"

"It is Mary Burnet," said she, in a soft whisper; and at the same time she let down a green veil over her face.

If Allanson's death-warrant had been announced to him at that moment, it could not have deprived him so completely of sense and motion. His visage changed into that of a corpse, his jaws fell down, and his eyes became glazed, so as apparently to throw no reflections inwardly. Mr. Welch, who had kept his eye steadily on them all the while, perceived his comrade's dilemma, and went up to him. "Allanson? Mr. Allanson? What is the matter with you, man?" said he. "Why, the girl has bewitched you, and turned you into a statue!"

Allanson made some sound in his throat, as if attempting to speak, but his tongue refused its office, and he only jabbered. Mr. Welch, conceiving that he was seized with some fit, or about to faint, supported him into the Johnston Arms; but he either could not, or would not grant him any explanation. Welch being, however, resolved to see the maiden in green once more, persuaded Allanson, after causing him to drink a good deal, to go out into the hiring-market again, in search of her. They ranged the market through and through, but the maiden in green was gone, and not to be found. She had vanished in the crowd the moment she divulged her name, and even though Welch had his eye fixed on her, he could not discover which way she went. Allanson appeared to be in a kind of stupor as well as terror, but when he found that she had left the market, he began to recover himself, and to look out again for the top of the market.

He soon found one more beautiful than the last. She was like a sylph, clothed in robes of pure snowy white, with green ribands. Again he pointed this new flower out to Mr. David Welch, who declared that such a perfect model of beauty he had never in his life seen. Allanson, being resolved to have this one at any wages, took her aside, and put the usual question: "Do you wish to hire, pretty maiden?"

"Yes, sir."

"Will you hire with me?"

"I care not though I do."

"What, then, are your wages to be? Come – say? And be reasonable; I am determined not to part with you for a trifle."

"My wages must be in a kind; I work on no other conditions. Pray, how are all the good people about Inverlawn?"

Allanson's breath began to cut, and a chillness to creep through his whole frame, and he answered, with a faltering tongue: "I thank you – much in their ordinary way."

"And your aged neighbours," rejoined she, "are they still alive and well?"

"I – I – I think they are," said he, panting for breath. "But I am at a loss to know whom I am indebted to for these kind recollections."

"What," said she, "have you so soon forgot Mary Burnet of Kirkstyle?"

Allanson started as if a bullet had gone through his heart. The lovely sylph-like form glided into the crowd, and left the astounded libertine once more standing like a rigid statue, until aroused by his friend, Mr. Welch. He tried a third fair one, and got the same answers, and the same name given. Indeed, the first time ever I heard the tale, it bore that he tried seven, who all turned out to be Mary Burnets of Kirkstyle; but I think it unlikely that he would try so many, as he must long ere that time have been sensible that he laboured under some power of enchantment. However, when nothing else would do, he helped himself to a good proportion of strong drink. While he was thus engaged, a phenomenon of beauty and grandeur came into the fair, that caught the sole attention of all present. This was a lovely dame, riding in a gilded chariot, with two livery-men before, and two behind, clothed in green and gold; and never sure was there so splendid a meteor seen in a Moffat fair. The word instantly circulated in the market, that this was the Lady Elizabeth Douglas, eldest daughter to the Earl of Morton, who then sojourned at Auchincastle, in the vicinity of Moffat, and which lady at that time was celebrated as a great beauty all over Scotland. She was afterwards Lady Keith; and the mention of this name in the tale, as it were by mere accident, fixes the era of it in the reign of James the Fourth, at the very time that fairies, brownies, and witches, were at the rifest in Scotland.

Every one in the market believed the lady to be the daughter of the Earl of Morton; and when she came to the Johnston Arms, a gentleman in green came out bareheaded, and received her out of the carriage. All the crowd gazed at such unparalleled beauty and grandeur, but none was half so much overcome as Allanson. He had never conceived aught half so lovely either in earth, or heaven, or fairyland; and while he stood in a burning fever of admiration, think of his astonishment, and the astonishment of the countless crowd that looked on, when this brilliant and matchless beauty beckoned him towards her! He could not believe his senses, but looked this way and that way to see how others regarded the affair but she beckoned him a second time, with such a winning courtesy and smile, that immediately he pulled off his beaver cap and hasted up to her; and without more ado she gave him her arm, and the two walked into the hostel.

Allanson conceived that he was thus distinguished by Lady Elizabeth Douglas, the flower of the land, and so did all the people of the market; and greatly they wondered who the young farmer could be that was thus particularly favoured; for it ought to have been mentioned that he had not one personal acquaintance in the fair save Mr. David Welch of Cariferan. The first thing the lady did was to inquire kindly after his health. Allanson thanked her ladyship with all the courtesy he was master of; and being by this time persuaded that she was in love with him, he became as light as if treading on the air. She next inquired after his father and mother. Oho? thought he to himself, poor creature, she is terribly in for it but her love shall not be thrown away upon a backward or ungrateful object. He answered her with great politeness, and at length began to talk of her noble father and young Lord William, but she cut him short by asking if he did not recognise her.

"Oh, yes! He knew who her ladyship was, and remembered that he had seen her comely face often before, although he could not, at that particular moment, recall to his memory the precise time or places of their meeting."

She next asked for his old neighbours of Kirkstyle, and if they were still in life and health Allanson felt as if his heart were a piece of ice. A chillness spread over his whole frame he sank back on a seat, and remained motionless; but the beautiful and adorable creature soothed him with kind words, till he again gathered courage to speak.

"What?" said he; "and has it been your own lovely self who has been playing tricks on me this whole day?"

"A first love is not easily extinguished, Mr. Allanson," said she. "You may guess from my appearance, that I have been fortunate in life; but, for all that, my first love for you has continued the same, unaltered and unchanged, and you must forgive the little freedoms I used to-day to try your affections, and the effects my appearance would have on you."

"It argues something for my good taste, however, that I never pitched on any face for beauty to-day but your own," said he. "But now that we have met once more, we shall not so easily part again. I will devote the rest of my life to you, only let me know the place of your abode."

"It is hard by," said she, "only a very little space from this and happy, happy, would I be to see you there to-night, were it proper or convenient. But my lord is at present from home and in a distant country."

"I should not conceive that any particular hindrance to my visit," said he.

With great apparent reluctance she at length consented to admit of his visit, and offered to leave one of her gentlemen, whom she could trust, to be his conductor; but this he positively refused. It was his desire, he said, that no eye of man should see him enter or leave her happy dwelling. She said he was a self-willed man, but should have his own way; and after giving him such directions as would infallibly lead him to her mansion, she mounted her chariot and was driven away.

Allanson was uplifted above every sublunary concern. Seeking out his friend, David Welch, he imparted to him his extraordinary good fortune, but he did not tell him that she was not the Lady Elizabeth Douglas. Welch insisted on accompanying him on the way, and refused to turn back till he came to the very point of the road next to the lady's splendid mansion; and in spite of all that Allanson could say, Welch remained there till he saw his comrade enter the court gate, which glowed with lights as innumerable as the stars of the firmament.

Allanson had promised to his father and mother to be home on the morning after the fair to breakfast. He came not either that day or the next; and the third day the old man mounted his white pony, and rode away towards Moffat in search of his son. He called at Cariferan on his way, and made inquiries at Mr. Welch. The latter manifested some astonishment that the young man had not returned; nevertheless he assured his father of his safety, and desired him to return home; and then with reluctance confessed that the young man was engaged in an amour with the Earl of Morton's beautiful daughter; that he had gone to the castle by appointment, and that he, David Welch, had accompanied him to the gate, and seen him enter, and it was apparent that his reception had been a kind one, since he had tarried so long.

Mr. Welch, seeing the old man greatly distressed, was persuaded to accompany him on his journey, as the last who had seen his son, and seen him enter the castle. On reaching Moffat they found his steed standing at the hostel, whither it had returned on the night of the fair, before the company broke up; but the owner had not been heard of since seen in company with Lady Elizabeth Douglas. The old man set out for Auchincastle, taking Mr. David Welch along with him; but long ere they reached the place, Mr. Welch assured him he would not find his son there, as it was nearly in a different direction that they rode on the evening of the fair. However, to the castle they went, and were admitted to the Earl, who, after hearing the old man's tale, seemed to consider him in a state of derangement. He sent for his daughter Elizabeth, and questioned her concerning her meeting with the son of the old respectable countryman – of her appointment with him on the night of the preceding Friday, and concluded by saying he hoped she had him still in safe concealment about the castle.

The lady, hearing her father talk in this manner, and seeing the serious and dejected looks of the old man, knew not what to say, and asked an explanation. But Mr. Welch put a stop to it by declaring to old Allanson that the Lady Elizabeth was not the lady with whom his son made the appointment, for he had seen her, and would engage to know her again among ten thousand; nor was that the castle towards which he had accompanied his son, nor any thing like it. "But go with me," continued he, "and, though I am a stranger in this district, I think I can take you to the very place."

They set out again; and Mr. Welch traced the road from Moffat, by which young Allanson and he had gone, until, after travelling several miles, they came to a place where a road struck off to the right at an angle. "Now I know we are right," said Welch; "for here we stopped, and your son intreated me to return, which I refused, and accompanied him to yon large tree, and a little way beyond it, from whence I saw him received in at the splendid gate. We shall be in sight of the mansion in three minutes."

They passed on to the tree, and a space beyond it; but then Mr. Welch lost the use of his speech, as he perceived that there was neither palace nor gate there, but a tremendous gulf; fifty fathoms deep, and a dark stream foaming and boiling below.

"How is this?" said old Allanson. "There is neither mansion nor habitation of man here!" Welch's tongue for a long time refused its office, and he stood like a statue, gazing on the altered and awful scene. "He only, who made the spirits of men," said he, at last, "and all the spirits that sojourn in the earth and air, can tell how his is. We are wandering in a world of enchantment, and have been influenced by some agencies above human nature, or without its pale; for here of a certainty did I take leave of your son – and there, in that direction, and apparently either on the verge of that gulf, or the space above it, did I see him received in at the court gate of a mansion, splendid beyond all conception. How can human comprehension make anything of this?"

They went forward to the verge, Mr. Welch leading the way to the very spot on which he saw the gate opened, and there they found marks where a horse had been plunging. Its feet had been over the brink, but it seemed to have recovered itself, and deep, deep down, and far within, lay the mangled corpse of John Allanson; and in this manner, mysterious beyond all example, terminated the career of that wicked and flagitious young man. What a beautiful moral may be extracted from this fairy tale!

But among all these turnings and windings, there is no account given, you will say, of the fate of Mary Burnet; for this last appearance of hers at Moffat seems to have been altogether a phantom or illusion.

Gentle and kind reader, I can give you no account of the fate of that maiden; for though the ancient fairy tale proceeds, it seems to me to involve her fate in ten times more mystery than what we have hitherto seen of it.

The yearly return of the day on which Mary was lost, was observed as a day of mourning by her aged and disconsolate parents – a day of sorrow, of fasting, and humiliation. Seven years came and passed away, and the seventh returning day of fasting and prayer was at hand. On the evening previous to it, old Andrew was moving along the sands of the loch, still looking for some relic of his beloved Mary, when he was aware of a little shrivelled old man, who came posting towards him. The creature was not above five spans in height, and had a face scarcely like that of a human creature; but he was, nevertheless, civil in his deportment, and sensible in speech. He bade Andrew a good evening, and asked him what he was looking for. Andrew answered, that he was looking for that which he should never find.

"Pray, what is your name, ancient shepherd?" said the stranger; "for methinks I should know something of you, and perhaps have a commission to you."

"Alas! why should you ask after my name?" said Andrew. "My name is now nothing to any one."

"Had not you once a beautiful daughter, named Mary?" said the stranger.

"It is a heartrending question, man," said Andrew; "but certes, I had once a beloved daughter named Mary."

"What became or her?" asked the stranger.

Andrew shook his head, turned round, and began to move away; it was a theme that his heart could not brook. He sauntered along the loch sands, his dim eye scanning every white pebble as he passed along. There was a hopelessness in his stooping form, his gait, his eye, his feature – in every step that he took there was a hopeless apathy. The dwarf followed him, and began to expostulate with him. "Old man, I see you are pining under some real or fancied affliction," said he. "But in continuing to do so, you are neither acting according to the dictates of reason nor true religion. What is man that he should fret, or the son of man that he should repine, under the chastening hand of his Maker?"

"I am far frae justifying myself," returned Andrew, surveying his shrivelled monitor with some degree of astonishment. "But there are some feelings that neither reason nor religion can o'er-master; and there are some that a parent may cherish without sin."

"I deny the position," said the stranger, "taken either absolutely or relatively. All repining under the Supreme decree is leavened with unrighteousness. But, subtleties aside, I ask you, as I did before, What became of your daughter?"

"Ask the Father of her spirit, and the framer of her body," said Andrew solemnly; "ask Him into whose hands I committed her from childhood. He alone knows what became of her, but I do not."

"How long is it since you lost her?"

"It is seven years to-morrow!"

"Ay! you remember the time well. And you have mourned for her all that while?"

"Yes; and I will go down to the grave mourning for my only daughter, the child of my age, and of all my affection. Oh, thou unearthly-looking monitor, knowest thou aught of my darling child? for if thou dost, thou wilt know that she was not like other women. There was a simplicity and a purity about my Mary, that was hardly consistent with our frail nature."

"Wouldst thou like to see her again?" said the dwarf.

Andrew turned round, his whole frame shaking as with a palsy, and gazed on the audacious imp. "See her again, creature!" cried he vehemently. "Would I like to see her again, sayest thou?"

"I said so," said the dwarf, "and I say further, Dost thou know this token? Look, and see if thou dost!"

Andrew took the token, and looked at it, then at the shrivelled stranger, and then at the token again; and at length he burst into tears, and wept aloud; but they were tears of joy, and his weeping seemed to have some breathings of laughter intermingled in it. And still as he kissed the token, he called out in broken and convulsive sentences "Yes, auld body, I do know it! – I do know it – I do know it! It is indeed the same golden Edward, with three holes in it, with which I presented my Mary on her birthday, in her eighteenth year, to buy a new suit for the holidays. But when she took it she said – ay, I mind weel what my bonny woman said. 'It is sae bonny and sae kenspeckle,' said she, 'that I think I'll keep it for the sake of the giver.' O dear, dear! Blessed little creature, tell me how she is, and where she is? Is she living, or is she dead?"

"She is living, and in good health," said the dwarf; "and better, and braver, and happier, and lovelier than ever; and if you make haste, you will see her and her family at Moffat tomorrow afternoon. They are to pass there on a journey, but it is an express one, and I am sent to you with that token, to inform you of the circumstance, that you may have it in your power to see and embrace your beloved daughter once before you die."

"And am I to meet my Mary at Moffat? Come away, little, dear, welcome body, thou blessed of heaven, come away, and taste of an auld shepherd's best cheer, and I'll gang foot for foot with you to

Moffat, and my auld wife shall gang foot for foot with us too. I tell you, little, blessed, and welcome crile, come alone with me."

"I may not tarry to enter your house, or taste of your cheer, good shepherd," said the being. "May plenty still be within your walls, and a thankful heart to enjoy it! But my directions are neither to taste meat nor drink in this country, but to haste back to her that sent me. Go – haste, and make ready, for you have no time to lose."

"At what time will she be there?" cried Andrew, flinging the plaid from him to run home with the tidings.

"Precisely when the shadow of the Holy Cross fails due east," cried the dwarf; and turning round, he hasted on his way.

When old Jean Linton saw her husband corning hobbling and running home without his plaid, and having his doublet flying wide open, she had no doubt that he had lost his wits; and, full of anxiety, she met him at the side of the kail-yard. "Gudeness preserve us a' in our right senses, Andrew Burnet, what's the matter wi' you, Andrew Burnet?"

"Stand out o' my gate, wife, for, d'ye see, I am rather in a haste, Jean Linton."

"I see that indeed, gudeman; but stand still, and tell me what has putten you in sic a haste. Ir ye dementit?"

"Na, na gudewife, Jean Linton, I'm no dementit – I'm only gaun away till Moffat."

"O, gudeness pity the poor auld body How can ye gang to Moffat, man? Or what have ye to do at Moffat? Dinna ye mind that the morn is the day o' our solemnity?"

"Haud out o' my gate, auld wife, and dinna speak o' solemnities to me. I'll keep it at Moffat the morn. Ay, gudewife, and ye shall keep it at Moffat, too. What d'ye think o' that, woman?

Too-whoo! ye dinna ken the metal that's in an auld body till it be tried."

"Andrew – Andrew Burnet!"

"Get awa' wi' your frightened looks, woman; and haste ye, gang and fling me out my Sabbath-day claes. And, Jean Linton, my woman, d'ye hear, gang and pit on your bridal gown, and your silk hood, for ye maun be at Moffat the morn too; and it is mair nor time we were awa'. Dinna look sae surprised, woman, till I tell ye, that our ain Mary is to meet us at Moffat the morn."

"Oh, Andrew I dinna sport wi' the feelings of an auld forsaken heart!"

"Gude forbid, my auld wife, that I should ever sport wi' feelings o' yours," cried Andrew, bursting into tears; "they are a' as sacred to me as breathings frae the Throne o' Grace. But it is true that I tell ye; our dear bairn is to meet us at Moffat the morn, wi' a son in every hand; and we maun e'en gang and see her aince again, and kiss her and bless her afore we dee."

The tears now rushed from the old woman's eyes like fountains, and dropped from her sorrow-worn cheeks to the earth, and then, as with a spontaneous movement, she threw her skirt over her head, kneeled down at her husband's feet, and poured out her soul in thanksgiving to her Maker. She then rose up, quite deprived of her senses through joy, and ran crouching away on the road, towards Moffat, as if hasting beyond her power to be at it. But Andrew brought her back; and they prepared themselves for their journey.

Kirkstyle being twenty miles from Moffat, they set out on the afternoon of Tuesday, the 16th of September; slept that night at a place called Turnbery Shiel, and were in Moffat next day by noon. Wearisome was the remainder of the day to that aged couple; they wandered about conjecturing by what road their daughter would come, and how she would come attended. "I have made up my mind on baith these matters," said Andrew; "at first I thought it was likely that she would come out of the east, because a' our blessings come frae that airt; but finding now that would be o'er near to the very road we hae come oursells, I now take it for granted she'll come frae the south; and I just think I see her leading a bonny boy in every hand, and a servant lass carrying a bit bundle ahint her."

The two now walked out on all the southern roads, in hopes to meet their Mary, but always returned to watch the shadow of the Holy Cross; and, by the time it fell due east, they could do nothing but stand in the middle of the street, and look round them in all directions. At length, about half a mile out on the Dumfries road, they perceived a poor beggar woman approaching with two children following close to her, and another beggar a good way behind. Their eyes were instantly riveted on these objects; for Andrew thought he perceived his friend the dwarf in the one that was behind; and now all other earthly objects were to them nothing, save these approaching beggars. At that moment a gilded chariot entered the village from the south, and drove by them at full speed, having two livery-men before, and two behind, clothed in green and gold, "Ach-wow! the vanity of worldly grandeur" ejaculated Andrew, as the splendid vehicle went thundering by; but neither he nor his wife deigned to look at it farther, their whole attention being fixed on the group of beggars. "Ay, it is just my woman," said Andrew, "it is just hersell; I ken her gang yet, sair pressed down wi' poortith although she be. But I dinna care how poor she be, for baith her and hers sall be welcome to my fireside as lang as I hae ane."

While their eyes were thus strained, and their hearts melting with tenderness and pity, Andrew felt something embracing his knees, and, on looking down, there was his Mary, blooming in splendour and beauty, kneeling at his feet. Andrew uttered a loud hysterical scream of joy, and clasped her to his bosom; and old Jean Linton stood trembling, with her arms spread, but durst not close them on so splendid a creature, till her daughter first enfolded her in a fond embrace, and then she hung upon her and wept. It was a wonderful event – a restoration without a parallel. They indeed beheld their Mary, their long-lost darling; they held her in their embraces, believed in her identity, and were satisfied. Satisfied, did I say? They were happy beyond the lot of mortals. She had just alighted from her chariot; and, perceiving her aged parents standing together, she ran and kneeled at their feet. They now retired into the hostel, where Mary presented her two sons to her father and mother. They spent the evening in every social endearment; and Mary loaded the good old couple with rich presents, watched over them till midnight, when they both fell into a deep and happy sleep, and then she remounted her chariot, and was driven away. If she was any more seen in Scotland, I never heard of it; but her parents rejoiced in the thoughts of her happiness till the day of their death.

The Screaming Skull of Greyfriars

W.T. Linskill

I never met a better fellow in the world than my old friend, Allan Beauchamp. He had been educated at Eton, and Magdalen at Oxford, after which he joined a crack regiment, and later on took it into his head to turn doctor. He was a great traveller and a magnificent athlete. There was no game in which he did not excel. Curiously enough, he hated music; he had no ear for it, and he did not know the difference between the airs of "Tommy, make room for your uncle" and "The Lost Chord." He was tremendously proud of his pedigree; he had descended from the de Beauchamps, and one of his ancestors, he gravely informed people, had helped Noah to get the wasps and elephants into the Ark. Another of them seems to have been not very far away in the Garden of Eden. In fact, they seem to have been quite prehistoric. He was quite cracked on the subject of brain transference, telepathy, spiritualism, ghosts, warnings, and the like, and on these points he was most uncanny and fearsome. The literature he had about them was blood curdling. He believed in dual personality, and in visions, horoscopes, and dreams. He showed me a pamphlet he had written, entitled "The Toad-faced Demon of Lone

Devil's Dyke." He was always flitting about Britain exploring haunted houses and castles, and sleeping in haunted rooms when it was possible. Some years ago Beauchamp and myself, accompanied by his faithful valet, rejoicing in the name of Pellingham Truffles, went to the Highlands for a bit of quiet and rest, and it was there I heard his curious story of the skull.

We were sitting over a cosy fire after dinner. It was snowing hard outside, and very cold. Our pipes were alight and our grog on the table, when Allan Beauchamp suddenly remarked – "It's a deuced curious thing for a man to be always followed about the place by a confounded grinning skull."

"Eh, what," I said, "who the deuce is being followed about by a skull? It's rubbish, and quite impossible."

"Not a bit," said my friend, "I've had a skull after me more or less for several years."

"It sounds like a remark a lunatic would make," I rejoined rather crossly. "Do not talk bunkum. You'll go dotty if you believe such infernal rot."

"It is not bunkum or rot a bit," said Allan, "It's gospel truth. Ask Truffles, ask Jack Weston, or Jimmy Darkgood, or any of my south country pals."

"I don't know Jack Weston or Jimmy Darkgood," I said, "but tell me the whole story, and some day, *if it's good*, I'll put it in the *St Andrews Citizen*."

"It's mostly about St Andrews," said Beauchamp, "so here goes, but shove on some coals first."

I did so, and then requested him to fire away.

"It was long, long ago, I think about the year 1513, that one of my ancestors, a man called Neville de Beauchamp, resided in Scotland. It seems he was an uncommonly wild dog, went in for racing and cards, and could take his wine and ale with any of them even in those hard-drinking days. He was known as Flash Neville. Later on he married a pretty girl, the daughter of a silk mercer in Perth, who, it seems, died (they said of a broken heart) two years after. Neville de Beauchamp was seized with awful remorse, and became shortly after a monk in Greyfriars Monastery at St Andrews. After Neville's wife's death, her relations seem to have been on the hunt after him, burning for revenge, and the girl's brother, a rough, wild dog in those stormy days, at last managed to track his quarry down in the monastery at St Andrews."

"Very interesting," I said, "that monastery stood very nearly on the site of the present infant school, and we found the well in 1880. Well, what did this brother do, eh?"

"It seems that one afternoon after vespers he forced his way into the Monastery Chapel, sought out Neville de Beauchamp, and slashed off his head with a sword in the aisle of the Kirk. Now a queer thing happened – his body fell on the floor, but the severed head, with a wild scream, flew up to the chapel ceiling and vanished through its roof."

"Mighty queer that," I said.

"The body was reverently buried," went on Allan, "but the head never was recovered, and, whirling through the air over the monastery, screaming and groaning most pitifully, it used to cause great terror to the monks and others o' nights. It was a well-known story, and few cared to venture in that locality after nightfall. The head soon became a skull, and since that time has always haunted some member of the house of Beauchamp. Now comes a strange thing. I went a few years ago and lived in rooms at St Andrews for a change, and while there I heard of my uncle's death somewhere abroad. I had never seen him, but I had frequently heard that he was very much perplexed and worried by the tender attentions paid him by the skull of Neville de Beauchamp, which was always turning up at odd times and in unexpected places."

"This is a grand tale," I said.

"Now I come on the job," said Allan, ruefully. "That uncle was the very last of our family, and I wondered if that skull would come my way. I felt very ill and nervous after I got the news of my uncle's death. A strange sense of depression and oppression overcame me, and I got very restless. One stormy evening I felt impelled by some strange influence to go out. I wandered about the place for several hours and got drenched. I felt as if I was walking in my sleep, or as if I had taken some drug or other. Then I had a sort of vision – I had just rounded the corner of North Bell Street."

"Now called Greyfriars Garden," I remarked.

"Yes! Well, when I got around that corner I saw a large, strange building before me. I opened a wicket gate and entered what I found to be the chapel; service was over, the lights were being extinguished, and the air was laden with incense. As I knelt in a corner of the chapel I saw the whole scene, the tragedy of which I had heard, enacted all over again. I saw that monk in the aisle, I saw a man rush in and cut off his head. I saw the body fall and the head fly up with a shriek to the roof. When I came to myself I found I was sitting on the low wall of the school. I was very cold and wet, and I got up to go home. As I rose I saw lying on the pavement at my feet what appeared to be a small football. I gave it a vicious kick, when to my horror it turned over and I saw it was a skull. It was gnashing its teeth and moaning. Then with a shriek it flew up in the air and vanished. A horrible thing.

Then I knew the worst. The skull of the monk Neville de Beauchamp had attached itself to me for life, I being the last of the race. Since then it is almost always with me."

"Where is it now?" I said, shuddering.

"Not very far away, you bet," he said.

"It's a most unpleasant tale," I said. "Good night, I'm off to bed after that."

I was in my first sleep about an hour afterwards, when a knock came at my door, and the valet came in.

"Sorry to disturb you, sir," he said, "but the skull has *just come back*. It's in the next room. Would you like to see it?"

"Certainly not," I roared. "Get away and let me go to sleep."

Then and there I firmly resolved to leave next morning. I hated skulls, and I fancied that probably it might take a fancy to me, and I had no desire to be followed about the country by a skull as if it was a fox terrier.

Next morning I went in to breakfast. "Where is that beastly skull?" I said to Allan.

"Oh, it's off again somewhere. Heaven knows where; but I have had another vision, a waking vision."

"What was it?"

"Well," said Allan, "I saw the skull and a white hand which seemed to beckon to me beside it. Then they slowly receded and in their place was what looked like a big sheet of paper. On it in large letters were the words – *Your friend, Jack Weston, is dead*. This morning I got this wire telling me of his sudden death. Read it."

That afternoon I left the Highlands and Allan Beauchamp.

Since then I have constant letters from him from his home in England. He has tried every means possible to get rid of that monk's skull; but they are of no avail, it always returns. So he has made the best he can of it, and keeps it in a locked casket in an empty room at the end of a wing of the old house. He says it keeps fairly quiet, but on stormy nights wails and gruesome shrieks are heard from the casket in that closed apartment.

I heard from him last week. He said: –

"DEAR W. T. L., – I don't think I mentioned that twice a year the skull of Neville de Beauchamp vanishes from its casket for a period of about two days. It is never away longer.

"I wonder if it still haunts its old monastery at St Andrews where its owner was slain. Do write and tell me if anyone now in that vicinity hears or sees the screaming skull of my ancestor, Neville de Beauchamp."

The Old Nurse's Story

George MacDonald

I set out one evening for the cottage of my old nurse, to bid her good-bye for many months, probably years. I was to leave the next day for Edinburgh, on my way to London, whence I had to repair by coach to my new abode – almost to me like the land beyond the grave, so little did I know about it, and so wide was the separation between it and my home. The evening was sultry when I began my walk, and before I arrived at its end, the clouds rising from all quarters of the horizon, and especially gathering around the peaks of the mountain, betokened the near approach of a thunderstorm. This was a great delight to me. Gladly would I take leave of my home with the memory of a last night of tumultuous magnificence; followed, probably, by a day of weeping rain, well suited to the mood of my own heart in bidding farewell to the best of parents and the dearest of homes. Besides, in common with most Scotchmen who are young and hardy enough to be unable to realise the existence of coughs and rheumatic fevers, it was a positive pleasure to me to be out in rain, hail, or snow.

"I am come to bid you good-bye, Margaret, and to hear the story which you promised to tell me before I left home: I go to-morrow."

"Do you go so soon, my darling? Well, it will be an awful night to tell it in; but, as I promised, I suppose I must."

At the moment, two or three great drops of rain, the first of the storm, fell down the wide chimney, exploding in the clear turf-fire.

"Yes, indeed you must," I replied.

After a short pause, she commenced. Of course she spoke in Gaelic; and I translate from my recollection of the Gaelic; but rather from the impression left upon my mind, than from any recollection of words. She drew her chair near the fire, which we had reason to fear would soon be put out by the falling rain, and began.

"How old the story is, I do not know. It has come down through many generations. My grandmother told it to me as I tell it to you; and her mother and my mother sat beside, never interrupting, but nodding their heads at every turn. Almost it ought to begin like the fairy tales, *Once upon a time*, – it took place so long ago; but it is too dreadful and too true to tell like a fairy tale. – There were two brothers, sons of the chief of our clan, but as different in appearance and disposition as two men could be. The elder was fair-haired and strong, much given to hunting and fishing; fighting too, upon occasion, I daresay, when they made a foray upon the Saxon, to get back a mouthful of their own. But he was gentleness itself to everyone about him, and the very soul of honour in all his doings. The younger was very dark in complexion, and tall and slender compared to his brother. He was very fond of book-learning, which, they say, was an uncommon taste in those times. He did not care for any sports or bodily exercises but one; and that, too, was unusual in these parts. It was horsemanship. He was a fierce rider, and as much at home in the saddle as in his study-chair. You may think that, so long ago, there was not much fit room for riding hereabouts; but, fit or not fit, he rode.

From his reading and riding, the neighbours looked doubtfully upon him, and whispered about the black art. He usually bestrode a great powerful black horse, without a white hair on him; and people said it was either the devil himself, or a demon-horse from the devil's own stud. What favoured this notion was that in or out of the stable, the brute would let no other than his master go near him. Indeed, no one would venture, after he had killed two men, and grievously maimed a third, tearing him with his teeth and hoofs like a wild beast. But to his master he was obedient as a hound, and would even tremble in his presence sometimes.

"The youth's temper corresponded to his habits. He was both gloomy and passionate. Prone to anger, he had never been known to forgive. Debarred from anything on which he had set his heart, he would have gone mad with longing if he had not gone mad with rage. His soul was like the night around us now, dark, and sultry, and silent, but lighted up by the red levin of wrath, and torn by the bellowings of thunder-passion. He must have his will: hell might have his soul. Imagine, then, the rage and malice in his heart, when he suddenly became aware that an orphan girl, distantly related to them, who had lived with them for nearly two years, and whom he had loved for almost all that period, was loved by his elder brother, and loved him in return. He flung his right hand above his head, and swore a terrible oath that if he might not, his brother should not, rushed out of the house, and galloped off among the hills.

"The orphan was a beautiful girl, tall, pale, and slender, with plentiful dark hair, which, when released from the snood, rippled down below her knees. Her appearance formed a strong contrast with that of her favoured lover, while there was some resemblance between her and the younger brother. This fact seemed, to his fierce selfishness, ground for a prior claim.

"It may appear strange that a man like him should not have had instant recourse to his superior and hidden knowledge, by means of which he might have got rid of his rival with far more of certainty and less of risk; but I presume that, for the moment, his passion overwhelmed his consciousness of skill. Yet I do not suppose that he foresaw the mode in which his hatred was about to operate. At the moment when he learned their mutual attachment, probably through a domestic, the lady was on her way to meet her lover as he returned from the day's sport. The appointed place was on the edge of a deep, rocky ravine, down in whose dark bosom brawled and foamed a little mountain torrent. You know the place, Duncan, my dear, I daresay."

(Here she gave me a minute description of the spot, with directions how to find it.)

"Whether any one saw what I am about to relate, or whether it was put together afterwards, I cannot tell. The story is like an old tree – so old that it has lost the marks of its growth. But this is how my grandmother told it to me. An evil chance led him in the right direction. The lovers, startled by the sound of the approaching horse, parted in opposite directions along a narrow mountain-path on the edge of the ravine. Into this path he struck at a point near where the lovers had met, but to opposite sides of which they had now receded; so that he was between them on the path. Turning his horse up the course of the stream, he soon came in sight of his brother on the ledge before him. With a suppressed scream of rage, he rode headlong at him, and, ere he had time to make the least defence, hurled him over the precipice. The helplessness of the strong man was uttered in one single despairing cry as he shot into the abyss.

Then all was still. The sound of his fall could not reach the edge of the gulf. Divining in a moment that the lady, whose name was Elsie, must have fled in the opposite direction, he reined his steed on his haunches. He could touch the precipice with his bridle-hand half outstretched; his sword-hand half outstretched would have dropped a stone to the bottom of the ravine. There was no room to wheel. One desperate practibility alone remained. Turning his horse's head towards the edge, he compelled him, by means of the powerful bit, to rear till he stood almost erect; and so, his body swaying over the gulf, with quivering and straining muscles, to turn on his hind legs. Having completed the half-circle, he let him drop, and urged him furiously in the opposite direction. It must have been by the devil's own care that he was able to continue his gallop along that ledge of rock.

"He soon caught sight of the maiden. She was leaning, half fainting, against the precipice. She had heard her lover's last cry, and, although it had conveyed no suggestion of his voice to her ear, she trembled from head to foot, and her limbs would bear her no farther. He checked his speed, rode gently up to her, lifted her unresisting, laid her across the shoulders of his horse, and, riding carefully till he reached a more open path, dashed again wildly along the mountain side. The lady's long hair was shaken loose, and dropped, trailing on the ground. The horse trampled upon it, and stumbled, half dragging her from the saddle-bow. He caught her, lifted her up, and looked at her face. She was dead. I suppose he went mad. He laid her again across the saddle before him, and rode on, reckless whither. Horse, and man, and maiden were found the next day, lying at the foot of a cliff, dashed to pieces. It was observed that a hind shoe of the horse was loose and broken. Whether this had been the cause of his fall, could not be told; but ever when he races, as race he will, till the day of doom, along that mountain side, his gallop is mingled with the clank of the loose and broken shoe. For, like the sin, the punishment is awful; he shall carry about for ages the phantom-body of the girl, knowing that her soul is away, sitting with the soul of his brother, down in the deep ravine, or scaling with him the topmost crags of the towering mountain peaks. There are some who, from time to time, see the doomed man careering along the face of the mountain, with the lady hanging across the steed; and they say it always betokens a storm, such as this which is now raving about us."

I had not noticed till now, so absorbed had I been in her tale, that the storm had risen to a very ecstasy of fury.

"They say, likewise, that the lady's hair is still growing; for, every time they see her, it is longer than before; and that now such is its length and the headlong speed of the horse, that it floats and streams out behind, like one of those curved clouds, like a comet's tail, far up in the sky; only the cloud is white, and the hair dark as night. And they say it will go on growing until the Last Day, when the horse will falter, and her hair will gather in; and the horse will fall, and the hair will twist, and twine, and wreathe itself like a mist of threads about him, and blind him to everything but her. Then the body will rise up within it, face to face with him, animated by a fiend, who, twining *her* arms around him, will drag him down to the bottomless pit.»

I may mention something which now occurred, and which had a strange effect on my old nurse. It illustrates the assertion that we see around us only what is within us; marvellous things enough will show themselves to the marvellous mood. During a short lull in the storm, just as she had finished her story, we heard the sound of iron-shod hoofs approaching the cottage. There was no bridle-way into the glen. A knock came to the door, and, on opening it, we saw an old man seated on a horse, with a long, slenderly-filled sack lying across the saddle before him. He said he had lost the path in the storm, and, seeing the light, had scrambled down to inquire his way. I perceived at once, from the scared and mysterious look of the old woman's eyes, that she was persuaded that this appearance had more than a little to do with the awful rider, the terrific storm, and myself who had heard the sound of the phantom hoofs. As he ascended the hill, she looked after him, with wide and pale but unshrinking eyes; then turning in, shut and locked the door behind her, as by a natural instinct. After two or three of her significant nods, accompanied by the compression of her lips, she said: –

"He need not think to take me in, wizard as he is, with his disguises. I can see him through them all. Duncan, my dear, when you suspect anything, do not be too incredulous. This human demon is, of course, a wizard still, and knows how to make himself, as well as anything he touches, take a quite different appearance from the real one; only every appearance must bear some resemblance, however distant, to the natural form. That man you saw at the door, was the phantom of which I have been telling you. What he is after now, of course, I cannot tell; but you must keep a bold heart, and a firm and wary foot, as you go home to-night."

I showed some surprise, I do not doubt, and, perhaps, some fear as well; but I only said: "How do you know him, Margaret?"

"I can hardly tell you," she replied; "but I do know him. I think he hates me. Often, of a wild night, when there is moonlight enough by fits, I see him tearing round this little valley, just on the top edge – all round; the lady's hair and the horse's mane and tail driving far behind, and mingling, vaporous, with the stormy clouds. About he goes, in wild careering gallop; now lost as the moon goes in, then visible far round when she looks out again – an airy, pale-grey spectre, which few eyes but mine could see; for, as far as I am aware, no one of the family but myself has ever possessed the double gift of seeing and hearing both. In this case I hear no sound, except now and then a clank from the broken shoe. But I did not mean to tell you that I had ever seen him. I am not a bit afraid of him. He cannot do more than he may. His power is limited; else ill enough would he work, the miscreant."

"But," said I, "what has all this, terrible as it is, to do with the fright you took at my telling you that I had heard the sound of the broken shoe? Surely you are not afraid of only a storm?"

"No, my boy; I fear no storm. But the fact is, that that sound is seldom heard, and never, as far as I know, by any of the blood of that wicked man, without betokening some ill to one of the family, and most probably to the one who hears it – but I am not quite sure about that. Only some evil it does portend, although a long time may elapse before it shows itself; and I have a hope it may mean some one else than you."

"Do not wish that," I replied. "I know no one better able to bear it than I am; and I hope, whatever it may be, that I only shall have to meet it. It must surely be something serious to be so foretold – it can hardly be connected with my disappointment in being compelled to be a pedagogue instead of a soldier."

"Do not trouble yourself about that, Duncan," replied she. "A soldier you must be. The same day you told me of the clank of the broken horseshoe, I saw you return wounded from battle, and fall fainting from your horse in the street of a great city – only fainting, thank God. But I have particular reasons for being uneasy at *your* hearing that boding sound. Can you tell me the day and hour of your birth?"

"No," I replied. "It seems very odd when I think of it, but I really do not know even the day."

"Nor any one else, which is stranger still," she answered.

"How does that happen, nurse?"

"We were in terrible anxiety about your mother at the time. So ill was she, after you were just born, in a strange, unaccountable way, that you lay almost neglected for more than an hour. In the very act of giving birth to you, she seemed to the rest around her to be out of her mind, so wildly did she talk; but I knew better. I knew that she was fighting some evil power; and what power it was, I knew full well; for twice, during her pains, I heard the click of the horseshoe. But no one could help her. After her delivery, she lay as if in a trance, neither dead, nor at rest, but as if frozen to ice, and conscious of it all the while. Once more I heard the terrible sound of iron; and, at the moment your mother started from her trance, screaming, 'My child! my child!' We suddenly became aware that no one had attended to the child, and rushed to the place where he lay wrapped in a blanket. Uncovering him, we found him black in the face, and spotted with dark spots upon the throat. I thought he was dead; but, with great and almost hopeless pains, we succeeded in making him breathe, and he gradually recovered. But his mother continued dreadfully exhausted. It seemed as if she had spent her life for her child's defence and birth. That was you, Duncan, my dear.

"I was in constant attendance upon her. About a week after your birth, as near as I can guess, just in the gloaming, I heard yet again the awful clank – only once. Nothing followed till about midnight. Your mother slept, and you lay asleep beside her. I sat by the bedside. A horror fell upon me suddenly, though I neither saw nor heard anything. Your mother started from her sleep with a cry, which sounded as if it came from far away, out of a dream, and did not belong to this world. My blood curdled with fear. She sat up in bed, with wide staring eyes, and half-open rigid lips, and, feeble as she was, thrust her arms straight out before her with great force, her hands open and lifted up, with the palms outwards. The whole action was of one violently repelling another. She began to talk wildly as she had done before you were born, but, though I seemed to hear and understand it all at the time, I could not recall a word of it afterwards. It was as if I had listened to it when half asleep. I attempted to soothe her, putting my arms round her, but she seemed quite unconscious of my presence, and my arms seemed powerless upon the fixed muscles of hers. Not that I tried to constrain her, for I knew that a battle was going on of some kind or other, and my interference might do awful mischief. I only tried to comfort and encourage her. All the time, I was in a state of indescribable cold and suffering, whether more bodily or mental I could not tell. But at length I heard yet again the clank of the shoe. A sudden peace seemed to fall upon my mind – or was it a warm, odorous wind that filled the room? Your mother dropped her arms, and turned feebly towards her baby. She saw that he slept a blessed sleep. She smiled like a glorified spirit, and fell back exhausted on the pillow. I went to the other side of the room to get a cordial. When I returned to the bedside, I saw at once that she was dead. Her face smiled still, with an expression of the uttermost bliss."

Nurse ceased, trembling as overcome by the recollection; and I was too much moved and awed to speak. At length, resuming the conversation, she said: "You see it is no wonder, Duncan, my dear, if, after all this, I should find, when I wanted to fix the date of your birth, that I could not determine the day or the hour when it took place. All was confusion in my poor brain. But it was strange that no one else could, any more than I. One thing only I can tell you about it. As I carried you across the room to lay you down – for I assisted at your birth – I happened to look up to the window. Then I saw what I did not forget, although I did not think of it again till many days after – a bright star was shining on the very tip of the thin crescent moon."

"Oh, then," said I, "it is possible to determine the day and the very hour when my birth took place."

"See the good of book-learning!" replied she. "When you work it out, just let me know, my dear, that I may remember it."

"That I will."

A silence of some moments followed. Margaret resumed:

"I am afraid you will laugh at my foolish fancies, Duncan; but in thinking over all these things, as you may suppose I often do, lying awake in my lonely bed, the notion sometimes comes to me: What if my Duncan be the youth whom his wicked brother hurled into the ravine, come again in a new body, to live out his life, cut short by his brother's hatred? If so, his persecution of you, and of your mother for your sake, is easy to understand. And if so, you will never be able to rest till you find your fere, wherever she may have been born on the face of the earth. For born she must be, long ere now, for you to find. I misdoubt me much, however, if you will find her without great conflict and suffering between, for the Powers of Darkness will be against you; though I have good hope that you will overcome at last. You must forgive the fancies of a foolish old woman, my dear."

I will not try to describe the strange feelings, almost sensations, that arose in me while listening to these extraordinary utterances, lest it should be supposed I was ready to believe all that Margaret narrated or concluded. I could not help doubting her sanity; but no more could I help feeling peculiarly moved by her narrative.

Few more words were spoken on either side, but, after receiving renewed exhortations to carefulness on the way home, I said good-bye to dear old nurse, considerably comforted, I must confess, that I was not doomed to be a tutor all my days; for I never questioned the truth of that vision and its consequent prophecy.

I went out into the midst of the storm, into the alternating throbs of blackness and radiance; now the possessor of no more room than what my body filled, and now isolated in world-wide space. And the thunder seemed to follow me, bellowing after me as I went.

Absorbed in the story I had heard, I took my way, as I thought, homewards. The whole country was well known to me. I should have said, before that night, that I could have gone home blindfold. Whether the lightning bewildered me and made me take a false turn, I cannot tell, for the hardest thing to understand, in intellectual as well as moral mistakes, is how we came to go wrong. But after wandering for some time, plunged in meditation, and with no warning whatever of the presence of inimical powers, a brilliant lightning-flash showed me that at least I was not near home. The light was prolonged for a second or two by a slight electric pulsation; and by that I distinguished a wide space of blackness on the ground in front of me. Once more wrapt in the folds of a thick darkness, I dared not move. Suddenly it occurred to me what the blackness was, and whither I had wandered. It was a huge quarry, of great depth, long disused, and half filled with water. I knew the place perfectly. A few more steps would have carried me over the brink. I stood still, waiting for the next flash, that I might be quite sure of the way I was about to take before I ventured to move. While I stood, I fancied I heard a single hollow plunge in the black water far below. When the lightning came, I turned, and took my path in another direction. After walking for some time across the heath, I fell. The fall became a roll, and down a steep declivity I went, over and over, arriving at the bottom uninjured.

Another flash soon showed me where I was – in the hollow valley, within a couple of hundred yards from nurse's cottage. I made my way towards it. There was no light in it, except the feeblest glow from the embers of her peat fire. "She is in bed," I said to myself, "and I will not disturb her." Yet something drew me towards the little window. I looked in. At first I could see nothing. At length, as I kept gazing, I saw something, indistinct in the darkness, like an outstretched human form.

By this time the storm had lulled. The moon had been up for some time, but had been quite concealed by tempestuous clouds. Now, however, these had begun to break up; and, while I stood looking into the cottage, they scattered away from the face of the moon, and a faint, vapoury gleam of her light, entering the cottage through a window opposite that at which I stood, fell directly on the face of my old nurse, as she lay on her back outstretched upon chairs, pale as death, and with her eyes closed. The light fell nowhere but on her face. A stranger to her habits would have thought that she was dead; but she had so much of the appearance she had had on a former occasion, that I concluded at once she was in one of her trances. But having often heard that persons in such a condition ought not to be disturbed, and feeling quite sure she knew best how to manage herself, I turned, though reluctantly, and left the lone cottage behind me in the night, with the death-like woman lying motionless in the midst of it.

I found my way home without any further difficulty, and went to bed, where I soon fell asleep, thoroughly wearied, more by the mental excitement I had been experiencing, than by the amount of bodily exercise I had gone through.

My sleep was tormented with awful dreams; yet, strange to say, I awoke in the morning refreshed and fearless. The sun was shining through the chinks in my shutters, which had been closed because of the storm, and was making streaks and bands of golden brilliancy upon the wall. I had dressed and completed my preparations long before I heard the steps of the servant who came to call me.

What a wonderful thing waking is! The time of the ghostly moonshine passes by, and the great positive sunlight comes. A man who dreams, and knows that he is dreaming, thinks he knows what waking is; but knows it so little that he mistakes, one after another, many a vague and dim change in his dream for an awaking. When the true waking comes at last, he is filled and overflowed with the power of its reality. So, likewise, one who, in the darkness, lies waiting for the light about to be struck, and trying to conceive, with all the force of his imagination, what the light will be like, is yet, when the reality flames up before him, seized as by a new and unexpected thing, different from and beyond all his imagining. He feels as if the darkness were cast to an infinite distance behind him. So shall it be with us when we wake from this dream of life into the truer life beyond, and find all our present notions of being thrown back as into a dim vapoury region of dreamland, where yet we thought we knew, and whence we looked forward into the present. This must be what Novalis means when he says: "Our life is not a dream; but it may become a dream, and perhaps ought to become one."

And so I look back upon the strange history of my past, sometimes asking myself: "Can it be that all this has really happened to the same *me*, who am now thinking about it in doubt and wonderment?"

The Sin-Eater
Fiona Macleod

SIN.

Taste this bread, this substance: tell me
Is it bread or flesh?

[The Senses approach.]

THE SMELL.

Its smell
Is the smell of bread.

SIN.

Touch, come. Why tremble?
Say what's this thou touchest?

THE TOUCH.

Bread.

SIN.

Sight, declare what thou discernest
In this object.

The Sight.

Bread alone.

Calderon, *Los Encantos de la Culpa*

A wet wind out of the south mazed and mooned through the sea-mist that hung over the Ross. In all the bays and creeks was a continuous weary lapping of water. There was no other sound anywhere.

Thus was it at daybreak; it was thus at noon; thus was it now in the darkening of the day. A confused thrusting and falling of sounds through the silence betokened the hour of the setting. Curlews wailed in the mist; on the seething limpet-covered rocks the skuas and terns screamed, or uttered hoarse, rasping cries. Ever and again the prolonged note of the oyster-catcher shrilled against the air, as an echo flying blindly along a blank wall of cliff. Out of weedy places, wherein the tide sobbed with long, gurgling moans, came at intervals the barking of a seal.

Inland, by the hamlet of Contullich, there is a reedy tarn called the Loch-a-chaoruinn. By the shores of this mournful water a man moved. It was a slow, weary walk that of the man Neil Ross. He had come from Duninch, thirty miles to the eastward, and had not rested foot, nor eaten, nor had word of man or woman, since his going west an hour after dawn.

At the bend of the loch nearest the clachan he came upon an old woman carrying peat. To his reiterated question as to where he was, and if the tarn were Feur-Lochan above Fionnaphort that is on the strait of Iona on the west side of the Ross of Mull, she did not at first make any answer. The rain trickled down her withered brown face, over which the thin gray locks hung limply. It was only in the deep-set eyes that the flame of life still glimmered, though that dimly.

The man had used the English when first he spoke, but as though mechanically. Supposing that he had not been understood, he repeated his question in the Gaelic.

After a minute's silence the old woman answered him in the native tongue, but only to put a question in return.

"I am thinking it is a long time since you have been in Iona?"

The man stirred uneasily.

"And why is that, mother?" he asked, in a weak voice hoarse with damp and fatigue; "how is it you will be knowing that I have been in Iona at all?"

"Because I knew your kith and kin there, Neil Ross."

"I have not been hearing that name, mother, for many a long year. And as for the old face o' you, it is unbeknown to me."

"I was at the naming of you, for all that. Well do I remember the day that Silis Macallum gave you birth; and I was at the house on the croft of Ballyrona when Murtagh Ross – that was your father – laughed. It was an ill laughing that."

"I am knowing it. The curse of God on him!"

"'Tis not the first, nor the last, though the grass is on his head three years agone now."

"You that know who I am will be knowing that I have no kith or kin now on Iona?"

"Ay; they are all under gray stone or running wave. Donald your brother, and Murtagh your next brother, and little Silis, and your mother Silis herself, and your two brothers of your father, Angus and Ian Macallum, and your father Murtagh Ross, and his lawful childless wife, Dionaid, and his sister Anna – one and all, they lie beneath the green wave or in the brown mould. It is said there is a curse upon all who live at Ballyrona. The owl builds now in the rafters, and it is the big sea-rat that runs across the fireless hearth."

"It is there I am going."

"The foolishness is on you, Neil Ross."

"Now it is that I am knowing who you are. It is old Sheen Macarthur I am speaking to."

"Tha mise...it is I."

"And you will be alone now, too, I am thinking, Sheen?"

"I am alone. God took my three boys at the one fishing ten years ago; and before there was moonrise in the blackness of my heart my man went. It was after the drowning of Anndra that my croft was taken from me. Then I crossed the Sound, and shared with my widow sister Elsie McVurie till *she* went; and then the two cows had to go; and I had no rent, and was old."

In the silence that followed, the rain dribbled from the sodden bracken and dripping loneroid. Big tears rolled slowly down the deep lines on the face of Sheen. Once there was a sob in her throat, but she put her shaking hand to it, and it was still.

Neil Ross shifted from foot to foot. The ooze in that marshy place squelched with each restless movement he made. Beyond them a plover wheeled, a blurred splatch in the mist, crying its mournful cry over and over and over.

It was a pitiful thing to hear – ah, bitter loneliness, bitter patience of poor old women. That he knew well. But he was too weary, and his heart was nigh full of its own burthen. The words could not come to his lips. But at last he spoke.

"Tha mo chridhe goirt," he said, with tears in his voice, as he put his hand on her bent shoulder; "my heart is sore."

She put up her old face against his.

"'S tha e ruidhinn mo chridhe," she whispered; "it is touching my heart you are."

After that they walked on slowly through the dripping mist, each dumb and brooding deep.

"Where will you be staying this night?" asked Sheen suddenly, when they had traversed a wide boggy stretch of land; adding, as by an afterthought – "Ah, it is asking you were if the tarn there were Feur-Lochan. No; it is Loch-a-chaoruinn, and the clachan that is near is Contullich."

"Which way?"

"Yonder, to the right."

"And you are not going there?"

"No. I am going to the steading of Andrew Blair. Maybe you are for knowing it? It is called the Baile-na-Chlais-nambuidheag."

"I do not remember. But it is remembering a Blair I am. He was Adam, the son of Adam, the son of Robert. He and my father did many an ill deed together."

"Ay, to the stones be it said. Sure, now, there was, even till this weary day, no man or woman who had a good word for Adam Blair."

"And why that...why till this day?"

"It is not yet the third hour since he went into the silence."

Neil Ross uttered a sound like a stifled curse. For a time he trudged wearily on.

"Then I am too late," he said at last, but as though speaking to himself. "I had hoped to see him face to face again, and curse him between the eyes. It was he who made Murtagh Ross break his troth to my mother, and marry that other woman, barren at that, God be praised! And they say ill of him, do they?"

"Ay, it is evil that is upon him. This crime and that, God knows; and the shadow of murder on his brow and in his eyes. Well, well, 'tis ill to be speaking of a man in corpse, and that near by. 'Tis Himself only that knows, Neil Ross."

"Maybe ay and maybe no. But where is it that I can be sleeping this night, Sheen Macarthur?"

"They will not be taking a stranger at the farm this night of the nights, I am thinking. There is no place else for seven miles yet, when there is the clachan, before you will be coming to Fionnaphort. There is the warm byre, Neil, my man; or, if you can bide by my peats, you may rest, and welcome, though there is no bed for you, and no food either save some of the porridge that is over."

"And that will do well enough for me, Sheen; and Himself bless you for it."

And so it was.

* * *

After old Sheen Macarthur had given the wayfarer food – poor food at that, but welcome to one nigh starved, and for the heartsome way it was given, and because of the thanks to God that was upon it before even spoon was lifted – she told him a lie. It was the good lie of tender love.

"Sure now, after all, Neil, my man," she said, "it is sleeping at the farm I ought to be, for Maisie Macdonald, the wise woman, will be sitting by the corpse, and there will be none to keep her company. It is there I must be going; and if I am weary, there is a good bed for me just beyond the dead-board, which I am not minding at all. So, if it is tired you are sitting by the peats, lie down on my bed there, and have the sleep; and God be with you."

With that she went, and soundlessly, for Neil Ross was already asleep, where he sat on an upturned claar, with his elbows on his knees, and his flame-lit face in his hands.

The rain had ceased; but the mist still hung over the land, though in thin veils now, and these slowly drifting seaward. Sheen stepped wearily along the stony path that led from her bothy to the farmhouse. She stood still once, the fear upon her, for she saw three or four blurred yellow gleams moving beyond her, eastward, along the dyke. She knew what they were – the corpse-lights that on the night of death go between the bier and the place of burial. More than once she had seen them before the last hour, and by that token had known the end to be near.

Good Catholic that she was, she crossed herself, and took heart. Then muttering

> *"Crois nan naoi aingeal leam*
> *'O mhullach mo chinn*
> *Gu craican mo bhonn."*

> *(The cross of the nine angels be about me,*
> *From the top of my head*
> *To the soles of my feet),*

she went on her way fearlessly.

When she came to the White House, she entered by the milk-shed that was between the byre and the kitchen. At the end of it was a paved place, with washing-tubs. At one of these stood a girl that served in the house – an ignorant lass called Jessie McFall, out of Oban. She was ignorant, indeed, not to know that to wash clothes with a newly dead body near by was an ill thing to do. Was it not a matter for the knowing that the corpse could hear, and might rise up in the night and clothe itself in a clean white shroud?

She was still speaking to the lassie when Maisie Macdonald, the deid-watcher, opened the door of the room behind the kitchen to see who it was that was come. The two old women nodded silently. It was not till Sheen was in the closed room, midway in which something covered with a sheet lay on a board, that any word was spoken.

"Duit sìth mòr, Beann Macdonald."

"And deep peace to you, too, Sheen; and to him that is there."

"Och, ochone, mise 'n diugh; 'tis a dark hour this."

"Ay; it is bad. Will you have been hearing or seeing anything?"

"Well, as for that, I am thinking I saw lights moving betwixt here and the green place over there."

"The corpse-lights?"

"Well, it is calling them that they are."

"I *thought* they would be out. And I have been hearing the noise of the planks – the cracking of the boards, you know, that will be used for the coffin to-morrow."

A long silence followed. The old women had seated themselves by the corpse, their cloaks over their heads. The room was fireless, and was lit only by a tall wax death-candle, kept against the hour of the going.

At last Sheen began swaying slowly to and fro, crooning low the while. "I would not be for doing that, Sheen Macarthur," said the deid-watcher in a low voice, but meaningly; adding, after a moment's pause, *"The mice have all left the house."*

Sheen sat upright, a look half of terror, half of awe in her eyes.

"God save the sinful soul that is hiding," she whispered.

Well she knew what Maisie meant. If the soul of the dead be a lost soul it knows its doom. The house of death is the house of sanctuary; but before the dawn that follows the death-night the soul must go forth, whosoever or whatsoever wait for it in the homeless, shelterless plains of air around and beyond. If it be well with the soul, it need have no fear; if it be not ill with the soul, it may fare forth with surety; but if it be ill with the soul, ill will the going be. Thus is it that the spirit of an evil man cannot stay, and yet dare not go; and so it strives to hide itself in secret places anywhere, in dark channels and blind walls; and the wise creatures that live near man smell the terror, and flee. Maisie repeated the saying of Sheen, then, after a silence, added:

"Adam Blair will not lie in his grave for a year and a day because of the sins that are upon him; and it is knowing that, they are here. He will be the Watcher of the Dead for a year and a day."

"Ay, sure, there will be dark prints in the dawn-dew over yonder."

Once more the old women relapsed into silence. Through the night there was a sighing sound. It was not the sea, which was too far off to be heard save in a day of storm. The wind it was, that was dragging itself across the sodden moors like a wounded thing, moaning and sighing.

Out of sheer weariness, Sheen twice rocked forward from her stool, heavy with sleep. At last Maisie led her over to the niche-bed opposite, and laid her down there, and waited till the deep furrows in the face relaxed somewhat, and the thin breath laboured slow across the fallen jaw.

"Poor old woman," she muttered, heedless of her own gray hairs and grayer years; "a bitter, bad thing it is to be old, old and weary. 'Tis the sorrow, that. God keep the pain of it!"

As for herself, she did not sleep at all that night, but sat between the living and the dead, with her plaid shrouding her. Once, when Sheen gave a low, terrified scream in her sleep, she rose, and in a loud voice cried, *"Sheeach-ad! Away with you!"* And with that she lifted the shroud from the dead man, and took the pennies off the eyelids, and lifted each lid; then, staring into these filmed wells, muttered an ancient incantation that would compel the soul of Adam Blair to leave the spirit of Sheen alone, and return to the cold corpse that was its coffin till the wood was ready.

The dawn came at last. Sheen slept, and Adam Blair slept a deeper sleep, and Maisie stared out of her wan, weary eyes against the red and stormy flares of light that came into the sky.

When, an hour after sunrise, Sheen Macarthur reached her bothy, she found Neil Ross, heavy with slumber, upon her bed. The fire was not out, though no flame or spark was visible; but she stooped and blew at the heart of the peats till the redness came, and once it came it grew. Having done this, she kneeled and said a rune of the morning, and after that a prayer, and then a prayer for the poor man Neil. She could pray no more because of the tears. She rose and put the meal and water into the pot for the porridge to be ready against his awaking. One of the hens that was there came and pecked at her ragged skirt. "Poor beastie," she said. "Sure, that will just be the way I am pulling at the white robe of the Mother o' God. 'Tis a bit meal for you, cluckie, and for me a healing hand upon my tears. O, och, ochone, the tears, the tears!"

It was not till the third hour after sunrise of that bleak day in that winter of the winters, that Neil Ross stirred and arose. He ate in silence. Once he said that he smelt the snow coming out of the north. Sheen said no word at all.

After the porridge, he took his pipe, but there was no tobacco. All that Sheen had was the pipeful she kept against the gloom of the Sabbath. It was her one solace in the long weary week. She gave him this, and held a burning peat to his mouth, and hungered over the thin, rank smoke that curled upward.

It was within half-an-hour of noon that, after an absence, she returned.

"Not between you and me, Neil Ross," she began abruptly, "but just for the asking, and what is beyond. Is it any money you are having upon you?"

"No."

"Nothing?"

"Nothing."

"Then how will you be getting across to Iona? It is seven long miles to Fionnaphort, and bitter cold at that, and you will be needing food, and then the ferry, the ferry across the Sound, you know."

"Ay, I know."

"What would you do for a silver piece, Neil, my man?"

"You have none to give me, Sheen Macarthur; and, if you had, it would not be taking it I would."

"Would you kiss a dead man for a crown-piece – a crown-piece of five good shillings?"

Neil Ross stared. Then he sprang to his feet.

"It is Adam Blair you are meaning, woman! God curse him in death now that he is no longer in life!"

Then, shaking and trembling, he sat down again, and brooded against the dull red glow of the peats.

But, when he rose, in the last quarter before noon, his face was white.

"The dead are dead, Sheen Macarthur. They can know or do nothing. I will do it. It is willed. Yes, I am going up to the house there. And now I am going from here. God Himself has my thanks to you, and my blessing too. They will come back to you. It is not forgetting you I will be. Good-bye."

"Good-bye, Neil, son of the woman that was my friend. A south wind to you! Go up by the farm. In the front of the house you will see what you will be seeing. Maisie Macdonald will be there. She will tell you what's for the telling. There is no harm in it, sure; sure, the dead are dead. It is praying for you I will be, Neil Ross. Peace to you!"

"And to you, Sheen."

And with that the man went.

* * *

When Neil Ross reached the byres of the farm in the wide hollow, he saw two figures standing as though awaiting him, but separate, and unseen of the other. In front of the house was a man he knew to be Andrew Blair; behind the milk-shed was a woman he guessed to be Maisie Macdonald.

It was the woman he came upon first.

"Are you the friend of Sheen Macarthur?" she asked in a whisper, as she beckoned him to the doorway.

"I am."

"I am knowing no names or anything. And no one here will know you, I am thinking. So do the thing and begone."

"There is no harm to it?"

"None."

"It will be a thing often done, is it not?"

"Ay, sure."

"And the evil does not abide?"

"No. The...the...person...the person takes them away, and..."

"Them?"

"For sure, man! Them...the sins of the corpse. He takes them away; and are you for thinking God would let the innocent suffer for the guilty? No...the person...the Sin-Eater, you know...takes them away on himself, and one by one the air of heaven washes them away till he, the Sin-Eater, is clean and whole as before."

"But if it is a man you hate...if it is a corpse that is the corpse of one who has been a curse and a foe...if..."

"Sst! Be still now with your foolishness. It is only an idle saying, I am thinking. Do it, and take the money and go. It will be hell enough for Adam Blair, miser as he was, if he is for knowing that five good shillings of his money are to go to a passing tramp because of an old, ancient silly tale."

Neil Ross laughed low at that. It was for pleasure to him.

"Hush wi' ye! Andrew Blair is waiting round there. Say that I have sent you round, as I have neither bite nor bit to give."

Turning on his heel, Neil walked slowly round to the front of the house. A tall man was there, gaunt and brown, with hairless face and lank brown hair, but with eyes cold and gray as the sea.

"Good day to you, an' good faring. Will you be passing this way to anywhere?"

"Health to you. I am a stranger here. It is on my way to Iona I am. But I have the hunger upon me. There is not a brown bit in my pocket. I asked at the door there, near the byres. The woman told me she could give me nothing – not a penny even, worse luck – nor, for that, a drink of warm milk. 'Tis a sore land this."

"You have the Gaelic of the Isles. Is it from Iona you are?"

"It is from the Isles of the West I come."

"From Tiree…from Coll?"

"No."

"From the Long Island…or from Uist…or maybe from Benbecula?"

"No."

"Oh well, sure it is no matter to me. But may I be asking your name?"

"Macallum."

"Do you know there is a death here, Macallum?"

"If I didn't I would know it now, because of what lies yonder."

Mechanically Andrew Blair looked round. As he knew, a rough bier was there, that was made of a dead-board laid upon three milking-stools. Beside it was a claar, a small tub to hold potatoes. On the bier was a corpse, covered with a canvas sheeting that looked like a sail.

"He was a worthy man, my father," began the son of the dead man, slowly; "but he had his faults, like all of us. I might even be saying that he had his sins, to the Stones be it said. You will be knowing, Macallum, what is thought among the folk…that a stranger, passing by, may take away the sins of the dead, and that, too, without any hurt whatever…any hurt whatever."

"Ay, sure."

"And you will be knowing what is done?"

"Ay."

"With the bread…and the water…?"

"Ay."

"It is a small thing to do. It is a Christian thing. I would be doing it myself, and that gladly, but the...the...passer-by who..."

"It is talking of the Sin-Eater you are?"

"Yes, yes, for sure. The Sin-Eater as he is called – and a good Christian act it is, for all that the ministers and the priests make a frowning at it – the Sin-Eater must be a stranger. He must be a stranger, and should know nothing of the dead man – above all, bear him no grudge."

At that Neil Ross's eyes lightened for a moment.

"And why that?"

"Who knows? I have heard this, and I have heard that. If the Sin-Eater was hating the dead man he could take the sins and fling them into the sea, and they would be changed into demons of the air that would harry the flying soul till Judgment-Day."

"And how would that thing be done?"

The man spoke with flashing eyes and parted lips, the breath coming swift. Andrew Blair looked at him suspiciously; and hesitated, before, in a cold voice, he spoke again.

"That is all folly, I am thinking, Macallum. Maybe it is all folly, the whole of it. But, see here, I have no time to be talking with you. If you will take the bread and the water you shall have a good meal if you want it, and...and...yes, look you, my man, I will be giving you a shilling too, for luck."

"I will have no meal in this house, Anndramhic-Adam; nor will I do this thing unless you will be giving me two silver half-crowns. That is the sum I must have, or no other."

"Two half-crowns! Why, man, for one half-crown..."

"Then be eating the sins o' your father yourself, Andrew Blair! It is going I am."

"Stop, man! Stop, Macallum. See here – I will be giving you what you ask."

"So be it. Is the…Are you ready?"

"Ay, come this way."

With that the two men turned and moved slowly towards the bier.

In the doorway of the house stood a man and two women; farther in, a woman; and at the window to the left, the serving-wench, Jessie McFall, and two men of the farm. Of those in the doorway, the man was Peter, the half-witted youngest brother of Andrew Blair; the taller and older woman was Catreen, the widow of Adam, the second brother; and the thin, slight woman, with staring eyes and drooping mouth, was Muireall, the wife of Andrew. The old woman behind these was Maisie Macdonald.

Andrew Blair stooped and took a saucer out of the claar. This he put upon the covered breast of the corpse. He stooped again, and brought forth a thick square piece of new-made bread. That also he placed upon the breast of the corpse. Then he stooped again, and with that he emptied a spoonful of salt alongside the bread.

"I must see the corpse," said Neil Ross simply.

"It is not needful, Macallum."

"I must be seeing the corpse, I tell you – and for that, too, the bread and the water should be on the naked breast."

"No, no, man; it…"

But here a voice, that of Maisie the wise woman, came upon them, saying that the man was right, and that the eating of the sins should be done in that way and no other.

With an ill grace the son of the dead man drew back the sheeting. Beneath it, the corpse was in a clean white shirt, a death-gown long ago prepared, that covered him from his neck to his feet, and left only the dusky yellowish face exposed.

While Andrew Blair unfastened the shirt and placed the saucer and the bread and the salt on the breast, the man beside him stood staring fixedly on the frozen features of the corpse. The new laird had to speak to him twice before he heard.

"I am ready. And you, now? What is it you are muttering over against the lips of the dead?"

"It is giving him a message I am. There is no harm in that, sure?"

"Keep to your own folk, Macallum. You are from the West you say, and we are from the North. There can be no messages between you and a Blair of Strathmore, no messages for *you* to be giving."

"He that lies here knows well the man to whom I am sending a message" – and at this response Andrew Blair scowled darkly. He would fain have sent the man about his business, but he feared he might get no other.

"It is thinking I am that you are not a Macallum at all. I know all of that name in Mull, Iona, Skye, and the near isles. What will the name of your naming be, and of your father, and of his place?"

Whether he really wanted an answer, or whether he sought only to divert the man from his procrastination, his question had a satisfactory result.

"Well, now, it's ready I am, Anndra-mhic-Adam."

With that, Andrew Blair stooped once more and from the claar brought a small jug of water. From this he filled the saucer.

"You know what to say and what to do, Macallum."

There was not one there who did not have a shortened breath because of the mystery that was now before them, and the fearfulness of it. Neil Ross drew himself up, erect, stiff, with white, drawn face. All who waited, save Andrew Blair, thought that the moving of his lips was because of the prayer that was slipping upon them, like the last lapsing of the ebb-tide. But Blair was watching him closely, and knew that it was no prayer which stole out against the blank air that was around the dead.

Slowly Neil Ross extended his right arm. He took a pinch of the salt and put it in the saucer, then took another pinch and sprinkled it upon the bread. His hand shook for a moment as he touched the saucer. But there was no shaking as he raised it towards his lips, or when he held it before him when he spoke.

"With this water that has salt in it, and has lain on thy corpse, O Adam mhic Anndra mhic Adam Mòr, I drink away all the evil that is upon thee…"

There was throbbing silence while he paused.

"…And may it be upon me and not upon thee, if with this water it cannot flow away."

Thereupon, he raised the saucer and passed it thrice round the head of the corpse sunways; and, having done this, lifted it to his lips and drank as much as his mouth would hold. Thereafter he poured the remnant over his left hand, and let it trickle to the ground. Then he took the piece of bread. Thrice, too, he passed it round the head of the corpse sunways.

He turned and looked at the man by his side, then at the others, who watched him with beating hearts.

With a loud clear voice he took the sins.

"*Thoir dhomh do ciontachd, O Adam mhic Anndra mhic Adam Mòr!* Give me thy sins to take away from thee! Lo, now, as I stand here, I break this bread that has lain on thee in corpse, and I am eating it, I am, and in that eating I take upon me the sins of thee, O man that was alive and is now white with the stillness!"

Thereupon Neil Ross broke the bread and ate of it, and took upon himself the sins of Adam Blair that was dead. It was a bitter swallowing, that. The remainder of the bread he crumbled in his hand, and threw it on the ground, and trod upon it. Andrew Blair gave a sigh of relief. His cold eyes lightened with malice.

"Be off with you, now, Macallum. We are wanting no tramps at the farm here, and perhaps you had better not be trying to get work this side Iona; for it is known as the Sin-Eater you will be, and that won't be for the helping, I am thinking! There – there are the two half-crowns for you...and may they bring you no harm, you that are *Scapegoat* now!

The Sin-Eater turned at that, and stared like a hill-bull. *Scapegoat!* Ay, that's what he was. Sin-Eater, Scapegoat! Was he not, too, another Judas, to have sold for silver that which was not for the selling? No, no, for sure Maisie Macdonald could tell him the rune that would serve for the easing of this burden. He would soon be quit of it.

Slowly he took the money, turned it over, and put it in his pocket.

"I am going, Andrew Blair," he said quietly, "I am going now. I will not say to him that is there in the silence, A chuid do Pharas da! – nor will I say to you, Gu'n gleidheadh Dia thu, – nor will I say to this dwelling that is the home of thee and thine, Gu'n beannaic-headh Dia an tigh!"

Here there was a pause. All listened. Andrew Blair shifted uneasily, the furtive eyes of him going this way and that, like a ferret in the grass.

"But, Andrew Blair, I will say this: when you fare abroad, *Droch caoidh ort!* and when you go upon the water, *Gaoth gun direadh ort!*

Ay, ay, Anndra-mhic-Adam, *Dia ad aghaidh 's ad aodann…agus bas dunach ort! Dhonas 's dholas ort, agus leat-sa!*"

The bitterness of these words was like snow in June upon all there. They stood amazed. None spoke. No one moved.

Neil Ross turned upon his heel, and, with a bright light in his eyes, walked away from the dead and the living. He went by the byres, whence he had come. Andrew Blair remained where he was, now glooming at the corpse, now biting his nails and staring at the damp sods at his feet.

When Neil reached the end of the milk-shed he saw Maisie Macdonald there, waiting.

"These were ill sayings of yours, Neil Ross," she said in a low voice, so that she might not be overheard from the house.

"So, it is knowing me you are."

"Sheen Macarthur told me."

"I have good cause."

"That is a true word. I know it."

"Tell me this thing. What is the rune that is said for the throwing into the sea of the sins of the dead? See here, Maisie Macdonald. There is no money of that man that I would carry a mile with me. Here it is. It is yours, if you will tell me that rune."

Maisie took the money hesitatingly. Then, stooping, she said slowly the few lines of the old, old rune.

"Will you be remembering that?"

"It is not forgetting it I will be, Maisie."

"Wait a moment. There is some warm milk here."

With that she went, and then, from within, beckoned to him to enter.

"There is no one here, Neil Ross. Drink the milk."

He drank; and while he did so she drew a leather pouch from some hidden place in her dress.

"And now I have this to give you."

She counted out ten pennies and two farthings.

"It is all the coppers I have. You are welcome to them. Take them, friend of my friend. They will give you the food you need, and the ferry across the Sound."

"I will do that, Maisie Macdonald, and thanks to you. It is not forgetting it I will be, nor you, good woman. And now, tell me, is it safe that I am? He called me a 'scapegoat', he, Andrew Blair! Can evil touch me between this and the sea?"

"You must go to the place where the evil was done to you and yours – and that, I know, is on the west side of Iona. Go, and God preserve you. But here, too, is a sian that will be for the safety."

Thereupon, with swift mutterings she said this charm: an old, familiar Sian against Sudden Harm:

> *"Sian a chuir Moire air Mac ort,*
> *Sian ro' marbhadh, sian ro' lot ort,*
> *Sian eadar a' chlioch 's a' ghlun,*
> *Sian nan Tri ann an aon ort,*
> *O mhullach do chinn gu bonn do chois ort:*
> *Sian seachd eadar a h-aon ort,*
> *Sian seachd eadar a dha ort,*
> *Sian seachd eadar a tri ort,*
> *Sian seachd eadar a ceithir ort,*
> *Sian seachd eadar a coig ort,*
> *Sian seachd eadar a sia ort,*

*Sian seachd paidir nan seach paidir dol deiseil ri
diugh narach ort, ga do ghleidheadh bho bheud 's
bho mhi-thapadh!"*

Scarcely had she finished before she heard heavy steps approaching.

"Away with you," she whispered, repeating in a loud, angry tone, "Away with you! *Seachad! Seachad!"*

And with that Neil Ross slipped from the milk-shed and crossed the yard, and was behind the byres before Andrew Blair, with sullen mien and swift, wild eyes, strode from the house.

It was with a grim smile on his face that Neil tramped down the wet heather till he reached the high road, and fared thence as through a marsh because of the rains there had been.

For the first mile he thought of the angry mind of the dead man, bitter at paying of the silver. For the second mile he thought of the evil that had been wrought for him and his. For the third mile he pondered over all that he had heard and done and taken upon him that day.

Then he sat down upon a broken granite heap by the way, and brooded deep till one hour went, and then another, and the third was upon him.

A man driving two calves came towards him out of the west. He did not hear or see. The man stopped; spoke again. Neil gave no answer. The drover shrugged his shoulders, hesitated, and walked slowly on, often looking back.

An hour later a shepherd came by the way he himself had tramped. He was a tall, gaunt man with a squint. The small, pale-blue eyes glittered out of a mass of red hair that almost covered his face. He stood still, opposite Neil, and leaned on his *cromak.*

"Latha math leat," he said at last; "I wish you good day."

Neil glanced at him, but did not speak.

"What is your name, for I seem to know you?"

But Neil had already forgotten him. The shepherd took out his snuff-mull, helped himself, and handed the mull to the lonely wayfarer. Neil mechanically helped himself.

"Am bheil thu 'dol do Fhionphort?" tried the shepherd again: "Are you going to Fionnaphort?"

"Tha mise 'dol a dh' I-challum-chille," Neil answered, in a low, weary voice, and as a man adream: "I am on my way to Iona."

"I am thinking I know now who you are. You are the man Macallum."

Neil looked, but did not speak. His eyes dreamed against what the other could not see or know. The shepherd called angrily to his dogs to keep the sheep from straying; then, with a resentful air, turned to his victim.

"You are a silent man for sure, you are. I'm hoping it is not the curse upon you already."

"What curse?"

"Ah, *that* has brought the wind against the mist! I was thinking so!"

"What curse?"

"You are the man that was the Sin-Eater over there?"

"Ay."

"The man Macallum?"

"Ay."

"Strange it is, but three days ago I saw you in Tobermory, and heard you give your name as Neil Ross to an Iona man that was there."

"Well?"

"Oh, sure, it is nothing to me. But they say the Sin-Eater should not be a man with a hidden lump in his pack."

"Why?"

"For the dead know, and are content. There is no shaking off any sins, then – for that man."

"It is a lie."

"Maybe ay and maybe no."

"Well, have you more to be saying to me? I am obliged to you for your company, but it is not needing it I am, though no offense."

"Och, man, there's no offense between you and me. Sure, there's Iona in me, too; for the father of my father married a woman that was the granddaughter of Tomais Macdonald, who was a fisherman there. No, no; it is rather warning you I would be."

"And for what?"

"Well, well, just because of that laugh I heard about."

"What laugh?"

"The laugh of Adam Blair that is dead."

Neil Ross stared, his eyes large and wild. He leaned a little forward. No word came from him. The look that was on his face was the question.

"Yes, it was this way. Sure, the telling of it is just as I heard it. After you ate the sins of Adam Blair, the people there brought out the coffin. When they were putting him into it, he was as stiff as a sheep dead in the snow – and just like that, too, with his eyes wide open. Well, someone saw you trampling the heather down the slope that is in front of the house, and said, 'It is the Sin-Eater!' With that, Andrew Blair sneered, and said – 'Ay, 'tis the scapegoat he is!' Then, after a while, he went on, 'The Sin-Eater they call him; ay, just so; and a bitter good bargain it is, too, if all's true that's thought true!' And with that he laughed, and then his wife that was behind him laughed, and then…"

"Well, what then?"

"Well, 'tis Himself that hears and knows if it is true! But this is the thing I was told: After that laughing there was a stillness and a dread. For all there saw that the corpse had turned its head and was looking after you as you went down the heather. Then, Neil Ross, if that be your true name, Adam Blair that was dead put up his white face against the sky, and laughed."

At this, Ross sprang to his feet with a gasping sob.

"It is a lie, that thing!" he cried, shaking his fist at the shepherd. "It is a lie."

"It is no lie. And by the same token, Andrew Blair shrank back white and shaking, and his woman had the swoon upon her, and who knows but the corpse might have come to life again had it not been for Maisie Macdonald, the deid-watcher, who clapped a handful of salt on his eyes, and tilted the coffin so that the bottom of it slid forward, and so let the whole fall flat on the ground, with Adam Blair in it sideways, and as likely as not cursing and groaning, as his wont was, for the hurt both to his old bones and his old ancient dignity."

Ross glared at the man as though the madness was upon him. Fear and horror and fierce rage swung him now this way and now that.

"What will the name of you be, shepherd?" he stuttered huskily.

"It is Eachainn Gilleasbuig I am to ourselves; and the English of that for those who have no Gaelic is Hector Gillespie; and I am Eachainn mac Ian mac Alasdair of Strathsheean that is where Sutherland lies against Ross."

"Then take this thing – and that is, the curse of the Sin-Eater! And a bitter bad thing may it be upon you and yours."

And with that Neil the Sin-Eater flung his hand up into the air, and then leaped past the shepherd, and a minute later was running through the frightened sheep, with his head low, and a white foam on his lips, and his eyes red with blood as a seal's that has the death-wound on it.

* * *

On the third day of the seventh month from that day, Aulay Macneill, coming into Balliemore of Iona from the west side of the island, said to old Ronald MacCormick, that was the father of his wife, that he had seen Neil Ross again, and that he was "absent" – for though he had spoken to him, Neil would not answer, but only gloomed at him from the wet weedy rock where he sat.

The going back of the man had loosed every tongue that was in Iona. When, too, it was known that he was wrought in some terrible way, if not actually mad, the islanders whispered that it was because of the sins of Adam Blair. Seldom or never now did they speak of him by his name, but simply as "The Sin-Eater." The thing was not so rare as to cause this strangeness, nor did many (and perhaps none did) think that the sins of the dead ever might or could abide with the living who had merely done a good Christian charitable thing. But there was a reason.

Not long after Neil Ross had come again to Iona, and had settled down in the ruined roofless house on the croft of Ballyrona, just like a fox or a wild-cat, as the saying was, he was given fishing-work to do by Aulay Macneill, who lived at Ard-an-teine, at the rocky north end of the machar or plain that is on the west Atlantic coast of the island.

One moonlit night, either the seventh or the ninth after the earthing of Adam Blair at his own place in the Ross, Aulay Macneill saw Neil Ross steal out of the shadow of Ballyrona and make for the sea. Macneill was there by the rocks, mending a lobster-creel. He had gone there because of the sadness. Well, when he saw the Sin-Eater, he watched.

Neil crept from rock to rock till he reached the last fang that churns the sea into yeast when the tide sucks the land just opposite.

Then he called out something that Aulay Macneill could not catch. With that he springs up, and throws his arms above him.

"Then," says Aulay when he tells the tale, "it was like a ghost he was. The moonshine was on his face like the curl o' a wave. White! there is no whiteness like that of the human face. It was whiter than the foam about the skerry it was; whiter than the moon shining; whiter than...well, as white as the painted letters on the black boards of the fishing-cobles. There he stood, for all that the sea was about him, the slip-slop waves leapin' wild, and the tide making, too, at that. He was shaking like a sail two points off the wind. It was then that, all of a sudden, he called in a womany, screamin' voice –

"'I am throwing the sins of Adam Blair into the midst of ye, white dogs o' the sea! Drown them, tear them, drag them away out into the black deeps! Ay, ay, ay, ye dancin' wild waves, this is the third time I am doing it, and now there is none left; no, not a sin, not a sin!

> "'O-hi O-ri, dark tide o' the sea,
> I am giving the sins of a dead man to thee!
> By the Stones, by the Wind, by the Fire, by the Tree,
> From the dead man's sins set me free, set me free!
> Adam mhic Anndra mhic Adam and me,
> Set us free! Set us free!'

"Ay, sure, the Sin-Eater sang that over and over; and after the third singing he swung his arms and screamed:

> "'And listen to me, black waters an' running tide,
> That rune is the good rune told me by Maisie the wise,
> And I am Neil the son of Silis Macallum
> By the black-hearted evil man Murtagh Ross,
> That was the friend of Adam mac Anndra, God against him!'

"And with that he scrambled and fell into the sea. But, as I am Aulay mac Luais and no other, he was up in a moment, an' swimmin' like a seal, and then over the rocks again, an' away back to that lonely roofless place once more, laughing wild at times, an' muttering an' whispering."

It was this tale of Aulay Macneill's that stood between Neil Ross and the isle-folk. There was something behind all that, they whispered one to another.

So it was always the Sin-Eater he was called at last. None sought him. The few children who came upon him now and again fled at his approach, or at the very sight of him. Only Aulay Macneill saw him at times, and had word of him.

After a month had gone by, all knew that the Sin-Eater was wrought to madness because of this awful thing: the burden of Adam Blair's sins would not go from him! Night and day he could hear them laughing low, it was said.

But it was the quiet madness. He went to and fro like a shadow in the grass, and almost as soundless as that, and as voiceless. More and more the name of him grew as a terror. There were few folk on that

wild west coast of Iona, and these few avoided him when the word
ran that he had knowledge of strange things, and converse, too, with
the secrets of the sea.

One day Aulay Macneill, in his boat, but dumb with amaze and
terror for him, saw him at high tide swimming on a long rolling wave
right into the hollow of the Spouting Cave. In the memory of man, no
one had done this and escaped one of three things: a snatching away
into oblivion, a strangled death, or madness. The islanders know
that there swims into the cave, at full tide, a Mar-Tarbh, a dreadful
creature of the sea that some call a kelpie; only it is not a kelpie, which
is like a woman, but rather is a sea-bull, offspring of the cattle that
are never seen. Ill indeed for any sheep or goat, ay, or even dog or
child, if any happens to be leaning over the edge of the Spouting Cave
when the Mar-tarv roars; for, of a surety, it will fall in and straightway
be devoured.

With awe and trembling Aulay listened for the screaming of the
doomed man. It was full tide, and the sea-beast would be there.

The minutes passed, and no sign. Only the hollow booming of
the sea, as it moved like a baffled blind giant round the cavern-
bases; only the rush and spray of the water flung up the narrow
shaft high into the windy air above the cliff it penetrates.

At last he saw what looked like a mass of seaweed swirled out on
the surge. It was the Sin-Eater. With a leap, Aulay was at his oars.
The boat swung through the sea. Just before Neil Ross was about
to sink for the second time, he caught him and dragged him into
the boat.

But then, as ever after, nothing was to be got out of the Sin-Eater
save a single saying: Tha e lamhan fuar! Tha e lamhan fuar! – "It
has a cold, cold hand!"

The telling of this and other tales left none free upon the island to look upon the "scapegoat" save as one accursed.

It was in the third month that a new phase of his madness came upon Neil Ross.

The horror of the sea and the passion for the sea came over him at the same happening. Oftentimes he would race along the shore, screaming wild names to it, now hot with hate and loathing, now as the pleading of a man with the woman of his love. And strange chants to it, too, were upon his lips. Old, old lines of forgotten runes were overheard by Aulay Macneill, and not Aulay only; lines wherein the ancient sea-name of the island, *Ioua,* that was given to it long before it was called Iona, or any other of the nine names that are said to belong to it, occurred again and again.

The flowing tide it was that wrought him thus. At the ebb he would wander across the weedy slabs or among the rocks, silent, and more like a lost duinshee than a man.

Then again after three months a change in his madness came. None knew what it was, though Aulay said that the man moaned and moaned because of the awful burden he bore. No drowning seas for the sins that could not be washed away, no grave for the live sins that would be quick till the day of the Judgment!

For weeks thereafter he disappeared. As to where he was, it is not for the knowing.

Then at last came that third day of the seventh month when, as I have said, Aulay Macneill told old Ronald MacCormick that he had seen the Sin-Eater again.

It was only a half-truth that he told, though. For, after he had seen Neil Ross upon the rock, he had followed him when he rose, and wandered back to the roofless place which he haunted now as of yore. Less wretched a shelter now it was, because of the summer that was come, though a cold, wet summer at that.

"Is that you, Neil Ross?" he had asked, as he peered into the shadows among the ruins of the house.

"That's not my name," said the Sin-Eater; and he seemed as strange then and there, as though he were a castaway from a foreign ship.

"And what will it be, then, you that are my friend, and sure knowing me as Aulay mac Luais – Aulay Macneill that never grudges you bit or sup?"

"I am Judas."

* * *

"And at that word," says Aulay Macneill, when he tells the tale, "at that word the pulse in my heart was like a bat in a shut room. But after a bit I took up the talk.

"'Indeed,' I said; 'and I was not for knowing that. May I be so bold as to ask whose son, and of what place?'

"But all he said to me was, *'I am Judas.'*

"Well, I said, to comfort him, 'Sure, it's not such a bad name in itself, though I am knowing some which have a more home-like sound.' But no, it was no good.

"'I am Judas. And because I sold the Son of God for five pieces of silver...'

"But here I interrupted him and said, 'Sure, now, Neil – I mean, Judas – it was eight times five.' Yet the simpleness of his sorrow prevailed, and I listened with the wet in my eyes.

"'I am Judas. And because I sold the Son of God for five silver shillings, He laid upon me all the nameless black sins of the world. And that is why I am bearing them till the Day of Days.'"

* * *

And this was the end of the Sin-Eater; for I will not tell the long story of Aulay Macneill, that gets longer and longer every winter; but only the unchanging close of it.

I will tell it in the words of Aulay.

* * *

"A bitter, wild day it was, that day I saw him to see him no more. It was late. The sea was red with the flamin' light that burned up the air betwixt Iona and all that is west of West. I was on the shore, looking at the sea. The big green waves came in like the chariots in the Holy Book. Well, it was on the black shoulder of one of them, just short of the ton o' foam that swept above it, that I saw a spar surgin' by.

"'What is that?' I said to myself. And the reason of my wondering was this: I saw that a smaller spar was swung across it. And while I was watching that thing another great billow came in with a roar, and hurled the double spar back, and not so far from me but I might have gripped it. But who would have gripped that thing if he were for seeing what I saw?

"It is Himself knows that what I say is a true thing.

"On that spar was Neil Ross, the Sin-Eater. Naked he was as the day he was born. And he was lashed, too – ay, sure, he was lashed to it by ropes round and round his legs and his waist and his left arm. It was the Cross he was on. I saw that thing with the fear upon me. Ah, poor drifting wreck that he was! *Judas on the Cross!* It was his *eric!*

"But even as I watched, shaking in my limbs, I saw that there was life in him still. The lips were moving, and his right arm was ever for swinging this way and that. 'Twas like an oar, working him off a lee shore; ay, that was what I thought.

"Then, all at once, he caught sight of me. Well he knew me, poor man, that has his share of heaven now, I am thinking!

"He waved, and called, but the hearing could not be, because of a big surge o' water that came tumbling down upon him. In the stroke of an oar he was swept close by the rocks where I was standing. In that flounderin', seethin' whirlpool I saw the white face of him for a moment, an' as he went out on the re-surge like a hauled net, I heard these words fallin' against my ears:

"'An eirig m'anama…In ransom for my soul!'

"And with that I saw the double-spar turn over and slide down the back-sweep of a drowning big wave. Ay, sure, it went out to the deep sea swift enough then. It was in the big eddy that rushes between Skerry-Mòr and Skerry-Beag. I did not see it again – no, not for the quarter of an hour, I am thinking. Then I saw just the whirling top of it rising out of the flying yeast of a great, black-blustering wave, that was rushing northward before the current that is called the Black-Eddy.

"With that you have the end of Neil Ross; ay, sure, him that was called the Sin-Eater. And that is a true thing; and may God save us the sorrow of sorrows.

"And that is all."

The Ghost of the Hindu Child
or, the Hauntings of the
White Dove Hotel
Elliott O'Donnell

In the course of many years' investigation of haunted houses, I have naturally come in contact with numerous people who have had first-hand experiences with the Occult. Nurse Mackenzie is one of these people. I met her for the first time last year at the house of my old friend, Colonel Malcolmson, whose wife she was nursing.

For some days I was hardly aware she was in the house, the illness of her patient keeping her in constant seclusion, but when Mrs. Malcolmson grew better, I not infrequently saw her, taking a morning "constitutional" in the beautiful castle grounds. It was on one of these occasions that she favoured me with an account of her psychical adventure.

It happened, she began, shortly after I had finished my term as probationer at St. K.'s Hospital, Edinburgh. A letter was received at the hospital one morning with the urgent request that two nurses should be sent to a serious case near St. Swithin's Street. As the letter was signed by a well-known physician in the town, it received immediate attention, and Nurse Emmett and I were dispatched, as day and night nurses respectively, to the scene of action. My hours on duty were from 9 p.m. till 9 a.m. The house in which the patient was located was the White Dove Hotel, a thoroughly respectable and well-managed establishment. The proprietor knew nothing about the invalid, except that her name was Vining, and that she had, at one period of her career, been an actress. He had noticed that she had looked ill on her arrival the previous week. Two days after her arrival, she had complained of feeling very ill, and the doctor, who had been summoned to attend her, said that she was suffering from a very loathsome Oriental disease, which, fortunately is, in this country, rare. The hotel, though newly decorated and equipped throughout with every up-to-date convenience, was in reality very old. It was one of those delightfully roomy erections that seem built for eternity rather than time, and for comfort rather than economy of space. The interior, with its oak-panelled walls, polished oak floors, and low ceilings, traversed with ponderous oaken beams, also impressed me pleasantly, whilst a flight of broad, oak stairs, fenced with balustrades a foot thick, brought me to a seemingly interminable corridor, into which the door of Miss Vining's room opened. It was a low, wainscoted apartment, and its deep-set window, revealing the thickness of the wall, looked out upon a dismal yard littered with brooms and buckets. Opposite the foot of the bed – a modern French bedstead, by the bye, whose brass fittings and somewhat flimsy hangings were strangely incongruous with their venerable surroundings – was an ingle, containing the smouldering relics of what had doubtless been intended for a fire, but which needed considerable coaxing before it could be converted from a pretence to a reality. There was no exit save by the doorway I had entered, and no furniture save a couple of rush-bottomed chairs and a table strewn with an untidy medley of writing materials and medicine bottles.

A feeling of depression, contrasting strangely with the effect produced on me by the cheerfulness of the hotel in general, seized me directly I entered the room. Despite the brilliancy of the electric light and the new and gaudy bed-hangings, the air was full of gloom – a gloom which, for the very reason that it was unaccountable, was the more alarming. I felt it hanging around me like the undeveloped shadow of something singularly hideous and repulsive, and, on my approaching the sick woman, it seemed to thrust itself in my way and force me back.

Miss Vining was decidedly good-looking; she had the typically theatrical features – neatly moulded nose and chin, curly yellow hair, and big, dreamy blue eyes that especially appeal to a certain class of men; like most women, however, I prefer something more solid, both physically and intellectually – I cannot stand "the pretty, pretty." She was, of course, far too ill to converse, and, beyond a few desultory and spasmodic ejaculations, maintained a rigid silence. As there was no occasion for me to sit close beside her, I drew up a chair before the fire, placing myself in such a position as to command a full view of the bed. My first night passed undisturbed by any incident, and in the morning the condition of my patient showed a slight improvement. It was eight o'clock in the evening when I came on duty again, and, the weather having changed during the day, the whole room echoed and re-echoed with the howling of the wind, which was raging round the house with demoniacal fury.

I had been at my post for a little over two hours – and had just registered my patient's temperature, when, happening to look up from the book I was reading, I saw to my surprise that the chair beside the head of the bed was occupied by a child – a tiny girl. How she had come into the room without attracting my attention was certainly extraordinary, and I could only suppose that the shrieking of the wind down the wide chimney had deadened the sound of the door and her footsteps.

I was naturally, of course, very indignant that she had dared to come in without rapping, and, getting up from my seat I was preparing to address her and bid her go, when she lifted a wee white hand and motioned me back. I obeyed because I could not help myself – her action was accompanied by a peculiar, – an unpleasantly peculiar, expression that held me spellbound; and without exactly knowing why, I stood staring at her, tongue-tied and trembling. As her face was turned towards the patient, and she wore, moreover, a very wide-brimmed hat, I could see nothing of her features; but from her graceful little figure and dainty limbs, I gathered that she was probably both beautiful and aristocratic. Her dress, though not perhaps of the richest quality, was certainly far from shoddy, and there was something in its style and make that suggested foreign nationality, – Italy – or Spain – or South America – or even the Orient, the probability of the latter being strengthened by her pose, which was full of the serpent-like ease which is characteristic of the East. I was so taken up with watching her that I forgot all about my patient, until a prolonged sigh from the bed reminded me of her existence. With an effort I then advanced, and was about to approach the bed, when the child, without moving her head, motioned me back, and – again I was helpless. The vision I had obtained of the sick woman, brief though it was, filled me with alarm. She was tossing to and fro on the blankets, and breathing in the most agonised manner as if in delirium, or enthralled by some particularly dreadful nightmare. Her condition so frightened me, that I made the most frantic efforts to overcome my inertia. I did not succeed, however, and at last, utterly overcome by my exertion, I closed my eyes. When I opened them again, the chair by the bed was vacant – the child had gone. A tremendous feeling of relief surged through me, and, jumping out of my seat, I hastened to the bedside – my patient was worse, the fever had increased, and she was delirious. I took her temperature. It was 104. I now sat close beside her, and my presence apparently had a soothing effect. She speedily grew calmer, and after taking her medicine gradually sank into a gentle sleep which lasted until late in the morning. When I left her she had altogether recovered from the relapse. I, of course, told the doctor of the child's visit, and he was very angry.

"Whatever happens, Nurse," he said, "take care that no one enters the room to-night; the patient's condition is far too critical for her to see any one, even her own daughter. You must keep the door locked."

Armed with this mandate, I went on duty the following night with a somewhat lighter heart, and, after locking the door, once again sat by the fire. During the day there had been a heavy fall of snow; the wind had abated, and the streets were now as silent as the grave.

Ten, eleven, and twelve o'clock struck, and my patient slept tranquilly. At a quarter to one, however, I was abruptly roused from a reverie by a sob, a sob of fear and agony that proceeded from the bed. I looked, and there – there, seated in the same posture as on the previous evening, was the child. I sprang to my feet with an exclamation of amazement. She raised her hand, and, as before, I collapsed – spellbound – paralysed. No words of mine can convey all the sensations I experienced as I sat there, forced to listen to the moaning and groaning of the woman whose fate had been entrusted to my keeping. Every second she grew worse, and each sound rang in my ears like the hammering of nails in her coffin. How long I endured such torment I cannot say, I dare not think, for, though the clock was within a few feet of me, I never once thought of looking at it. At last the child rose, and, moving slowly from the bed, advanced with bowed head towards the window. The spell was broken. With a cry of indignation I literally bounded over the carpet and faced the intruder.

"Who are you?" I hissed. "Tell me your name instantly! How dare you enter this room without my permission?"

As I spoke she slowly raised her head. I snatched at her hat. It melted away in my hands, and, to my unspeakable terror, my undying terror, I looked into the face of a corpse! – the corpse of a Hindu child, with a big, gaping cut in its throat. In its lifetime the child had, without doubt, been lovely; it was now horrible – horrible with all the ghastly disfigurements, the repellent disfigurements, of a long consignment to the grave. I fainted, and, on recovering, found my ghostly visitor had vanished, and that my patient was dead. One of her hands was thrown across her eyes, as if to shut out some object on which she feared to look, whilst the other grasped the counterpane convulsively.

It fell to my duty to help pack up her belongings, and among her letters was a large envelope bearing the postmark "Quetta." As we were on the look-out for some clue as to the address of her relatives, I opened it. It was merely the cabinet-size photograph of a Hindu child, but I recognised the dress immediately – it was that of my ghostly visitor. On the back of it were these words: "Natalie. May God forgive us both."

Though we made careful inquiries for any information as to Natalie and Miss Vining in Quetta, and advertised freely in the leading London papers, we learned nothing, and in time we were forced to let the matter drop. As far as I know, the ghost of the Hindu child has never been seen again, but I have heard that the hotel is still haunted – haunted by a woman.

Glamis Castle

Elliott O'Donnell

Of all the hauntings in Scotland, none has gained such widespread notoriety as the hauntings of Glamis Castle, the seat of the Earl of Strathmore and Kinghorne in Forfarshire.

Part of the castle – that part which is the more frequently haunted – is of ancient though uncertain date, and if there is any truth in the tradition that Duncan was murdered there by Macbeth, must, at any rate, have been in existence at the commencement of the eleventh century. Of course, extra buildings have, from time to time, been added, and renovations made; but the original structure remains pretty nearly the same as it always has been, and is included in a square tower that occupies a central position, and commands a complete view of the entire castle.

Within this tower – the walls of which are fifteen feet thick – there is a room, hidden in some unsuspected quarter, that contains a secret (the keynote to one, at least, of the hauntings) which is known only to the Earl, his heir (on the attainment of his twenty-first birthday), and the factor of the estate.

In all probability, the mystery attached to this room would challenge but little attention, were it not for the fact that unearthly noises, which at the time were supposed to proceed from this chamber, have been heard by various visitors sleeping in the Square Tower.

The following experience is said to have happened to a lady named Bond. I append it more or less in her own words.

* * *

It is a good many years since I stayed at Glamis. I was, in fact, but little more than a child, and had only just gone through my first season in town. But though young, I was neither nervous nor imaginative; I was inclined to be what is termed stolid, that is to say, extremely matter-of-fact and practical. Indeed, when my friends exclaimed, "You don't mean to say you are going to stay at Glamis! Don't you know it's haunted?" I burst out laughing.

"Haunted!" I said, "how ridiculous! There are no such things as ghosts. One might as well believe in fairies."

Of course I did not go to Glamis alone – my mother and sister were with me; but whereas they slept in the more modern part of the castle, I was, at my own request, apportioned a room in the Square Tower.

I cannot say that my choice had anything to do with the secret chamber. That, and the alleged mystery, had been dinned into my ears so often that I had grown thoroughly sick of the whole thing. No, I wanted to sleep in the Square Tower for quite a different reason, a reason of my own. I kept an aviary; the tower was old; and I naturally hoped its walls would be covered with ivy and teeming with birds' nests, some of which I might be able to reach – and, I am ashamed to say, plunder – from my window.

Alas, for my expectations! Although the Square Tower was so ancient that in some places it was actually crumbling away – not the sign of a leaf, not the vestige of a bird's nest could I see anywhere; the walls were abominably, brutally bare. However, it was not long before my disappointment gave way to delight; for the air that blew in through the open window was so sweet, so richly scented with heather and honeysuckle, and the view of the broad, sweeping, thickly wooded grounds so indescribably charming, that, despite my inartistic and unpoetical nature, I was entranced – entranced as I had never been before, and never have been since. "Ghosts!" I said to myself, "ghosts! how absurd! how preposterously absurd! such an adorable spot as this can only harbour sunshine and flowers."

I well remember, too – for, as I have already said, I was not poetical – how much I enjoyed my first dinner at Glamis. The long journey and keen mountain air had made me hungry, and I thought I had never tasted such delicious food – such ideal salmon (from the Esk) and such heavenly fruit. But I must tell you that, although I ate heartily, as a healthy girl should, by the time I went to bed I had thoroughly digested my meal, and was, in fact, quite ready to partake of a few oatmeal biscuits I found in my dressing-case, and remembered having bought at Perth. It was about eleven o'clock when my maid left me, and I sat for some minutes wrapped in my dressing gown, before the open window. The night was very still, and save for an occasional rustle of the wind in the distant tree-tops, the hooting of an owl, the melancholy cry of a peewit and the hoarse barking of a dog, the silence was undisturbed.

The interior of my room was, in nearly every particular, modern. The furniture was not old; there were no grim carvings; no grotesquely-fashioned tapestries on the walls; no dark cupboards; no gloomy corners; – all was cosy and cheerful, and when I got into bed no thought of bogle or mystery entered my mind.

In a few minutes I was asleep, and for some time there was nothing but a blank – a blank in which all identity was annihilated. Then suddenly I found myself in an oddly-shaped room with a lofty ceiling, and a window situated at so great a distance from the black oaken floor as to be altogether inaccessible from within. Feeble gleams of phosphorescent light made their way through the narrow panes, and served to render distinct the more prominent objects around; but my eyes struggled in vain to reach the remoter angles of the wall, one of which inspired me with terror such as I had never felt before. The walls were covered with heavy draperies that were sufficient in themselves to preclude the possibility of any save the loudest of sounds penetrating without.

The furniture, if such one could call it, puzzled me. It seemed more fitted for the cell of a prison or lunatic asylum, or even for a kennel, than for an ordinary dwelling-room. I could see no chair, only a coarse deal table, a straw mattress, and a kind of trough. An air of irredeemable gloom and horror hung over and pervaded everything. As I stood there, I felt I was waiting for something – something that was concealed in the corner of the room I dreaded. I tried to reason with myself, to assure myself that there was nothing there that could hurt me, nothing that could even terrify me, but my efforts were in vain – my fears grew. Had I had some definite knowledge as to the cause of my alarm I should not have suffered so much, but it was my ignorance of what was there, of what I feared, that made my terror so poignant. Each second saw the agony of my suspense increase. I dared not move. I hardly dare breathe, and I dreaded lest the violent pulsation of my heart should attract the attention of the Unknown Presence and precipitate its coming out. Yet despite the perturbation of my mind, I caught myself analysing my feelings. It was not danger

I abhorred so much, as its absolute effect – fright. I shuddered at the
bare thought of what result the most trivial incident – the creaking of
a board, ticking of a beetle, or hooting of an owl – might have on the
intolerable agitation of my soul.

In this unnerved and pitiable condition I felt that the period was
bound to come, sooner or later, when I should have to abandon life
and reason together in the most desperate of struggles with – fear.

At length, something moved. An icy chill ran through my
frame, and the horror of my anticipations immediately reached its
culminating point. The Presence was about to reveal itself.

The gentle rubbing of a soft body on the floor, the crack of a bony
joint, breathing, another crack, and then – was it my own excited
imagination – or the disturbing influence of the atmosphere – or the
uncertain twilight of the chamber that produced before me, in the
stygian darkness of the recess, the vacillating and indistinct outline of
something luminous, and horrid? I would gladly have risked futurity
to have looked elsewhere – I could not. My eyes were fixed – I was
compelled to gaze steadily in front of me.

Slowly, very slowly, the thing, whatever it was, took shape. Legs
– crooked, misshapen, human legs. A body – tawny and hunched.
Arms – long and spidery, with crooked, knotted fingers. A head –
large and bestial, and covered with a tangled mass of grey hair that
hung around its protruding forehead and pointed ears in ghastly
mockery of curls. A face – and herein was the realisation of all my
direst expectations – a face – white and staring, piglike in formation,
malevolent in expression; a hellish combination of all things foul and
animal, and yet withal not without a touch of pathos.

As I stared at it aghast, it reared itself on its haunches after the
manner of an ape, and leered piteously at me. Then, shuffling

forward, it rolled over, and lay sprawled out like some ungainly turtle – and wallowed, as for warmth, in the cold grey beams of early dawn.

At this juncture the handle of the chamber door turned, some one entered, there was a loud cry – and I awoke – awoke to find the whole tower, walls and rafters, ringing with the most appalling screams I have ever heard, – screams of some thing or of some one – for there was in them a strong element of what was human as well as animal – in the greatest distress.

Wondering what it meant, and more than ever terrified, I sat up in bed and listened, – listened whilst a conviction – the result of intuition, suggestion, or what you will, but a conviction all the same – forced me to associate the sounds with the thing in my dream. And I associate them still.

* * *

It was, I think, in the same year – in the year that the foregoing account was narrated to me – that I heard another story of the hauntings at Glamis, a story in connection with a lady whom I will call Miss Macginney. I append her experience as nearly as possible as she is stated to have told it.

* * *

I seldom talk about my adventure, Miss Maginney announced, because so many people ridicule the superphysical, and laugh at the mere mention of ghosts. I own I did the same myself till I stayed at Glamis; but a week there quite cured me of scepticism, and I came away a confirmed believer.

The incident occurred nearly twenty years ago – shortly after my return from India, where my father was then stationed.

It was years since I had been to Scotland, indeed I had only once crossed the border and that when I was a babe; consequently I was delighted to receive an invitation to spend a few weeks in the land of my birth. I went to Edinburgh first – I was born in Drumsheugh Gardens – and thence to Glamis.

It was late in the autumn, the weather was intensely cold, and I arrived at the castle in a blizzard. Indeed, I do not recollect ever having been out in such a frightful storm. It was as much as the horses could do to make headway, and when we reached the castle we found a crowd of anxious faces eagerly awaiting us in the hall.

Chilled! I was chilled to the bone, and thought I never should thaw. But the huge fires and bright and cosy atmosphere of the rooms – for the interior of Glamis was modernised throughout – soon set me right, and by tea time I felt nicely warm and comfortable.

My bedroom was in the oldest part of the castle – the Square Tower – but although I had been warned by some of the guests that it might be haunted, I can assure you that when I went to bed no subject was farther from my thoughts than the subject of ghosts. I returned to my room at about half-past eleven. The storm was then at its height – all was babel and confusion – impenetrable darkness mingled with the wildest roaring and shrieking; and when I peeped through my casement window I could see nothing – the panes were shrouded in snow – snow which was incessantly dashed against them with cyclonic fury. I fixed a comb in the window-frame so as not to be kept awake by the constant jarring; and with the caution characteristic of my sex looked into the wardrobe and under the bed for burglars – though Heaven knows what I should have done had I found one there – placed a candlestick and matchbox on the table by my bedside, lest the roof or window should be blown in during the night or any other catastrophe happen, and after all these preparations got into bed. At this period of my life I was a sound sleeper, and, being somewhat unusually tired after my journey, I was soon in a dreamless slumber. What awoke me I cannot say, but I came to myself with a violent start, such as might have been occasioned by a loud noise. Indeed, that was, at first, my impression, and I strained my ears to try and ascertain the cause of it. All was, however, silent. The storm had abated, and the castle and grounds were wrapped in an almost preternatural hush. The sky had cleared, and the room was partially illuminated by a broad stream of silvery light that filtered softly in through the white and tightly drawn blinds. A feeling that there was something unnatural in the air, that the stillness was but the prelude to some strange and startling event, gradually came over me. I strove to reason with myself, to argue that the feeling was wholly due to the novelty of my surroundings, but my efforts were fruitless. And soon there stole upon me a sensation to which I had been hitherto an utter stranger – I became afraid. An irrepressible tremor pervaded my frame, my teeth chattered, my blood froze. Obeying an impulse – an impulse I could not resist, I lifted myself up from the pillows, and, peering fearfully into the shadowy glow that lay directly in front of me – listened. Why I listened I do not know, saving that an instinctive spirit prompted me. At first I could hear nothing, and then, from a direction I could not define, there came a noise, low, distinct, uninterpretative. It was repeated in rapid succession, and speedily construed itself into the sound of mailed footsteps racing up the long flight of stairs at the end of the corridor leading to my room. Dreading to think what it might be, and seized with a wild sentiment of self-preservation, I made frantic endeavours to get out of bed and barricade my door. My limbs, however, refused to move. I was paralysed. Nearer and nearer drew the sounds; and I could at length distinguish, with a clearness that petrified my very soul, the banging and clanging of sword scabbards, and the panting and gasping of men, sore pressed in a wild and desperate race. And then the meaning of it all came to me with hideous abruptness – it was a case of pursued and pursuing – the race was for – LIFE. Outside my door the fugitive halted, and from the noise he made in trying to draw his breath, I knew he was dead beat. His antagonist, however, gave him but scant time for recovery. Bounding at him with prodigious leaps, he struck him a blow that sent him reeling with such tremendous force against the door, that the panels, although composed of the stoutest oak, quivered and strained like flimsy matchboard.

The blow was repeated; the cry that rose in the victim's throat was converted into an abortive gurgling groan; and I heard the ponderous battle-axe carve its way through helmet, bone, and brain. A moment later came the sound of slithering armour; and the corpse, slipping sideways, toppled to the ground with a sonorous clang.

A silence too awful for words now ensued. Having finished his hideous handiwork, the murderer was quietly deliberating what to do next; whilst my dread of attracting his attention was so great that I scarcely dare breathe. This intolerable state of things had already lasted for what seemed to me a lifetime, when, glancing involuntarily at the floor, I saw a stream of dark-looking fluid lazily lapping its way to me from the direction of the door. Another moment and it would reach my shoes. In my dismay I shrieked aloud. There was a sudden stir without, a significant clatter of steel, and the next moment – despite the fact that it was locked – the door slowly opened. The limits of my endurance had now happily been reached, the over-taxed valves of my heart could stand no more – I fainted. On my awakening to consciousness it was morning, and the welcome sun rays revealed no evidences of the distressing drama. I own I had a hard tussle before I could make up my mind to spend another night in that room; and my feelings as I shut the door on my retreating maid, and prepared to get into bed, were not the most enviable. But nothing happened, nor did I again experience anything of the sort till the evening before I left. I had lain down all the afternoon – for I was tired after a long morning's tramp on the moors, a thing I dearly love – and I was thinking it was about time to get up, when a dark shadow suddenly fell across my face.

I looked up hastily, and there, standing by my bedside and bending over me, was a gigantic figure in bright armour.

Its visor was up, and what I saw within the casque is stamped for ever on my memory. It was the face of the dead – the long since dead – with the expression – the subtly hellish expression – of the living. As I gazed helplessly at it, it bent lower. I threw up my hands to ward it off. There was a loud rap at the door. And as my maid softly entered to tell me tea was ready – it vanished.

* * *

The third account of the Glamis hauntings was told me as long ago as the summer of 1893. I was travelling by rail from Perth to Glasgow, and the only other occupant of my compartment was an elderly gentleman, who, from his general air and appearance, might have been a dominie, or member of some other learned profession. I can see him in my mind's eye now – a tall, thin man with a premature stoop. He had white hair, which was brushed forward on either side of his head in such a manner as suggested a wig; bushy eyebrows; dark, piercing eyes; and a stern, though somewhat sad, mouth. His features were fine and scholarly; he was clean-shaven. There was something about him – something that marked him from the general horde – something that attracted me, and I began chatting with him soon after we left Perth.

In the course of a conversation, that was at all events interesting to me, I adroitly managed to introduce the subject of ghosts – then, as ever, uppermost in my thoughts.

* * *

Well, he said, I can tell you of something rather extraordinary that my mother used to say happened to a friend of hers at Glamis. I have no doubt you are well acquainted with the hackneyed stories in connection with the hauntings at the castle; for example, Earl Beardie playing cards with the Devil, and The Weeping Woman without Hands or Tongue. You can read about them in scores of books and magazines. But what befell my mother's friend, whom I will call Mrs. Gibbons – for I have forgotten her proper name – was apparently of a novel nature. The affair happened shortly before Mrs. Gibbons died, and I always thought that what took place might have been, in some way, connected with her death.

She had driven over to the castle one day – during the absence of the owner – to see her cousin, who was in the employ of the Earl and Countess. Never having been at Glamis before, but having heard so much about it, Mrs. Gibbons was not a little curious to see that part of the building, called the Square Tower, that bore the reputation of being haunted.

Tactfully biding an opportunity, she sounded her relative on the subject, and was laughingly informed that she might go anywhere about the place she pleased, saving to one spot, namely, "Bluebeard's Chamber"; and there she could certainly never succeed in poking her nose, as its locality was known only to three people, all of whom were pledged never to reveal it. At the commencement of her tour of inspection, Mrs. Gibbons was disappointed – she was disappointed in the Tower. She had expected to see a gaunt, grim place, crumbling to pieces with age, full of blood-curdling, spiral staircases, and deep, dark dungeons; whereas everything was the reverse. The walls were in an excellent state of preservation – absolutely intact; the rooms bright and cheerful and equipped in the most modern style; there were no dungeons, at least none on view, and the passages and staircases were suggestive of nothing more alarming than – bats! She was accompanied for some time by her relative, but, on the latter being called away, Mrs. Gibbons continued her rambles alone. She had explored the lower premises, and was leisurely examining a handsomely furnished apartment on the top floor, when, in crossing from one side of the room to the other, she ran into something. She looked down – nothing was to be seen. Amazed beyond description, she thrust out her hands, and they alighted on an object, which she had little difficulty in identifying. It was an enormous cask or barrel lying in a horizontal position.

She bent down close to where she felt it, but she could see nothing – nothing but the well-polished boards of the floor. To make sure again that the barrel was there, she gave a little kick – and drew back her foot with a cry of pain. She was not afraid – the sunshine in the room forbade fear – only exasperated. She was certain a barrel was there – that it was objective – and she was angry with herself for not seeing it. She wondered if she were going blind; but the fact that other objects in the room were plainly visible to her, discountenanced such an idea. For some minutes she poked and jabbed at the Thing, and then, seized with a sudden and uncontrollable panic, she turned round and fled. And as she tore out of the room, along the passage and down the seemingly interminable flight of stairs, she heard the barrel behind her in close pursuit-bump – bump – bump!

At the foot of the staircase Mrs. Gibbons met her cousin, and, as she clutched the latter for support, the barrel shot past her, still continuing its descent – bump – bump – bump! (though the steps as far as she could see had ended) – till the sounds gradually dwindled away in the far distance.

Whilst the manifestations lasted, neither Mrs. Gibbons nor her cousin spoke; but the latter, as soon as the sounds had ceased, dragged Mrs. Gibbons away, and, in a voice shaking with terror, cried: "Quick, quick – don't, for Heaven's sake, look round – worse has yet to come." And, pulling Mrs. Gibbons along in breathless haste, she unceremoniously hustled her out of the Tower.

"That was no barrel!" Mrs. Gibbons's cousin subsequently remarked by way of explanation. "I saw it – I have seen it before. Don't ask me to describe it. I dare not – I dare not even think of it. Whenever it appears, a certain thing happens shortly afterwards. Don't, don't on any account say a word about it to any one here." And Mrs. Gibbons, my mother told me, came away from Glamis a thousand times more curious than she was when she went.

* * *

The last story I have to relate is one I heard many years ago, when I was staying near Balmoral. A gentleman named Vance, with strong antiquarian tastes, was staying at an inn near the Strathmore estate, and, roaming abroad one afternoon, in a fit of absent-mindedness entered the castle grounds. It so happened – fortunately for him – that the family were away, and he encountered no one more formidable than a man he took to be a gardener, an uncouth-looking fellow, with a huge head covered with a mass of red hair, hawk-like features, and high cheek-bones, high even for a Scot. Struck with the appearance of the individual, Mr. Vance spoke, and, finding him wonderfully civil, asked whether, by any chance, he ever came across any fossils, when digging in the gardens.

"I dinna ken the meaning of fossils," the man replied. "What are they?"

Mr. Vance explained, and a look of cunning gradually pervaded the fellow's features. "No!" he said, "I've never found any of those things, but if you'll give me your word to say nothing about it, I'll show you something I once dug up over yonder by the Square Tower."

"Do you mean the Haunted Tower? – the Tower that is supposed to contain the secret room?" Mr. Vance exclaimed.

An extraordinary expression – an expression such as Mr. Vance found it impossible to analyse – came into the man's eyes. "Yes! that's it!" he nodded. "What people call – and rightly call – the Haunted Tower. I got it from there. But don't you say naught about it!"

Mr. Vance, whose curiosity was roused, promised, and the man, politely requesting him to follow, led the way to a cottage that stood near by, in the heart of a gloomy wood. To Mr. Vance's astonishment the treasure proved to be the skeleton of a hand – a hand with abnormally large knuckles, and the first joint – of both fingers and thumb – much shorter than the others. It was the most extraordinarily shaped hand Mr. Vance had ever seen, and he did not know in the least how to classify it. It repelled, yet interested him, and he eventually offered the man a good sum to allow him to keep it. To his astonishment the money was refused. "You may have the thing, and welcome," the fellow said. "Only, I advise you not to look at it late at night; or just before getting into bed. If you do, you may have bad dreams."

"I will take my chance of that!" Mr. Vance laughed. "You see, being a hard-headed cockney, I am not superstitious. It is only you Highlanders, and your first cousins the Irish, who believe nowadays in bogles, omens, and such-like»; and, packing the hand carefully in his knapsack, Mr. Vance bid the strange-looking creature good morning, and went on his way.

For the rest of the day the hand was uppermost in his thoughts – nothing had ever fascinated him so much. He sat pondering over it the whole evening, and bedtime found him still examining it – examining it upstairs in his room by candlelight. He had a hazy recollection that some clock had struck twelve, and he was beginning to feel that it was about time to retire, when, in the mirror opposite him, he caught sight of the door – it was open.

"By Jove! that's odd!" he said to himself. "I could have sworn I shut and bolted it." To make sure, he turned round – the door was closed. "An optical delusion," he murmured; "I will try again."

He looked into the mirror – the door reflected in it was – open. Utterly at a loss to know how to explain the phenomenon, he leaned forward in his seat to examine the glass more carefully, and as he did so he gave a start. On the threshold of the doorway was a shadow – black and bulbous. A cold shiver ran down Mr. Vance's spine, and just for a moment he felt afraid, terribly afraid; but he quickly composed himself – it was nothing but an illusion – there was no shadow there in reality – he had only to turn round, and the thing would be gone. It was amusing – entertaining. He would wait and see what happened.

The shadow moved. It moved slowly through the air like some huge spider, or odd-shaped bird. He would not acknowledge that there was anything sinister about it – only something droll – excruciatingly droll. Yet it did not make him laugh. When it had drawn a little nearer, he tried to diagnose it, to discover its material counterpart in one of the objects around him; but he was obliged to acknowledge his attempts were failures – there was nothing in the room in the least degree like it. A vague feeling of uneasiness gradually crept over him – was the thing the shadow of something with which he was familiar, but could not just then recall to mind – something he feared – something that was sinister? He struggled against the idea, he dismissed it as absurd; but it returned – returned, and took deeper root as the shadow drew nearer. He wished the house was not quite so silent – that he could hear some indication of life – anything – anything for companionship, and to rid him of the oppressive, the very oppressive, sense of loneliness and isolation.

Again a thrill of terror ran through him.

"Look here!" he exclaimed aloud, glad to hear the sound of his own voice. "Look here! if this goes on much longer I shall begin to think I'm going mad. I have had enough, and more than enough, of magic mirrors for one night – it's high time I got into bed." He strove to rise from his chair – to move; he was unable to do either; some strange, tyrannical force held him a prisoner.

A change now took place in the shadow; the blurr dissipated, and the clearly defined outlines of an object – an object that made Mr. Vance perfectly sick with apprehension – slowly disclosed themselves. His suspicions were verified – it was the HAND! – the hand – no longer skeleton, but covered with green, mouldering flesh – feeling its way slyly and stealthily towards him – towards the back of his chair! He noted the murderous twitching of its short, flat finger-tips, the monstrous muscles of its hideous thumb, and the great, clumsy hollows of its clammy palm. It closed in upon him; its cold, slimy, detestable skin touched his coat – his shoulder – his neck – his head! It pressed him down, squashed, suffocated him! He saw it all in the glass – and then an extraordinary thing happened. Mr. Vance suddenly became animated. He got up and peeped furtively round. Chairs, bed, wardrobe, had all disappeared – so had the bedroom – and he found himself in a small, bare, comfortless, queerly constructed apartment without a door, and with only a narrow slit of a window somewhere near the ceiling.

He had in one of his hands a knife with a long, keen blade, and his whole mind was bent on murder. Creeping stealthily forward, he approached a corner of the room, where he now saw, for the first time – a mattress – a mattress on which lay a huddled-up form. What the Thing was – whether human or animal – Mr. Vance did not know – did not care – all he felt was that it was there for him to kill – that he loathed and hated it – hated it with a hatred such as nothing else could have produced. Tiptoeing gently up to it, he bent down, and, lifting his knife high above his head, plunged it into the Thing's body with all the force he could command.

* * *

He recrossed the room, and found himself once more in his apartment at the inn. He looked for the skeleton hand – it was not where he had left it – it had vanished. Then he glanced at the mirror, and on its brilliantly polished surface saw – not his own face – but the face of the gardener, the man who had given him the hand! Features, colour, hair – all – all were identical – wonderfully, hideously identical – and as the eyes met his, they smiled – devilishly.

* * *

Early the next day, Mr. Vance set out for the spinney and cottage; they were not to be found – nobody had ever heard of them. He continued his travels, and some months later, at a loan collection of pictures in a gallery in Edinburgh, he came to an abrupt – a very abrupt – halt, before the portrait of a gentleman in ancient costume. The face seemed strangely familiar – the huge head with thick, red hair – the hawk-like features – the thin and tightly compressed lips. Then, in a trice, it all came back to him: the face he looked at was that of the uncouth gardener – the man who had given him the hand. And to clinch the matter, the eyes – leered.

The Open Door
Margaret Oliphant

I took the house of Brentwood on my return from India in 18—, for the temporary accommodation of my family, until I could find a permanent home for them. It had many advantages which made it peculiarly appropriate. It was within reach of Edinburgh; and my boy Roland, whose education had been considerably neglected, could ride in and out to school; which was thought to be better for him than either leaving home altogether or staying there always with a tutor. The lad was doubly precious to us, being the only one left to us of many; and he was fragile in body, we believed, and deeply sensitive in mind. The two girls also found at Brentwood everything they wanted. They were near enough to Edinburgh to have masters and lessons as many as they required for completing that never-ending education which the young people seem to require nowadays.

Brentwood stands on that fine and wealthy slope of country – one of the richest in Scotland – which lies between the Pentland Hills and the Firth. In clear weather you could see the blue gleam of the great estuary on one side of you; and on the other the blue heights. Edinburgh – with its two lesser heights, the Castle and the Calton Hill, its spires and towers piercing through the smoke, and Arthur's

Seat lying crouched behind, like a guardian no longer very needful, taking his repose beside the well-beloved charge, which is now, so to speak, able to take care of itself without him – lay at our right hand.

The village of Brentwood, with its prosaic houses, lay in a hollow almost under our house. Village architecture does not flourish in Scotland. Still a cluster of houses on different elevations, with scraps of garden coming in between, a hedgerow with clothes laid out to dry, the opening of a street with its rural sociability, the women at their doors, the slow wagon lumbering along, gives a centre to the landscape. In the park which surrounded the house were the ruins of the former mansion of Brentwood, – a much smaller and less important house than the solid Georgian edifice which we inhabited. The ruins were picturesque, however, and gave importance to the place. Even we, who were but temporary tenants, felt a vague pride in them, as if they somehow reflected a certain consequence upon ourselves. The old building had the remains of a tower, – an indistinguishable mass of masonwork, overgrown with ivy; and the shells of the walls attached to this were half filled up with soil. At a little distance were some very commonplace and disjointed fragments of buildings, one of them suggesting a certain pathos by its very commonness and the complete wreck which it showed. This was the end of a low gable, a bit of grey wall, all incrusted with lichens, in which was a common door-way. Probably it had been a servants' entrance, a backdoor, or opening into what are called "the offices" in Scotland. No offices remained to be entered, – pantry and kitchen had all been swept out of being; but there stood the door-way open and vacant, free to all the winds, to the rabbits, and every wild creature. It struck my eye, the first time I went to Brentwood, like a melancholy comment upon a life that was over. A door that led to nothing, – closed once, perhaps, with anxious care, bolted and guarded, now void of any meaning. It impressed me, I remember, from the first; so perhaps it may be said that my mind was prepared to attach to it an importance which nothing justified.

The summer was a very happy period of repose for us all; and it was when the family had settled down for the winter, when the days were short and dark, and the rigorous reign of frost upon us, that the incidents occurred which alone could justify me in intruding upon the world my private affairs.

I was absent in London when these events began. In London an old Indian plunges back into the interests with which all his previous life has been associated, and meets old friends at every step. I had been circulating among some half-dozen of these and had missed some of my home letters. It is never safe to miss one's letters. In this transitory life, as the Prayer-book says, how can one ever be certain what is going to happen? All was well at home. I knew exactly (I thought) what they would have to say to me: "The weather has been so fine, that Roland has not once gone by train, and he enjoys the ride beyond anything." "Dear papa, be sure that you don't forget anything, but bring us so-and-so, and so-and-so," – a list as long as my arm. Dear girls and dearer mother! I would not for the world have forgotten their commissions, or lost their little letters!

When I got back to my club, however, three or four letters were lying for me, upon some of which I noticed the "immediate," "urgent," which old-fashioned people and anxious people still believe will influence the post-office and quicken the speed of the mails. I was about to open one of these, when the club porter brought me two telegrams, one of which, he said, had arrived the night before. I opened, as was to be expected, the last first, and this was what I read: "Why don't you come or answer? For God's sake, come. He is much worse." This was a thunderbolt to fall upon a man's head who had one only son, and he the light of his eyes! The other telegram, which I opened with hands trembling so much that I lost time by my haste, was to much the same purpose: "No better; doctor afraid of brain-fever. Calls for you day and night. Let nothing detain you." The first thing I did was to look up the time-tables to see if there was any way of getting off sooner than by the night-train, though I knew well enough there was not; and then I read the letters, which furnished, alas! too clearly, all the details. They told me that the boy had been pale for some time, with a scared look. His mother had noticed it before I left home, but would not say anything to alarm me. This look had increased day by day; and soon it was observed that Roland came home at a wild gallop through the park, his pony panting and in foam, himself "as white as a sheet," but with the perspiration streaming from his forehead. For a long time he had resisted all questioning, but at length had developed such strange changes of mood, showing a reluctance to go to school, a desire to be fetched in the carriage at night, – which was a ridiculous piece of luxury, – an unwillingness to go out into the grounds, and nervous start at every sound, that his mother had insisted upon an explanation. When the boy – our boy Roland, who had never known what fear was – began to talk to her of voices he had heard in the park, and shadows that had appeared to him among the ruins, my wife promptly put him to bed and sent for Dr. Simson, which, of course, was the only thing to do.

I hurried off that evening, as may be supposed, with an anxious heart. How I got through the hours before the starting of the train, I cannot tell. We must all be thankful for the quickness of the railway when in anxiety; but to have thrown myself into a post-chaise as soon as horses could be put to, would have been a relief. I got to Edinburgh very early in the blackness of the winter morning, and scarcely dared look the man in the face, at whom I gasped, "What news?" My wife had sent the brougham for me, which I concluded, before the man spoke, was a bad sign. His answer was that stereotyped answer which leaves the imagination so wildly free, – "Just the same." Just the same! What might that mean? The horses seemed to me to creep along the long dark country road. As we dashed through the park, I thought I heard some one moaning among the trees, and clenched my fist at him (whoever he might be) with fury. Why had the fool of a woman at the gate allowed any one to come in to disturb the quiet of the place? If I had not been in such hot haste to get home, I think I should have stopped the carriage and got out to see what tramp it was that had made an entrance, and chosen my grounds, of all places in the world, – when my boy was ill! – to grumble and groan in. But I had no reason to complain of our slow pace here. The horses flew like lightning along the intervening path, and drew up at the door all panting, as if they had run a race. My wife stood waiting to receive me, with a pale face, and a candle in her hand, which made her look paler still as the wind blew the flame about. "He is sleeping," she said in a whisper, as if her voice might wake him. And I replied, when I could find my voice, also in a whisper, as though the jingling of the horses' furniture and the sound of their hoofs must not have been more dangerous. I stood on the steps with her a moment, almost afraid to go in, now that I was here; and it seemed to me that I saw without observing, if I may so say, that the horses were unwilling to turn round, though their stables lay that way, or that the men were unwilling. These things occurred to me afterwards, though at the moment I was not capable of anything but to ask questions and to hear of the condition of the boy.

I looked at him from the door of his room, for we were afraid to go near, lest we should disturb that blessed sleep. It looked like actual sleep, not the lethargy into which my wife told me he would sometimes fall. She told me everything in the next room, which communicated with his, rising now and then and going to the door of the communication; and in this there was much that was very startling and confusing to the mind. It appeared that ever since the winter began – since it was early dark, and night had fallen before his return from school – he had been hearing voices among the ruins; at first only a groaning, he said, at which his pony was as much alarmed as he was, but by degrees a voice. The tears ran down my wife's cheeks as she described to me how he would start up in the night and cry out. "Oh, mother, let me in! oh, mother, let me in!" with a pathos which rent her heart. And she sitting there all the time, only longing to do everything his heart could desire! But though she would try to soothe him, crying, "You are at home, my darling. I am here. Don't you know me? Your mother is here!" he would only stare at her, and after a while spring up again with the same cry. At other times he would be quite reasonable, she said, asking eagerly when I was coming, but declaring that he must go with me as soon as I did so, "to let them in." "The doctor thinks his nervous system must have received a shock," my wife said. "Oh, Henry, can it be that we have pushed him on too much with his work – a delicate boy like Roland? And what is his work in comparison with his health? Even you would think little of honours or prizes if it hurt the boy's health." Even I! – as if I were an inhuman father sacrificing my child to my ambition. But I would not increase her trouble by taking any notice.

There was just daylight enough to see his face when I went to him; and what a change in a fortnight! He was paler and more worn, I thought, than even in those dreadful days in the plains before we left India. His hair seemed to me to have grown long and lank; his eyes were like blazing lights projecting out of his white face. He got hold of my hand in a cold and tremulous clutch, and waved to everybody to go away. "Go away – even mother," he said; "go away." This went to her heart; for she did not like that even I should have more of the boy's confidence than herself; but my wife has never been a woman to think of herself, and she left us alone. "Are they all gone?" he said eagerly. "They would not let me speak. The doctor treated me as if I were a fool. You know I am not a fool, papa."

"Yes, yes, my boy, I know. But you are ill, and quiet is so necessary. You are not only not a fool, Roland, but you are reasonable and understand. When you are ill you must deny yourself; you must not do everything that you might do being well."

He waved his thin hand with a sort of indignation. "Then, father, I am not ill," he cried. "Oh, I thought when you came you would not stop me, – you would see the sense of it! What do you think is the matter with me, all of you? Simson is well enough; but he is only a doctor. What do you think is the matter with me? I am no more ill than you are. A doctor, of course, he thinks you are ill the moment he looks at you – that's what he's there for – and claps you into bed."

"Which is the best place for you at present, my dear boy."

"I made up my mind," cried the little fellow, "that I would stand it till you came home. I said to myself, I won't frighten mother and the girls. But now, father," he cried, half jumping out of bed, "it's not illness: it's a secret."

His eyes shone so wildly, his face was so swept with strong feeling, that my heart sank within me. It could be nothing but fever that did it, and fever had been so fatal. I got him into my arms to put him back into bed. "Roland," I said, humouring the poor child, which I knew was the only way, "if you are going to tell me this secret to do any good, you know you must be quite quiet, and not excite yourself. If you excite yourself, I must not let you speak."

"Yes, father," said the boy. He was quiet directly, like a man, as if he quite understood. When I had laid him back on his pillow, he looked up at me with that grateful, sweet look with which children, when they are ill, break one's heart, the water coming into his eyes in his weakness. "I was sure as soon as you were here you would know what to do," he said.

"To be sure, my boy. Now keep quiet, and tell it all out like a man." To think I was telling lies to my own child! for I did it only to humour him, thinking, poor little fellow, his brain was wrong.

"Yes, father. Father, there is some one in the park, – some one that has been badly used."

"Hush, my dear; you remember there is to be no excitement. Well, who is this somebody, and who has been ill-using him? We will soon put a stop to that."

"Ah," cried Roland, "but it is not so easy as you think. I don't know who it is. It is just a cry. Oh, if you could hear it! It gets into my head in my sleep. I heard it as clear – as clear; and they think that I am dreaming, or raving perhaps," the boy said, with a sort of disdainful smile.

This look of his perplexed me; it was less like fever than I thought. "Are you quite sure you have not dreamed it, Roland?" I said.

"Dreamed? – that!" He was springing up again when he suddenly bethought himself, and lay down flat, with the same sort of smile on his face. "The pony heard it, too," he said. "She jumped as if she had been shot. If I had not grasped at the reins – for I was frightened, father—"

"No shame to you, my boy," said I, though I scarcely knew why.

"If I hadn't held to her like a leech, she'd have pitched me over her head, and never drew breath till we were at the door. Did the pony dream it?" he said, with a soft disdain, yet indulgence for my foolishness. Then he added slowly, "It was only a cry the first time, and all the time before you went away. I wouldn't tell you, for it was so wretched to be frightened. I thought it might be a hare or a rabbit snared, and I went in the morning and looked; but there was nothing. It was after you went I heard it really first; and this is what he says." He raised himself on his elbow close to me, and looked me in the face: "Oh, mother, let me in! oh, mother, let me in!" As he said the words a mist came over his face, the mouth quivered, the soft features all melted and changed, and when he had ended these pitiful words, dissolved in a shower of heavy tears.

Was it a hallucination? Was it the fever of the brain? Was it the disordered fancy caused by great bodily weakness? How could I tell? I thought it wisest to accept it as if it were all true.

"This is very touching, Roland," I said.

"Oh, if you had just heard it, father! I said to myself, if father heard it he would do something; but mamma, you know, she's given over to Simson, and that fellow's a doctor, and never thinks of anything but clapping you into bed."

"We must not blame Simson for being a doctor, Roland."

"No, no," said my boy, with delightful toleration and indulgence; "oh, no: that's the good of him; that's what he's for; I know that. But you – you are different; you are just father; and you'll do something – directly, papa, directly; this very night."

"Surely," I said. "No doubt it is some little lost child."

He gave me a sudden, swift look, investigating my face as though to see whether, after all, this was everything my eminence as "father" came to, – no more than that. Then he got hold of my shoulder, clutching it with his thin hand: "Look here," he said, with a quiver in his voice: "suppose it wasn't – living at all!"

"My dear boy, how then could you have heard it?" I said.

He turned away from me with a pettish exclamation, – "As if you didn't know better than that!"

"Do you want to tell me it is a ghost?" I said.

Roland withdrew his hand; his countenance assumed an aspect of great dignity and gravity; a slight quiver remained about his lips. "Whatever it was – you always said we were not to call names. It was something – in trouble. Oh, father, in terrible trouble!"

"But, my boy," I said (I was at my wits' end), "if it was a child that was lost, or any poor human creature – but, Roland, what do you want me to do?"

"I should know if I was you," said the child eagerly. "That is what I always said to myself, – Father will know. Oh, papa, papa, to have to face it night after night, in such terrible, terrible trouble, and never to be able to do it any good! I don't want to cry; it's like a baby, I know; but what can I do else? Out there all by itself in the ruin, and nobody to help it! I can't bear it!" cried my generous boy. And in his weakness he burst out, after many attempts to restrain it, into a great childish fit of sobbing and tears.

I do not know that I was ever in a greater perplexity in my life; and afterwards, when I thought of it, there was something comic in it too. It is bad enough to find your child's mind possessed with the conviction that he had seen, or heard, a ghost; but that he should require you to go instantly and help that ghost was the most bewildering experience that had ever come my way. I did my best to console my boy without giving any promise of this astonishing kind; but he was too sharp for me; he would have none of my caresses. With sobs breaking in at intervals upon his voice, and the rain-drops hanging on his eyelids, he yet returned to the charge.

"It will be there now! – it will be there all the night! Oh, think, papa, – think if it was me! I can't rest for thinking of it. Don't!" he cried, putting away my hand, – "don't! You go and help it, and mother can take care of me."

"But, Roland, what can I do?"

My boy opened his eyes, which were large with weakness and fever, and gave me a smile such, I think, as sick children only know the secret of. "I was sure you would know as soon as you came. I always said, 'Father will know.' And mother," he cried, with a softening of repose upon his face, his limbs relaxing, his form sinking with a luxurious ease in his bed, – "mother can come and take care of me."

I called her, and saw him turn to her with the complete dependence of a child; and then I went away and left them, as perplexed a man as any in Scotland. I must say, however, I had this consolation, that my mind was greatly eased about Roland. He might be under a hallucination; but his head was clear enough, and I did not think him so ill as everybody else did. The girls were astonished even at the ease with which I took it. "How do you think he is?" they said in a breath, coming round me, laying hold of me. "Not half so ill as I expected," I said; "not very bad at all." "Oh, papa, you are a darling!" cried Agatha, kissing me, and crying upon my shoulder; while little Jeanie, who was as pale as Roland, clasped both her arms round mine, and could not speak at all. I knew nothing about it, not half so much as Simson; but they believed in me: they had a feeling that all would go right now. God is very good to you when your children look to you like that. It makes one humble, not proud. I was not worthy of it; and then I recollected that I had to act the part of a father to Roland's ghost, – which made me almost laugh, though I might just as well have cried. It was the strangest mission that ever was intrusted to mortal man.

It was then I remembered suddenly the looks of the men when they turned to take the brougham to the stables in the dark that morning. They had not liked it, and the horses had not liked it. I remembered that even in my anxiety about Roland I had heard them tearing along the avenue back to the stables, and had made a memorandum mentally that I must speak of it. It seemed to me that the best thing I could do was to go to the stables now and make a few inquiries. The coachman was the head of this little colony, and it was to his house I went to pursue my investigations. He was a native of the district, and had taken care of the place in the absence of the family for years; it was impossible but that he must know everything that was going on, and all the traditions of the place. The men, I could see, eyed me anxiously when I thus appeared at such an hour among them, and followed me with their eyes to Jarvis's house, where he lived alone with his old wife, their children being all married and out in the world. Mrs. Jarvis met me with anxious questions. How was the poor young gentleman? But the others knew, I could see by their faces, that not even this was the foremost thing in my mind.

After a while I elicited without much difficulty the whole story. In the opinion of the Jarvises, and of everybody about, the certainty that the place was haunted was beyond all doubt. As Sandy and his wife warmed to the tale, one tripping up another in their eagerness to tell everything, it gradually developed as distinct a superstition as I ever heard, and not without poetry and pathos. How long it was since the voice had been heard first, nobody could tell with certainty. Jarvis's opinion was that his father, who had been coachman at Brentwood before him, had never heard anything about it, and that the whole thing had arisen within the last ten years, since the complete dismantling of the old house; which was a wonderfully modern date for a tale so well authenticated. According to these witnesses, and to several whom I questioned afterwards, and who were all in perfect agreement, it was only in the months of November and December that "the visitation" occurred. During these months, the darkest of the year, scarcely a night passed without the recurrence of these inexplicable cries. Nothing, it was said, had ever been seen, – at least, nothing that could be identified. Some people, bolder or more imaginative than the others, had seen the darkness moving, Mrs. Jarvis said, with unconscious poetry. It began when night fell, and continued at intervals till day broke. Very often it was only an inarticulate cry and moaning, but sometimes the words which had taken possession of my poor boy's fancy had been distinctly audible, – "Oh, mother, let me in!" The Jarvises were not aware that there had ever been any investigation into it. The estate of Brentwood had lapsed into the hands of a distant branch of the family, who had lived but little there; and of the many people who had taken it, as I had done, few had remained through two Decembers. And nobody had taken the trouble to make a very close examination into the facts.

"No, no," Jarvis said, shaking his head, "No, no, Cornel. Wha wad set themsels up for a laughin'-stock to a' the country-side, making a wark about a ghost? Naebody believes in ghosts. It bid to be the wind in the trees, the last gentleman said, or some effec' o' the water wrastlin' among the rocks. He said it was a' quite easy explained; but he gave up the hoose. And when you cam, Cornel, we were awfu' anxious you should never hear. What for should I have spoiled the bargain and hairmed the property for no-thing?"

"Do you call my child's life nothing?" I said in the trouble of the moment, unable to restrain myself. "And instead of telling this all to me, you have told it to him, – to a delicate boy, a child unable to sift evidence or judge for himself, a tender-hearted young creature—"

I was walking about the room with an anger all the hotter that I felt it to be most likely quite unjust. My heart was full of bitterness against the stolid retainers of a family who were content to risk other people's children and comfort rather than let a house lie empty. If I had been warned I might have taken precautions, or left the place, or sent Roland away, a hundred things which now I could not do; and here I was with my boy in a brain-fever, and his life, the most precious life on earth, hanging in the balance, dependent on whether or not I could get to the reason of a commonplace ghost-story!

"Cornel," said Jarvis solemnly, "and *she'll* bear me witness, – the young gentleman never heard a word from me – no, nor from either groom or gardner; I'll gie ye my word for that. In the first place, he's no a lad that invites ye to talk. There are some that are, and that arena. Some will draw ye on, till ye've tellt them a' the clatter of the toun, and a' ye ken, and whiles mair. But Maister Roland, his mind's fu' of his books. He's aye civil and kind, and a fine lad; but no that sort. And ye see it's for a' our interest, Cornel, that you should stay

at Brentwood. I took it upon me mysel to pass the word, – 'No a
syllable to Maister Roland, nor to the young leddies – no a syllable.'
The women-servants, that have little reason to be out at night, ken
little or nothing about it. And some think it grand to have a ghost
so long as they're no in the way of coming across it. If you had
been tellt the story to begin with, maybe ye would have thought
so yourself."

This was true enough. I should not have been above the idea of
a ghost myself! Oh, yes, I claim no exemption. The girls would have
been delighted. I could fancy their eagerness, their interest, and
excitement. No; if we had been told, it would have done no good, –
we should have made the bargain all the more eagerly, the fools that
we are.

"Come with me, Jarvis," I said hastily, "and we'll make an attempt
at least to investigate. Say nothing to the men or to anybody. Be ready
for me about ten o'clock."

"Me, Cornel!" Jarvis said, in a faint voice. I had not been looking
at him in my own preoccupation, but when I did so, I found that the
greatest change had come over the fat and ruddy coachman. "Me,
Cornel!" he repeated, wiping the perspiration from his brow. "There's
nothin' I wouldna do to pleasure ye, Cornel, but if ye'll reflect that I
am no used to my feet. With a horse atween my legs, or the reins in
my hand, I'm maybe nae worse than other men; but on fit, Cornel
– it's no the – bogles; – but I've been cavalry, ye see," with a little
hoarse laugh, "a' my life. To face a thing ye dinna understan' – on your
feet, Cornel."

"He believes in it, Cornel, and you dinna believe in it," the
woman said.

"Will you come with me?" I said, turning to her.

She jumped back, upsetting her chair in her bewilderment. "Me!" with a scream, and then fell into a sort of hysterical laugh. "I wouldna say but what I would go; but what would the folk say to hear of Cornel Mortimer with an auld silly woman at his heels?"

The suggestion made me laugh too, though I had little inclination for it. "I'm sorry you have so little spirit, Jarvis," I said. "I must find some one else, I suppose."

Jarvis, touched by this, began to remonstrate, but I cut him short. My butler was a soldier who had been with me in India, and was not supposed to fear anything, – man or devil, – certainly not the former; and I felt that I was losing time. The Jarvises were too thankful to get rid of me. They attended me to the door with the most anxious courtesies. Outside, the two grooms stood close by, a little confused by my sudden exit. I don't know if perhaps they had been listening, – at least standing as near as possible, to catch any scrap of the conversation. I waved my hand to them as I went past, in answer to their salutations, and it was very apparent to me that they also were glad to see me go.

And it will be thought very strange, but it would be weak not to add, that I myself, though bent on the investigation I have spoken of, pledged to Roland to carry it out, and feeling that my boy's health, perhaps his life, depended on the result of my inquiry, – I felt the most unaccountable reluctance, now that it was dark, to pass the ruins on my way home. My curiosity was intense; and yet it was all my mind could do to pull my body along. I dare say the scientific people would describe it the other way, and attribute my cowardice to the state of my stomach. I went on; but if I had followed my impulse, I should have turned and bolted. Everything in me seemed to cry out against it; my heart thumped, my pulses all began, like sledge-hammers, beating against my ears and every sensitive part. It was very dark, as I have said; the old house, with its shapeless tower, loomed a heavy mass through the darkness, which was only not entirely so solid as itself. On the other hand, the great dark cedars of which we were so proud seemed to fill up the night. My foot strayed out of the path in my confusion and the gloom together, and I brought myself up with a cry as I felt myself knocked against something solid. What was it? The contact with hard stone and lime and prickly bramble-bushes restored me a little to myself. "Oh, it's only the old gable," I said aloud, with a little laugh to reassure myself. The rough feeling of the stones reconciled me. As I groped about thus, I shook off my visionary folly. What so easily explained as that I should have strayed from the path in the darkness? This brought me back to common existence, as if I had been shaken by a wise hand out of all the silliness of superstition. How silly it was, after all! What did it matter which path I took? I laughed again, this time with better heart, when suddenly, in a moment, the blood was chilled in my veins, a shiver stole along my spine, my faculties seemed to forsake me. Close by me, at my side, at my feet, there was a sigh. No, not a groan, not a moaning, not anything so tangible, – a perfectly soft, faint, inarticulate sigh. I sprang back, and my heart stopped beating. Mistaken! no, mistake was impossible. I heard it as clearly as I hear myself speak; a long, soft, weary sigh, as if drawn to the utmost, and emptying out a load of sadness that filled the breast. To hear this in the solitude, in the dark, in the night (though it was still early), had an effect which I cannot describe. I feel it now, – something cold creeping over me up into my hair, and down to my feet, which refused to move. I cried out, with a trembling voice, "Who is there?" as I had done before; but there was no reply.

I got home I don't quite know how; but in my mind there was no longer any indifference as to the thing, whatever it was, that haunted these ruins. My scepticism disappeared like a mist. I was as firmly determined that there was something as Roland was. I did not for a moment pretend to myself that it was possible I could be deceived; there were movements and noises which I understood all about, – cracklings of small branches in the frost, and little rolls of gravel on the path, such as have a very eerie sound sometimes, and perplex you with wonder as to who has done it, *when there is no real mystery*; but I assure you all these little movements of nature don't affect you one bit *when there is something*. I understood *them*. I did not understand the sigh. That was not simple nature; there was meaning in it, feeling, the soul of a creature invisible. This is the thing that human nature trembles at, – a creature invisible, yet with sensations, feelings, a power somehow of expressing itself. Bagley was in the hall as usual when I went in. He was always there in the afternoon, always with the appearance of perfect occupation, yet, so far as I know, never doing anything. The door was open, so that I hurried in without any pause, breathless; but the sight of his calm regard, as he came to help me off with my overcoat, subdued me in a moment. Anything out of the way, anything incomprehensible, faded to nothing in the presence of Bagley. You saw and wondered how *he* was made: the parting of his hair, the tie of his white neckcloth, the fit of his trousers, all perfect as works of art: but you could see how they were done, which makes all the difference. I flung myself upon him, so to speak, without waiting to note the extreme unlikeness of the man to anything of the kind I meant. "Bagley," I said, "I want you to come out with me tonight to watch for—"

"Poachers, Colonel?" he said, a gleam of pleasure running all over him.

"No, Bagley; a great deal worse," I cried.

"Yes, Colonel; at what hour, sir?" the man said; but then I had not told him what it was.

It was ten o'clock when we set out. All was perfectly quiet indoors. My wife was with Roland, who had been quite calm, she said, and who (though, no doubt, the fever must run its course) had been better ever since I came. I told Bagley to put on a thick greatcoat over his evening coat, and did the same myself, with strong boots; for the soil was like a sponge, or worse. Talking to him, I almost forgot what we were going to do. It was darker even than it had been before, and Bagley kept very close to me as we went along. I had a small lantern in my hand, which gave us a partial guidance. We had come to the corner where the path turns. On one side was the bowling-green, which the girls had taken possession of for their croquet-ground, – a wonderful enclosure surrounded by high hedges of holly, three hundred years old and more; on the other, the ruins. Both were black as night; but before we got so far, there was a little opening in which we could just discern the trees and the lighter line of the road. I thought it best to pause there and take breath. "Bagley," I said, "there is something about these ruins I don't understand. It is there I am going. Keep your eyes open and your wits about you. Be ready to pounce upon any stranger you see, – anything, man or woman. Don't hurt, but seize – anything you see." "Colonel," said Bagley, with a little tremor in his breath, "they do say there's things there – as is neither man nor woman." There was no time for words. "Are you game to follow me, my man? that's the question," I said. Bagley fell in without a word, and saluted. I knew then I had nothing to fear.

We went, so far as I could guess, exactly as I had come, when I heard that sigh. The darkness, however, was so complete that all marks, as of trees or paths, disappeared. One moment we felt our feet on the gravel, another sinking noiselessly into the slippery grass, that was all. I had shut up my lantern, not wishing to scare any one, whoever it might be. Bagley followed, it seemed to me, exactly in my footsteps as I made my way, as I supposed, towards the mass of the ruined house. We seemed to take a long time groping along seeking this; the squash of the wet soil under our feet was the only thing that marked our progress. After a while I stood still to see, or rather feel, where we were. The darkness was very still, but no stiller than is usual in a winter's night. The sounds I have mentioned – the crackling of twigs, the roll of a pebble, the sound of some rustle in the dead leaves, or creeping creature on the grass – were audible when you listened, all mysterious enough when your mind is disengaged, but to me cheering now as signs of the livingness of nature, even in the death of the frost. As we stood still there came up from the trees in the glen the prolonged hoot of an owl. Bagley started with alarm, being in a state of general nervousness, and not knowing what he was afraid of. But to me the sound was encouraging and pleasant, being so comprehensible. "An owl," I said, under my breath. "Y – es, Colonel," said Bagley, his teeth chattering. We stood still about five minutes, while it broke into the still brooding of the air, the sound widening out in circles, dying upon the darkness. This sound, which is not a cheerful one, made me almost gay. It was natural, and relieved the tension of the mind. I moved on with new courage, my nervous excitement calming down.

When all at once, quite suddenly, close to us, at our feet, there broke out a cry. I made a spring backwards in the first moment of surprise and horror, and in doing so came sharply against the same rough masonry and brambles that had struck me before. This new sound came upwards from the ground, – a low, moaning, wailing voice, full of suffering and pain. The contrast between it and the hoot of the owl was indescribable, – the one with a wholesome wildness and naturalness that hurt nobody; the other, a sound that made one's blood curdle, full of human misery. With a great deal of fumbling, – for in spite of everything I could do to keep up my courage my hands shook, – I managed to remove the slide of my lantern. The light leaped out like something living, and made the place visible in a moment. We were what would have been inside the ruined building had anything remained but the gable-wall which I have described. It was close to us, the vacant door-way in it going out straight into the blackness outside. The light showed the bit of wall, the ivy glistening upon it in clouds of dark green, the bramble-branches waving, and below, the open door, – a door that led to nothing. It was from this the voice came which died out just as the light flashed upon this strange scene. There was a moment's silence, and then it broke forth again. The sound was so near, so penetrating, so pitiful, that, in the nervous start I gave, the light fell out of my hand. As I groped for it in the dark my hand was clutched by Bagley, who, I think, must have dropped upon his knees; but I was too much perturbed myself to think much of this. He clutched at me in the confusion of his terror, forgetting all his usual decorum. "For God's sake, what is it, sir?" he gasped. If I yielded, there was evidently an end of both of us. "I can't tell," I said, "any more than you; that's what we've got to find out. Up, man, up!" I pulled him to his feet. "Will you go round and examine the other side, or will you stay here with the lantern?" Bagley gasped at me with a face of horror. "Can't we stay together, Colonel?" he said; his knees were trembling under him. I pushed him against the corner of the wall, and put the light into his hands. "Stand fast till I come back; shake yourself together, man; let nothing pass you," I said. The voice was within two or three feet of us; of that there could be no doubt.

I went myself to the other side of the wall, keeping close to it. The light shook in Bagley's hand, but, tremulous though it was, shone out through the vacant door, one oblong block of light marking all the crumbling corners and hanging masses of foliage. Was that something dark huddled in a heap by the side of it? I pushed forward across the light in the door-way, and fell upon it with my hands; but it was only a juniper-bush growing close against the wall. Meanwhile, the sight of my figure crossing the door-way had brought Bagley's nervous excitement to a height; he flew at me, gripping my shoulder. "I've got him, Colonel! I've got him!" he cried, with a voice of sudden exultation. He thought it was a man, and was at once relieved. But at the moment the voice burst forth again between us, at our feet, – more close to us than any separate being could be. He dropped off from me, and fell against the wall, his jaw dropping as if he were dying. I suppose, at the same moment, he saw that it was me whom he had clutched. I for my part, had scarcely more command of myself. I snatched the light out of his hand, and flashed it all about me wildly. Nothing, – the juniper-bush which I thought I had never seen before, the heavy growth of the glistening ivy, the brambles waving. It was close to my ears now, crying, crying, pleading as if for life. Either I heard the same words Roland had heard, or else, in my excitement, his imagination got possession of mine. The voice went on, growing into distinct articulation, but wavering about, now from one point, now from another, as if the owner of it were moving slowly back and forward. "Mother! mother!" and then an outburst of wailing. As my mind steadied, getting accustomed (as one's mind gets accustomed to anything), it seemed to me as if some uneasy, miserable creature was pacing up and down before a closed door. Sometimes – but that must have been excitement – I thought I heard a sound like knocking, and then another burst, "Oh, mother! mother!" All this close, close to the space where I was standing with my lantern, now before me, now behind me: a creature restless, unhappy, moaning, crying, before the vacant door-way, which no one could either shut or open more.

"Do you hear it, Bagley? do you hear what it is saying?" I cried, stepping in through the door-way. He was lying against the wall, his eyes glazed, half dead with terror. He made a motion of his lips as if to answer me, but no sounds came; then lifted his hand with a curious imperative movement as if ordering me to be silent and listen. And how long I did so I cannot tell. It began to have an interest, an exciting hold upon me, which I could not describe. It seemed to call up visibly a scene any one could understand, – a something shut out, restlessly wandering to and fro; sometimes the voice dropped, as if throwing itself down, sometimes wandered off a few paces, growing sharp and clear. "Oh, mother, let me in! oh, mother, mother, let me in! oh, let me in." Every word was clear to me. No wonder the boy had gone wild with pity. I tried to steady my mind upon Roland, upon his conviction that I could do something, but my head swam with the excitement, even when I partially overcame the terror. At last the words died away, and there was a sound of sobs and moaning. I cried out, "In the name of God who are you?" with a kind of feeling in my mind that to use the name of God was profane, seeing that I did not believe in ghosts or anything supernatural; but I did it all the same, and waited, my heart giving a leap of terror lest there should be a reply. Why this should have been I cannot tell, but I had a feeling that if there was an answer it would be more than I could bear. But there was no answer, the moaning went on, and then, as if it had been real, the voice rose a little higher again, the words recommenced, "Oh, mother, let me in! oh, mother, let me in!" with an expression that was heart-breaking to hear.

As if it had been real! What do I mean by that? I suppose I got less alarmed as the thing went on. I began to recover the use of my senses, – I seemed to explain it all to myself by saying that this had once happened, that it was a recollection of a real scene. Why there should have seemed something quite satisfactory and composing in this explanation I cannot tell, but so it was. I began to listen almost as if it had been a play, forgetting Bagley, who, I almost think, had fainted, leaning against the wall. I was started out of this strange spectatorship that had fallen upon me by the sudden rush of something which made my heart jump once more, a large black figure in the doorway waving its arms. "Come in! come in! come in!" it shouted out hoarsely at the top of a deep bass voice, and then poor Bagley fell down senseless across the threshold. He was less sophisticated than I, – he had not been able to bear it any longer. I took him for something supernatural, as he took me, and it was some time before I awoke to the necessities of the moment. I remembered only after, that from the time I began to give my attention to the man, I heard the other voice no more. It was some time before I brought him to. It must have been a strange scene: the lantern making a luminous spot in the darkness, the man's white face lying on the black earth, I over him, doing what I could for him. Probably I should have been thought to be murdering him had any one seen us. When at last I succeeded in pouring a little brandy down his throat, he sat up and looked about him wildly. "What's up?" he said; then recognizing me, tried to struggle to his feet with a faint "Beg your pardon, Colonel." I got him home as best I could, making him lean upon my arm. The great fellow was as weak as a child. Fortunately he did not for some time remember what had happened. From the time Bagley fell the voice had stopped, and all was still.

* * *

"You've got an epidemic in your house, Colonel," Simson said to me next morning. "What's the meaning of it all? Here's your butler raving about a voice. This will never do, you know; and so far as I can make out, you are in it too."

"Yes, I am in it, Doctor. I thought I had better speak to you. Of course you are treating Roland all right, but the boy is not raving, he is as sane as you or me. It's all true."

"As sane as – I – or you. I never thought the boy insane. He's got cerebral excitement, fever. I don't know what you've got. There's something very queer about the look of your eyes."

"Come," said I, "you can't put us all to bed, you know. You had better listen and hear the symptoms in full."

The Doctor shrugged his shoulders, but he listened to me patiently. He did not believe a word of the story, that was clear; but he heard it all from beginning to end. "My dear fellow," he said, "the boy told me just the same. It's an epidemic. When one person falls a victim to this sort of thing, it's as safe as can be, – there's always two or three."

"Then how do you account for it?" I said.

"Oh, account for it! – that's a different matter; there's no accounting for the freaks our brains are subject to. If it's delusion, if it's some trick of the echoes or the winds, – some phonetic disturbance or other—"

"Come with me tonight and judge for yourself," I said.

Upon this he laughed aloud, then said, "That's not such a bad idea; but it would ruin me forever if it were known that John Simson was ghost-hunting."

"There it is," said I; "you dart down on us who are unlearned with your phonetic disturbances, but you daren't examine what the thing really is for fear of being laughed at. That's science!"

"It's not science, – it's common-sense," said the Doctor. "The thing has delusion on the front of it. It is encouraging an unwholesome tendency even to examine. What good could come of it? Even if I am convinced, I shouldn't believe."

"I should have said so yesterday; and I don't want you to be convinced or to believe," said I. "If you prove it to be a delusion, I shall be very much obliged to you for one. Come; somebody must go with me."

"You are cool," said the Doctor. "You've disabled this poor fellow of yours, and made him – on that point – a lunatic for life; and now you want to disable me. But, for once, I'll do it. To save appearance, if you'll give me a bed, I'll come over after my last rounds."

It was agreed that I should meet him at the gate, and that we should visit the scene of last night's occurrences before we came to the house, so that nobody might be the wiser. It was scarcely possible to hope that the cause of Bagley's sudden illness should not somehow steal into the knowledge of the servants at least, and it was better that all should be done as quietly as possible. The day seemed to me a very long one. I had to spend a certain part of it with Roland, which was a terrible ordeal for me, for what could I say to the boy? The improvement continued, but he was still in a very precarious state, and the trembling vehemence with which he turned to me when his mother left the room filled me with alarm. "Father?" he said quietly. "Yes, my boy, I am giving my best attention to it; all is being done that I can do. I have not come to any conclusion – yet. I am neglecting nothing you said," I cried. What I could not do was to give his active mind any encouragement to dwell upon the mystery. It was a hard predicament, for some satisfaction had to be given him. He looked at me very wistfully, with the great blue eyes which shone so large and brilliant out of his white and worn face. "You must trust me," I said. "Yes, father. Father understands," he said to himself, as if to soothe some inward doubt. I left him as soon as I could. He was about the most precious thing I had on earth, and his health my first thought; but yet somehow, in the excitement of this other subject, I put that aside, and preferred not to dwell upon Roland, which was the most curious part of it all.

That night at eleven I met Simson at the gate. He had come by train, and I let him in gently myself. I had been so much absorbed in the coming experiment that I passed the ruins in going to meet him, almost without thought, if you can understand that. I had my lantern; and he showed me a coil of taper which he had ready for use. "There is nothing like light," he said in his scoffing tone. It was a very still night, scarcely a sound, but not so dark. We could keep the path without difficulty as we went along. As we approached the spot we could hear a low moaning, broken occasionally by a bitter cry. "Perhaps that is your voice," said the Doctor; "I thought it must be something of the kind. That's a poor brute caught in some of these infernal traps of yours; you'll find it among the bushes somewhere." I said nothing. I felt no particular fear, but a triumphant satisfaction in what was to follow. I led him to the spot where Bagley and I had stood on the previous night. All was silent as a winter night could be,

– so silent that we heard far off the sound of the horses in the stables, the shutting of a window at the house. Simson lighted his taper and went peering about, poking into all the corners. We looked like two conspirators lying in wait for some unfortunate traveller; but not a sound broke the quiet. The moaning had stopped before we came up; a star or two shone over us in the sky, looking down as if surprised at our strange proceedings. Dr. Simson did nothing but utter subdued laughs under his breath. "I thought as much," he said. "It is just the same with tables and all other kinds of ghostly apparatus; a sceptic's presence stops everything. When I am present nothing ever comes off. How long do you think it will be necessary to stay here? Oh, I don't complain; only when *you* are satisfied I am – quite."

I will not deny that I was disappointed beyond measure by this result. It made me look like a credulous fool. It gave the Doctor such a pull over me as nothing else could. I should point all his morals for years to come; and his materialism, his scepticism, would be increased beyond endurance. "It seems, indeed," I said, "that there is to be no—" "Manifestation," he said, laughing; "that is what all the mediums say. No manifestations, in consequence of the presence of an unbeliever." His laugh sounded very uncomfortable to me in the silence; and it was now near midnight. But that laugh seemed the signal; before it died away the moaning we had heard before was resumed. It started from some distance off, and came towards us, nearer and nearer, like some one walking along and moaning to himself. There could be no idea now that it was a hare caught in a trap. The approach was slow, like that of a weak person, with little halts and pauses. We heard it coming along the grass straight towards the vacant door-way. Simson had been a little startled by the first sound. He said hastily, "That child has no business to be out so late." But he felt, as well as I, that this was no child's voice. As it came nearer, he grew silent, and, going to the door-way with his taper, stood looking out towards the sound. The taper being unprotected blew about in the night air, though there was scarcely any wind. I threw the light of my lantern steady and white across the same space. It was in a blaze of light in the midst of the blackness. A little icy thrill had gone over me at the first sound, but as it came close, I confess that my only feeling was satisfaction. The scoffer could scoff no more. The light touched his own face, and showed a very perplexed countenance. If he was afraid, he concealed it with great success, but he was perplexed. And then all that had happened on the previous night was enacted once more. It fell strangely upon me with a sense of repetition. Every cry, every sob seemed the same as before. I listened almost without any emotion at all in my own person, thinking of its effect upon Simson. He maintained a very bold front, on the whole. All that coming and going of the voice was, if our ears could be trusted, exactly in front of the vacant, blank door-way, blazing full of light, which caught and shone in the glistening leaves of the great hollies at a little distance. Not a rabbit could have crossed the turf without being seen; but there was nothing. After a time, Simson, with a certain caution and bodily reluctance, as it seemed to me, went out with his roll of taper into this space. His figure showed against the holly in full outline. Just at this moment the voice sank, as was its custom, and seemed to fling itself down at the door. Simson recoiled violently, as if some one had come up against him, then turned, and held his taper low, as if examining something. "Do you see anybody?" I cried in a whisper, feeling the chill of nervous panic steal over me at this action. "It's nothing but a – confounded juniper-bush," he said. This I knew very well to be nonsense, for the juniper-bush was on the other side. He went about after this, round and round, poking his taper everywhere, then returned to me on the inner side of the wall. He scoffed no longer; his face was contracted and pale. "How long does this go on?" he whispered to me, like a man who does not wish to interrupt some one who is speaking. I had become too much perturbed myself to remark whether the successions and changes of the voice were the same as last night. It suddenly went out in the air almost as he was speaking, with a soft reiterated sob dying away. If there had been anything to be seen, I should have said that the person was at that moment crouching on the ground close to that door.

We walked home very silent afterwards. It was only when we were in sight of the house that I said, "What do you think of it?" "I can't tell what to think of it," he said quickly. He took – though he was a very temperate man – not the claret I was going to offer him, but some brandy from the tray, and swallowed it almost undiluted. "Mind you, I don't believe a word of it," he said, when he had lighted his candle; "but I can't tell what to think," he turned round to add, when he was half-way upstairs.

All of this, however, did me no good with the solution of my problem. I was to help this weeping, sobbing thing, which was already to me as distinct a personality as anything I knew; or what should I say to Roland? It was on my heart that my boy would die if I could not find some way of helping this creature. You may be surprised that I should speak of it in this way. I did not know if it was man or woman; but I no more doubted that it was a soul in pain than I doubted my own being; and it was my business to soothe this pain, – to deliver it, if that was possible. Was ever such a task given to an anxious father trembling for his only boy? I felt in my heart, fantastic as it may appear, that I must fulfil this somehow, or part with my child; and you may conceive that rather than do that I was ready to die. But even my dying would not have advanced me, unless by bringing me into the same world with that seeker at the door.

* * *

Next morning Simson was out before breakfast, and came in with evident signs of the damp grass on his boots, and a look of worry and weariness, which did not say much for the night he had passed. He improved a little after breakfast, and visited his two patients, – for Bagley was still an invalid. I went out with him on his way to the train, to hear what he had to say about the boy. "He is going on very well," he said; "there are no complications as yet. But mind you, that's not a boy to be trifled with, Mortimer. Not a word to him about last night." I had to tell him then of my last interview with Roland, and of the impossible demand he had made upon me, by which, though he tried to laugh, he was much discomposed, as I could see. "We must just perjure ourselves all round," he said, "and swear you exorcised it"; but the man was too kind-hearted to be satisfied with that. "It's frightfully serious for you, Mortimer. I can't laugh as I should like to. I wish I saw a way out of it, for your sake. By the way," he added shortly, "didn't you notice that juniper-bush on the left-hand side?" "There was one on the right hand of the door. I noticed you made that mistake last night." "Mistake!" he cried, with a curious low laugh, pulling up the collar of his coat as though he felt the cold, – "there's no juniper there this morning, left or right. Just go and see." As he stepped into the train a few minutes after, he looked back upon me and beckoned me for a parting word. "I'm coming back tonight," he said.

I don't think I had any feeling about this as I turned away from that common bustle of the railway which made my private preoccupations feel so strangely out of date. There had been a distinct satisfaction in my mind before, that his scepticism had been so entirely defeated. But the more serious part of the matter pressed upon me now. I went straight from the railway to the manse, which stood on a little plateau on the side of the river opposite to the woods of Brentwood. The minister was one of a class which is not so common in Scotland as it used to be. He was a man of good family, well educated in the Scotch way, strong in philosophy, not so strong in Greek, strongest of all in experience, – a man who had "come across," in the course of his life, most people of note that had ever been in Scotland, and who was said to be very sound in doctrine, without infringing the toleration with which old men, who are good men, are generally endowed. He was old-fashioned; perhaps he did not think so much about the troublous problems of theology as many of the young men, nor ask himself any hard questions about the Confession of Faith; but he understood human nature, which is perhaps better. He received me with a cordial welcome. "Come away, Colonel Mortimer," he said; "I'm all the more glad to see you, that I feel it's a good sign for the boy. He's doing well? – God be praised, – and the Lord bless him and keep him. He has many a poor body's prayers, and that can do nobody harm."

"He will need them all, Dr. Moncrieff," I said, "and your counsel, too." And I told him the story, – more than I had told Simson. The old clergyman listened to me with many suppressed exclamations, and at the end the water stood in his eyes.

"That's just beautiful," he said. "I do not mind to have heard anything like it; it's as fine as Burns when he wished deliverance to one – that is prayed for in no kirk. Ay, ay! so he would have you console the poor lost spirit? God bless the boy! There's something more than common in that, Colonel Mortimer. And also the faith of him in his father! – I would like to put that into a sermon." Then the old gentleman gave me an alarmed look, and said, "No, no; I was not meaning a sermon; but I must write it down for the 'Children's Record.'" I saw the thought that passed through his mind. Either he thought, or he feared I would think, of a funeral sermon. You may believe this did not make me more cheerful.

I can scarcely say that Dr. Moncrieff gave me any advice. How could any one advise on such a subject? But he said, "I think I'll come too. I'm an old man; I'm less liable to be frightened than those that are further off the world unseen. It behooves me to think of my own journey there. I've no cut-and-dry beliefs on the subject. I'll come too; and maybe at the moment the Lord will put into our heads what to do."

This gave me a little comfort, – more than Simson had given me. To be clear about the cause of it was not my grand desire. It was another thing that was in my mind, – my boy. As for the poor soul at the open door, I had no more doubt, as I have said, of its existence than I had of my own. It was no ghost to me. I knew the creature, and it was in trouble. That was my feeling about it, as it was Roland's. To hear it first was a great shock to my nerves, but not now; a man will get accustomed to anything. But to do something for it was the great problem; how was I to be serviceable to a being that was invisible, that was mortal no longer? "Maybe at the moment the Lord will put it into our heads." This is very old-fashioned phraseology, and a week before, most likely, I should have smiled (though always with kindness) at Dr. Moncrieff's credulity; but there was a great comfort, whether rational or otherwise I cannot say, in the mere sound of the words.

The road to the station and the village lay through the glen, not by the ruins; but though the sunshine and the fresh air, and the beauty of the trees, and the sound of the water were all very soothing to the spirits, my mind was so full of my own subject that I could not refrain from turning to the right hand as I got to the top of the glen, and going straight to the place which I may call the scene of all my thoughts. It was lying full in the sunshine, like all the rest of the world. The ruined gable looked due east, and in the present aspect of the sun the light streamed down through the door-way as our lantern had done, throwing a flood of light upon the damp grass beyond. There was a strange suggestion in the open door, – so futile, a kind of emblem of vanity: all free around, so that you could go where you pleased, and yet that semblance of an enclosure, – that way of entrance, unnecessary, leading to nothing. And why any creature should pray and weep to get in – to nothing, or be kept out – by nothing! You could not dwell upon it, or it made your brain go round. I remembered, however, what Simson said about the juniper, with a little smile on my own mind as to the inaccuracy of recollection which even a scientific man will be guilty of. I could see now the light of my lantern gleaming upon the wet glistening surface of the spiky leaves at the right hand, – and he ready to go to the stake for it that it was the left! I went round to make sure. And then I saw what he had said. Right or left there was no juniper at all! I was confounded by this, though it was entirely a matter of detail: nothing at all, – a bush of brambles waving, the grass growing up to the very walls. But after all, though it gave me a shock for a moment, what did that matter? There were marks as if a number of footsteps had been up and down in front of the door, but these might have been our steps; and all was bright and peaceful and still. I poked about the other ruin – the larger ruins of the old house – for some time, as I had done before. There were marks upon the grass here and there – I could not call them footsteps – all about; but that told for nothing one way or another. I had examined the ruined rooms closely the first day. They were half-filled up with soil and debris, withered brackens and bramble, – no refuge for any one there. It vexed me that Jarvis should see me coming from that spot when he came up to me for his orders. I don't know whether my nocturnal expeditions had got wind among the servants. But there was a significant look in his face. Something in it I felt was like my own sensation when Simson in the midst of his scepticism was struck dumb. Jarvis felt satisfied that his veracity had been put beyond question. I never spoke to a servant of mine in such a peremptory tone before. I sent him away "with a flea in his lug," as the man described it afterwards. Interference of any kind was intolerable to me at such a moment.

But what was strangest of all was, that I could not face Roland. I did not go up to his room, as I would have naturally done, at once. This the girls could not understand. They saw there was some mystery in it. "Mother has gone to lie down," Agatha said; "he has had such a good night." "But he wants you so, papa!" cried little Jeanie, always with her two arms embracing mine in a pretty way she had. I was obliged to go at last, but what could I say? I could only kiss him, and tell him to keep still, – that I was doing all I could. There is something mystical about the patience of a child. "It will come all right, won't it, father?" he said. "God grant it may! I hope so, Roland." "Oh, yes, it will come all right." Perhaps he understood that in the midst of my anxiety I could not stay with him as I should have done otherwise.

But the girls were more surprised than it is possible to describe. They looked at me with wondering eyes. "If I were ill, papa, and you only stayed with me a moment, I should break my heart," said Agatha. But the boy had a sympathetic feeling. He knew that of my own will I would not have done it. I shut myself up in the library, where I could not rest, but kept pacing up and down like a caged beast. What could I do? and if I could do nothing, what would become of my boy? These were the questions that, without ceasing, pursued each other through my mind.

Simson came out to dinner, and when the house was all still, and most of the servants in bed, we went out and met Dr. Moncrieff, as we had appointed, at the head of the glen. Simson, for his part, was disposed to scoff at the Doctor. "If there are to be any spells, you know, I'll cut the whole concern," he said. I did not make him any reply. I had not invited him; he could go or come as he pleased. He was very talkative, far more so than suited my humour, as we went on. "One thing is certain, you know; there must be some human agency," he said. "It is all bosh about apparitions. I never have investigated the laws of sound to any great extent, and there's a great deal in ventriloquism that we don't know much about." "If it's the same to you," I said, "I wish you'd keep all that to yourself, Simson. It doesn't suit my state of mind." "Oh, I hope I know how to respect idiosyncrasy," he said. The very tone of his voice irritated me beyond measure. These scientific fellows, I wonder people put up with them as they do, when you have no mind for their cold-blooded confidence. Dr. Moncrieff met us about eleven o'clock, the same time as on the previous night. He was a large man, with a venerable countenance and white hair, – old, but in full vigour, and thinking less of a cold night walk than many a younger man. He had his lantern, as I had. We were fully provided with means of lighting the place, and we were all of us resolute men. We had a rapid consultation as we went up, and the result was that we divided to different posts. Dr. Moncrieff remained inside the wall – if you can call that inside where there was no wall but one. Simson placed himself on the side next the ruins, so as to intercept any communication with the old house, which was what his mind was fixed upon. I was posted on the other side. To say that nothing could come near without being seen was self-evident. It had been so also on the previous night. Now, with our three lights in the midst of the darkness, the whole place seemed illuminated. Dr. Moncrieff's lantern, which was a large one, without any means of shutting up, – an old-fashioned lantern with a pierced and ornamental top, – shone steadily, the rays shooting out of it upward into the gloom. He placed it on the grass, where the middle of the room, if this had been a room, would have been. The usual effect of the light streaming out of the door-way was prevented by the illumination which Simson and I on either side supplied. With these differences, everything seemed as on the previous night.

And what occurred was exactly the same, with the same air of repetition, point for point, as I had formerly remarked. I declare that it seemed to me as if I were pushed against, put aside, by the owner of the voice as he paced up and down in his trouble, – though these are perfectly futile words, seeing that the stream of light from my lantern, and that from Simson's taper, lay broad and clear, without a shadow, without the smallest break, across the entire breadth of the grass. But just as it threw itself sobbing at the door (I cannot use other words), there suddenly came something which sent the blood coursing through my veins, and my heart into my mouth. It was a voice inside the wall, – my minister's well-known voice. I would have been prepared for it in any kind of adjuration, but I was not prepared for what I heard. It came out with a sort of stammering, as if too much moved for utterance. "Willie, Willie! Oh, God preserve us! is it you?"

I made a dash round to the other side of the wall. The old minister was standing where I had left him, his shadow thrown vague and large upon the grass by the lantern which stood at his feet. I lifted my own light to see his face. He was very pale, his eyes wet and glistening, his mouth quivering with parted lips. He neither saw nor heard me. His whole being seemed absorbed in anxiety and tenderness. He held out his hands, which trembled, but it seemed to me with eagerness, not fear. He went on speaking all the time. "Willie, if it is you, – and it's you, if it is not a delusion of Satan, – Willie, lad! why come ye here frighting them that know you not? Why came ye not to me? Your mother's gone with your name on her lips. Do you think she would ever close her door on her own lad? Do ye think the Lord will close the door, ye faint-hearted creature? No! – I forbid ye! I forbid ye!" cried the old man. The sobbing voice had begun to resume its cries. He made a step forward, calling out the last words in a voice of command. "I forbid ye! Cry out no more to man. Go home, ye wandering spirit! go home! Do you hear me? – me that christened ye, that have struggled with ye, that have wrestled for ye with the Lord!" Here the loud tones of his voice sank into tenderness. "And her too, poor woman! poor woman! her you are calling upon. She's no here. You'll find her with the Lord. Go there and seek her, not here. Do you hear me, lad? go after her there. He'll let you in, though it's late. Man, take heart! if you will lie and sob and greet, let it be at heaven's gate, and no your poor mother's ruined door."

He stopped to get his breath; and the voice had stopped, not as it had done before, when its time was exhausted and all its repetitions said, but with a sobbing catch in the breath as if overruled. Then the minister spoke again, "Are you hearing me, Will? Oh, laddie, you've liked the beggarly elements all your days. Be done with them now. Go home to the Father – the Father! Are you hearing me?" Here the old man sank down upon his knees, his face raised upwards, his hands held up with a tremble in them, all white in the light in the midst of the darkness. I resisted as long as I could, though I cannot tell why; then I, too, dropped upon my knees. Simson all the time stood in the door-way, with an expression in his face such as words could not tell, his under lip dropped, his eyes wild, staring. It seemed to be to him, that image of blank ignorance and wonder, that we were praying. All the time the voice, with a low arrested sobbing, lay just where he was standing, as I thought.

"Lord," the minister said, – "Lord, take him into Thy everlasting habitations. The mother he cries to is with Thee. Who can open to him but Thee? Lord, when is it too late for Thee, or what is too hard for Thee? Lord, let that woman there draw him inower! Let her draw him inower!"

I sprang forward to catch something in my arms that flung itself wildly within the door. The illusion was so strong, that I never paused till I felt my forehead graze against the wall and my hands clutch the ground, – for there was nobody there to save from falling, as in my foolishness I thought. Simson held out his hand to me to help me up. He was trembling and cold, his lower lip hanging, his speech almost inarticulate. "It's gone," he said, stammering, – "it's gone!"

As long as I live I will never forget the shining of the strange lights, the blackness all round, the kneeling figure with all the whiteness of the light concentrated on its white venerable head and uplifted hands. I never knew how long we stood, like sentinels guarding him at his prayers. But at last the old minister rose from his knees, and standing up at his full height, raised his arms, as the Scotch manner is at the end of a religious service, and solemnly gave the apostolical benediction, – to what? to the silent earth, the dark woods, the wide breathing atmosphere; for we were but spectators gasping an Amen!

It seemed to me that it must be the middle of the night, as we all walked back. It was in reality very late. Dr. Moncrieff himself was the first to speak. "I must be going," he said; "I will go down the glen, as I came."

"But not alone. I am going with you, Doctor."

"Well, I will not oppose it. I am an old man, and agitation wearies more than work. Yes; I'll be thankful of your arm. Tonight, Colonel, you've done me more good turns than one."

I pressed his hand on my arm, not feeling able to speak. But Simson, who turned with us, and who had gone along all this time with his taper flaring, in entire unconsciousness, became himself, sceptical and cynical. "I should like to ask you a question," he said. "Do you believe in Purgatory, Doctor? It's not in the tenets of the Church, so far as I know."

"Sir," said Dr. Moncrieff, "an old man like me is sometimes not very sure what he believes. There is just one thing I am certain of – and that is the loving-kindness of God."

"But I thought that was in this life. I am no theologian—"

"Sir," said the old man again, with a tremor in him which I could feel going over all his frame, "if I saw a friend of mine within the gates of hell, I would not despair but his Father would take him by the hand still, if he cried like *you*."

"I allow it is very strange, very strange. I cannot see through it. That there must be human agency, I feel sure. Doctor, what made you decide upon the person and the name?"

The minister put out his hand with the impatience which a man might show if he were asked how he recognized his brother. "Tuts!" he said, in familiar speech; then more solemnly, "How should I not recognize a person that I know better – far better – than I know you?"

"Then you saw the man?"

Dr. Moncrieff made no reply. He moved his hand again with a little impatient movement, and walked on, leaning heavily on my arm. We parted with him at his own door, where his old housekeeper appeared in great perturbation, waiting for him. "Eh, me, minister! the young gentleman will be worse?" she cried.

"Far from that – better. God bless him!" Dr. Moncrieff said.

I think if Simson had begun again to me with his questions, I should have pitched him over the rocks as we returned up the glen; but he was silent, by a good inspiration. And the sky was clearer than it had been for many nights, shining high over the trees, with here and there a star faintly gleaming through the wilderness of dark and bare branches. We went up to the boy's room when we went in. There we found the complete hush of rest. My wife looked up out of a doze, and gave me a smile; "I think he is a great deal better; but you are very late," she said in a whisper, shading the light with her hand that the Doctor might see his patient. The boy had got back something like his own colour. He woke as we stood all round his bed. His eyes had the happy, half-awakened look of childhood, glad to shut again, yet pleased with the interruption and glimmer of the light. I stooped over him and kissed his forehead, which was moist and cool. "All is well, Roland," I said. He looked up at me with a glance of pleasure, and took my hand and laid his cheek upon it, and so went to sleep.

* * *

For some nights after, I watched among the ruins, spending all the dark hours up to midnight patrolling about the bit of wall which was associated with so many emotions; but I heard nothing, and saw nothing beyond the quiet course of nature; nor, so far as I am aware, has anything been heard again. Dr. Moncrieff gave me the history of the youth, whom he never hesitated to name. I did not ask, as Simson did, how he recognized him. He had been a prodigal, – weak, foolish, easily imposed upon, and "led away," as people say. All that we had heard had passed actually in life, the Doctor said. The young man had come home thus a day or two after his mother died, – who was no more than housekeeper in the old house, – and distracted with the news, had thrown himself down at the door and called upon her to let him in. The old man could scarcely speak of it for tears. He was not terrified, as I had been myself, and all the rest of us. It was no "ghost," as I fear we all vulgarly considered it, to him, – but a poor creature whom he knew under these conditions, just as he had known him in the flesh, having no doubt of his identity. And to Roland it was the same. This spirit in pain, – if it was a spirit, – this voice out of the unseen, – was a poor fellow-creature in misery, to be succoured and helped out of his trouble, to my boy. He spoke to me quite frankly about it when he got better. "I knew father would find out some way," he said. And this was when he was strong and well, and all idea that he would turn hysterical or become a seer of visions had happily passed away.

* * *

I must add one curious fact, which does not seem to me to have any relation to the above, but which Simson made great use of, as the human agency which he was determined to find somehow. One Sunday afternoon Simson found a little hole, – for it was more a hole than a room, – entirely hidden under the ivy and ruins, in which there was a quantity of straw laid in a corner, as if some one had made a bed there, and some remains of crusts about the floor. Some one had lodged there, and not very long before, he made out; and that this unknown being was the author of all the mysterious sounds we heard he is convinced. "I was puzzled myself, – I could not make it out, – but I always felt convinced human agency was at the bottom of it. And here it is, – and a clever fellow he must have been," the Doctor says. There is no argument with men of this kind.

Bagley left my service as soon as he got well. He assured me it was no want of respect, but he could not stand "them kind of things"; and the man was so shaken and ghastly that I was glad to give him a present and let him go. For my own part, I made a point of staying out the time – two years – for which I had taken Brentwood; but I did not renew my tenancy. By that time we had settled, and found for ourselves a pleasant home of our own.

I must add, that when the Doctor defies me, I can always bring back gravity to his countenance, and a pause in his railing, when I remind him of the juniper-bush. To me that was a matter of little importance. I could believe I was mistaken. I did not care about it one way or other; but on his mind the effect was different. The miserable voice, the spirit in pain, he could think of as the result of ventriloquism, or reverberation, or – anything you please: an elabourate prolonged hoax, executed somehow by the tramp that had found a lodging in the old tower; but the juniper-bush staggered him. Things have effects so different on the minds of different men.

Wandering Willie's Tale

Sir Walter Scott

Ye maun have heard of Sir Robert Redgauntlet of that Ilk, who lived in these parts before the dear years. The country will lang mind him; and our fathers used to draw breath thick if ever they heard him named. He was out wi' the Hielandmen in Montrose's time; and again he was in the hills wi' Glencairn in the saxteen hundred and fifty-twa; and sae when King Charles the Second came in, wha was in sic favour as the Laird of Redgauntlet? He was knighted at Lonon court, wi' the King's ain sword; and being a redhot prelatist, he came down here, rampauging like a lion, with commissions of lieutenancy (and of lunacy, for what I ken), to put down a' the Whigs and Covenanters in the country. Wild wark they made of it; for the Whigs were as dour as the Cavaliers were fierce, and it was which should first tire the other. Redgauntlet was aye for the strong hand; and his name is kend as wide in the country as Claverhouse's or Tam Dalyell's. Glen, nor dargle, nor mountain, nor cave, could hide the puir hill-folk when Redgauntlet was out with bugle and bloodhound after them, as if they had been sae mony deer. And troth when they fand them, they didna mak muckle mair ceremony than a Hielandman wi' a roebuck – It was just, "Will ye tak the test?" – if not, "Make ready – present – fire!" – and there lay the recusant.

Far and wide was Sir Robert hated and feared. Men thought he had a direct compact with Satan – that he was proof against steel – and that bullets happed aff his buff-coat like hailstanes from a hearth – that he had a mear that would turn a hare on the side of Carrifragawns – and muckle to the same purpose, of whilk mair anon. The best blessing they wared on him was, "Deil scowp wi' Redgauntlet!" He wasna a bad maister to his ain folk, though, and was weel aneugh liked by his tenants; and as for the lackies and troopers that rade out wi' him to the persecutions, as the Whigs caa'd those killing times, they wad hae drunken themsells blind to his health at ony time.

Now you are to ken that my gudesire lived on Redgauntlet's grund – they ca' the place Primrose-Knowe. We had lived on the grund, and under the Redgauntlets, since the riding days, and lang before. It was a pleasant bit; and I think the air is callerer and fresher there than ony where else in the country. It's a' deserted now; and I sat on the broken door-cheek three days since, and was glad I couldna see the plight the place was in; but that's a' wide o' the mark. There dwelt my gudesire, Steenie Steenson, a rambling, rattling chiel he had been in his young days, and could play weel on the pipes; he was famous at "Hoopers and Girders" – a' Cumberland couldna touch him at "Jockie Lattin" – and he had the finest finger for the backlilt between Berwick and Carlisle. The like o' Steenie wasna the sort that they made Whigs o'. And so he became a Tory, as they ca' it, which we now ca' Jacobites, just out of a kind of needcessity, that he might belang to some side or other. He had nae ill-will to the Whig bodies, and liked little to see the blude rin, though, being obliged to follow Sir Robert in hunting and hosting, watching and warding, he saw muckle mischief, and maybe did some, that he couldna avoid.

Now Steenie was a kind of favourite with his master, and kend a' the folks about the Castle, and was often sent for to play the pipes when they were at their merriment. Auld Dougal MacCallum, the butler, that had followed Sir Robert through gude and ill, thick and thin, pool and stream, was specially fond of the pipes, and aye gae my gudesire his gude word wi' the Laird; for Dougal could turn his master round his finger.

Weel, round came the Revolution, and it had like to have broken the hearts baith of Dougal and his master. But the change was not a'thegether sae great as they feared, and other folk thought for. The Whigs made an unco crawing what they wad do with their auld enemies, and in special wi' Sir Robert Redgauntlet. But there were ower mony great folks dipped in the same doings, to mak a spick and span new warld. So Parliament passed it a' ower easy; and Sir Robert, bating that he was held to hunting foxes instead of Covenanters, remained just the man he was. His revel was as loud, and his hall as weel lighted, as ever it had been, though maybe he lacked the fines of the nonconformists, that used to come to stock his larder and cellar; for it is certain he began to be keener about the rents than his tenants used to find him before, and they behoved to be prompt to the rent-day, or else the Laird wasna pleased. And he was sic an awsome body, that naebody cared to anger him; for the oaths he swore, and the rage that he used to get into, and the looks that he put on, made men sometimes think him a devil incarnate.

Weel, my gudesire was nae manager – no that he was a very great misguider – but he hadna the saving gift, and he got twa terms' rent in arrear. He got the first brash at Whitsunday put ower wi' fair word and piping; but when Martinmas came, there was a summons from the grund-officer to come wi' the rent on a day preceese, or else Steenie behoved to flit. Sair wark he had to get the siller; but he was weel-freended, and at last he got the haill scraped thegether – a thousand merks – the maist of it was from a neighbour they caa'd Laurie Lapraik – a sly tod. Laurie had walth o' gear – could hunt wi' the hound and rin wi' the hare – and be Whig or Tory, saunt or sinner, as the wind stood. He was a professor in this Revolution warld, but he liked an orra sough of this warld, and a tune on the pipes weel aneugh at a by time; and abune a', he thought he had a gude security for the siller he lent my gudesire ower the stocking at Primrose-Knowe.

Away trots my gudesire to Redgauntlet Castle, wi' a heavy purse and a light heart, glad to be out of the Laird's danger. Weel, the first thing he learned at the Castle was, that Sir Robert had fretted himself into a fit of the gout, because he did not appear before twelve o'clock. It wasna a'thegether for sake of the money, Dougal thought; but because he didna like to part wi' my gudesire aff the grund. Dougal was glad to see Steenie, and brought him into the great oak parlour, and there sat the Laird his leesome lane, excepting that he had beside him a great, ill-favoured jackanape, that was a special pet of his; a cankered beast it was, and mony an ill-natured trick it played – ill to please it was, and easily angered – ran about the haill castle, chattering and yowling, and pinching, and biting folk, especially before ill-weather, or disturbances in the state. Sir Robert caa'd it Major Weir, after the warlock that was burnt; and few folk liked either the name or the conditions of the creature – they thought there was something in it by ordinary – and my gudesire was not just easy in his mind when the door shut on him, and he saw himself in the room wi' naebody but the Laird, Dougal MacCallum, and the Major, a thing that hadna chanced to him before.

Sir Robert sat, or, I should say, lay, in a great armchair, wi' his grand velvet gown, and his feet on a cradle; for he had baith gout and gravel, and his face looked as gash and ghastly as Satan's. Major Weir sat opposite to him, in a red laced coat, and the Laird's wig on his head; and aye as Sir Robert girned wi' pain, the jackanape girned too, like a sheep's-head between a pair of tangs – an ill-faur'd, fearsome couple they were. The Laird's buff-coat was hung on a pin behind him, and his broadsword and his pistols within reach; for he keepit up the auld fashion of having the weapons ready, and a horse saddled day and night, just as he used to do when he was able to loup on horseback, and away after ony of the hill-folk he could get speerings of. Some said it was for fear of the Whigs taking vengeance, but I judge it was just his auld custom – he wasna gien to fear ony thing. The rental-book, wi' its black cover and brass clasps, was lying beside him; and a book of sculduddry sangs was put betwixt the leaves, to keep it open at the place where it bore evidence against the Goodman of Primrose-Knowe, as behind the hand with his mails and duties. Sir Robert gave my gudesire a look, as if he would have withered his heart in his bosom. Ye maun ken he had a way of bending his brows, that men saw the visible mark of a horse-shoe in his forehead, deep-dinted, as if it had been stamped there.

"Are ye come light-handed, ye son of a toom whistle?" said Sir Robert. "Zounds! if you are—"

My gudesire, with as gude a countenance as he could put on, made a leg, and placed the bag of money on the table wi' a dash, like a man that does something clever. The Laird drew it to him hastily – "Is it all here, Steenie, man?"

"Your honour will find it right," said my gudesire.

"Here, Dougal," said the Laird, "gie Steenie a tass of brandy down stairs, till I count the siller and write the receipt."

But they werena weel out of the room, when Sir Robert gied a yelloch that garr'd the Castle rock. Back ran Dougal – in flew the livery men – yell on yell gied the Laird, ilk ane mair awfu' than the ither. My gudesire knew not whether to stand or flee, but he ventured back into the parlour, where a' was gaun hirdy-girdie – naebody to say "come in," or "gae out." Terribly the Laird roared for cauld water to his feet, and wine to cool his throat; and hell, hell, hell, and its flames, was aye the word in his mouth. They brought him water, and when they plunged his swoln feet into the tub, he cried out it was burning; and folk say that it *did* bubble and sparkle like a seething caldron. He flung the cup at Dougal's head, and said he had given him blood instead of burgundy; and, sure aneugh, the lass washed clotted blood aff the carpet the neist day. The jackanape they caa'd Major Weir, it jibbered and cried as if it was mocking its master; my gudesire's head was like to turn – he forgot baith siller and receipt, and down stairs he banged; but as he ran, the shrieks came faint and fainter; there was a deep-drawn shivering groan, and word gaed through the Castle, that the Laird was dead.

Weel, away came my gudesire, wi' his finger in his mouth, and his best hope was, that Dougal had seen the money-bag, and heard the Laird speak of writing the receipt. The young Laird, now Sir John, came from Edinburgh, to see things put to rights. Sir John and his father never gree'd weel. Sir John had been bred an advocate, and afterwards sat in the last Scots Parliament and voted for the Union, having gotten, it was thought, a rug of the compensations – if his father could have come out of his grave, he would have brained him for it on his awn hearthstane. Some thought it was easier counting with the auld rough Knight than the fair-spoken young ane – but mair of that anon.

Dougal MacCallum, poor body, neither grat nor graned, but gaed about the house looking like a corpse, but directing, as was his duty, a' the order of the grand funeral. Now, Dougal looked aye waur and waur when night was coming, and was aye the last to gang to his bed, whilk was in a little round just opposite the chamber of dais, whilk his master occupied while he was living, and where he now lay in state, as they caa'd it, weel-a-day! The night before the funeral, Dougal could keep his awn counsel nae langer; he cam doun with his proud spirit, and fairly asked auld Hutcheon to sit in his room with him for an hour. When they were in the round, Dougal took ae tass of brandy to himsell, and gave another to Hutcheon, and wished him all health and lang life, and said that, for himsell, he wasna lang for this world; for that, every night since Sir Robert's death, his silver call had sounded from the state-chamber, just as it used to do at nights in his lifetime, to call Dougal to help to turn him in his bed. Dougal said, that being alone with the dead on that floor of the tower (for naebody cared to wake Sir Robert Redgauntlet like another corpse), he had never daured to answer the call, but that now his conscience checked him for neglecting his duty; for, "though death breaks service," said MacCallum, "it shall never break my service to Sir Robert; and I will answer his next whistle, so be you will stand by me, Hutcheon."

Hutcheon had nae will to the wark, but he had stood by Dougal in battle and broil, and he wad not fail him at this pinch; so down the carles sat ower a stoup of brandy, and Hutcheon, who was something of a clerk, would have read a chapter of the Bible; but

Dougal would hear naething but a blaud of Davie Lindsay, whilk was the waur preparation.

When midnight came, and the house was quiet as the grave, sure aneugh the silver whistle sounded as sharp and shrill as if Sir Robert was blowing it, and up gat the twa auld serving-men, and tottered into the room where the dead man lay. Hutcheon saw aneugh at the first glance; for there were torches in the room, which showed him the foul fiend, in his ain shape, sitting on the Laird's coffin! Over he cowped as if he had been dead. He could not tell how lang he lay in a trance at the door, but when he gathered himself, he cried on his neighbour, and getting nae answer, raised the house, when Dougal was found lying dead within twa steps of the bed where his master's coffin was placed. As for the whistle, it was gaen anes and aye; but mony a time was it heard at the top of the house on the bartizan, and amang the auld chimneys and turrets, where the howlets have their nests. Sir John hushed the matter up, and the funeral passed over without mair bogle-wark.

But when a' was ower, and the Laird was beginning to settle his affairs, every tenant was called up for his arrears, and my gudesire for the full sum that stood against him in the rental-book. Weel, away he trots to the Castle, to tell his story, and there he is introduced to Sir John, sitting in his father's chair, in deep mourning, with weepers and hanging cravat, and a small walking rapier by his side, instead of the auld broadsword, that had a hundred-weight of steel about it, what with blade, chape, and basket-hilt. I have heard their communing so often tauld ower, that I almost think I was there mysell, though I couldna be born at the time. (In fact, Alan, my companion mimicked, with a good deal of humour, the flattering, conciliating tone of the tenant's address, and the hypocritical melancholy of the Laird's reply. His grandfather, he said, had, while he spoke, his eye fixed on the rental-book, as if it were a mastiff-dog that he was afraid would spring up and bite him.)

"I wuss ye joy, sir, of the head seat, and the white loaf, and the braid lairdship. Your father was a kind man to friends and followers; muckle grace to you, Sir John, to fill his shoon – his boots, I suld say, for he seldom wore shoon, unless it were muils when he had the gout."

"Ay, Steenie," quoth the Laird, sighing deeply and putting his napkin to his een, "his was a sudden call, and he will be missed in the country; no time to set his house in order – weel prepared Godward, no doubt, which is the root of the matter – but left us behind a tangled hesp to wind, Steenie. – Hem! hem! We maun go to business, Steenie; much to do, and little time to do it in."

Here he opened the fatal volume. I have heard of a thing they call Doomsday-book – I am clear it has been a rental of back-ganging tenants.

"Stephen," said Sir John, still in the same soft, sleekit tone of voice – "Stephen Stevenson, or Steenson, ye are down here for a year's rent behind the hand – due at last term."

Stephen. "Please your honour, Sir John, I paid it to your father."

Sir John. "Ye took a receipt then, doubtless, Stephen; and can produce it?"

Stephen. "Indeed I hadna time, an it like your honour; for nae sooner had I set doun the siller, and just as his honour Sir Robert, that's gaen, drew it till him to count it, and write out the receipt, he was ta'en wi' the pains that removed him."

"That was unlucky," said Sir John, after a pause. "But you maybe paid it in the presence of somebody. I want but a *talis qualis* evidence, Stephen. I would go ower strictly to work with no poor man."

Stephen. "Troth, Sir John, there was naebody in the room but Dougal MacCallum the butler. But, as your honour kens, he has e'en followed his auld master."

"Very unlucky again, Stephen," said Sir John, without altering his voice a single note. "The man to whom ye paid the money is dead – and the man who witnessed the payment is dead too – and the siller, which should have been to the fore, is neither seen nor heard tell of in the repositories. How am I to believe a' this?"

Stephen. "I dinna ken, your honour; but there is a bit memorandum note of the very coins; for, God help me! I had to borrow out of twenty purses; and I am sure that ilka man there set down will take his grit oath for what purpose I borrowed the money."

Sir John. "I have little doubt ye *borrowed* the money, Steenie. It is the *payment* to my father that I want to have some proof of."

Stephen. "The siller maun be about the house, Sir John. And since your honour never got it, and his honour that was canna have ta'en it wi' him, maybe some of the family may have seen it."

Sir John. "We will examine the servants, Stephen; that is but reasonable."

But lackey and lass, and page and groom, all denied stoutly that they had ever seen such a bag of money as my gudesire described. What was waur, he had unluckily not mentioned to any living soul of them his purpose of paying his rent. Ae quean had noticed something under his arm, but she took it for the pipes.

Sir John Redgauntlet ordered the servants out of the room, and then said to my gudesire, "Now, Steenie, ye see you have fair play;

and, as I have little doubt ye ken better where to find the siller than ony other body, I beg, in fair terms, and for your own sake, that you will end this fasherie; for, Stephen, ye maun pay or flit."

"The Lord forgie your opinion," said Stephen, driven almost to his wit's end – "I am an honest man."

"So am I, Stephen," said his honour; "and so are all the folks in the house, I hope. But if there be a knave amongst us, it must be he that tells the story he cannot prove." He paused, and then added, mair sternly, "If I understand your trick, sir, you want to take advantage of some malicious reports concerning things in this family, and particularly respecting my father's sudden death, thereby to cheat me out of the money, and perhaps take away my character, by insinuating that I have received the rent I am demanding. – Where do you suppose this money to be? – I insist upon knowing."

My gudesire saw everything look sae muckle against him, that he grew nearly desperate – however, he shifted from one foot to another, looked to every corner of the room and made no answer.

"Speak out, sirrah," said the Laird, assuming a look of his father's, a very particular ane, which he had when he was angry – it seemed as if the wrinkles of his frown made that self-same fearful shape of a horse's shoe in the middle of his brow; – "Speak out, sir! I *will* know your thoughts; – do you suppose that I have this money?"

"Far be it frae me to say so," said Stephen.

"Do you charge any of my people with having taken it?"

"I wad be laith to charge them that may be innocent," said my gudesire; "and if there be anyone that is guilty, I have nae proof."

"Somewhere the money must be, if there is a word of truth in your story," said Sir John; "I ask where you think it is – and demand a correct answer?"

"In hell, if you *will* have my thoughts of it," said my gudesire, driven to extremity, – "in hell! with your father, his jackanape, and his silver whistle."

Down the stairs he ran (for the parlour was nae place for him after such a word), and he heard the Laird swearing blood and wounds behind him, as fast as ever did Sir Robert, and roaring for the bailie and the baron-officer.

Away rode my gudesire to his chief creditor (him they caa'd Laurie Lapraik), to try if he could make ony thing out of him; but when he tauld his story, he got but the warst word in his wame – thief, beggar, and dyvour, were the saftest terms; and to the boot of these hard terms, Laurie brought up the auld story of his dipping his hand in the blood of God's saunts, just as if a tenant could have helped riding with the Laird, and that a laird like Sir Robert Redgauntlet. My gudesire was, by this time, far beyond the bounds of patience, and, while he and Laurie were at deil speed the liars, he was wanchancie aneugh to abuse Lapraik's doctrine as weel as the man, and said things that garr'd folk's flesh grue that heard them; – he wasna just himsell, and he had lived wi' a wild set in his day.

At last they parted, and my gudesire was to ride hame through the wood of Pitmurkie, that is a' fou of black firs, as they say. – I ken the wood, but the firs may be black or white for what I can tell. – At the entry of the wood there is a wild common, and on the edge of the common, a little lonely change-house, that was keepit then by an ostler-wife, they suld hae caa'd her Tibbie Faw, and there puir Steenie cried for a mutchkin of brandy, for he had had no refreshment the haill day. Tibbie was earnest wi' him to take a bite of meat, but he couldna think o't, nor would he take his foot out of the stirrup, and took off the brandy wholely at twa draughts, and named a toast at each: – the first was, the memory of Sir Robert Redgauntlet, and might he never lie quiet in his grave till he had righted his poor bond-tenant; and the second was, a health to Man's Enemy, if he would but get him back the pock of siller, or tell him what came o't, for he saw the haill world was like to regard him as a thief and a cheat, and he took that waur than even the ruin of his house and hauld.

On he rode, little caring where. It was a dark night turned, and the trees made it yet darker, and he let the beast take its ain road through the wood; when, all of a sudden, from tired and wearied that it was before, the nag began to spring, and flee, and stend, that my gudesire could hardly keep the saddle. – Upon the whilk, a horseman, suddenly riding up beside him, said, "That's a mettle beast of yours, freend; will you sell him?" – So saying, he touched the horse's neck with his riding-wand, and it fell into its auld heigh-ho of a stumbling trot. "But his spunk's soon out of him, I think," continued the stranger, "and that is like mony a man's courage, that thinks he wad do great things till he come to the proof."

My gudesire scarce listened to this, but spurred his horse, with "Gude e'en to you, freend."

But it's like the stranger was ane that doesna lightly yield his point; for, ride as Steenie liked, he was aye beside him at the self-same pace. At last my gudesire, Steenie Steenson, grew half angry; and, to say the truth, half feared.

"What is it that ye want with me, freend?" he said. "If ye be a robber, I have nae money; if ye be a leal man, wanting company, I have nae heart to mirth or speaking; and if ye want to ken the road, I scarce ken it mysell."

"If you will tell me your grief," said the stranger, "I am one that, though I have been sair miscaa'd in the world, am the only hand for helping my freends."

So my gudesire, to ease his ain heart, mair than from any hope of help, told him the story from beginning to end.

"It's a hard pinch," said the stranger; "but I think I can help you."

"If you could lend the money, sir, and take a lang day – I ken nae other help on earth," said my gudesire.

"But there may be some under the earth," said the stranger. "Come, I'll be frank wi' you; I could lend you the money on bond, but you would maybe scruple my terms. Now, I can tell you, that your auld Laird is disturbed in his grave by your curses, and the wailing of your family, and if ye daur venture to go to see him, he will give you the receipt."

My gudesire's hair stood on end at this proposal, but he thought his companion might be some humorsome chield that was trying to frighten him, and might end with lending him the money. Besides, he was bauld wi' brandy, and desperate wi' distress; and he said, he had courage to go to the gate of hell, and a step farther, for that receipt. – The stranger laughed.

Weel, they rode on through the thickest of the wood, when, all of a sudden, the horse stopped at the door of a great house; and, but that he knew the place was ten miles off, my father would have thought he was at Redgauntlet Castle. They rode into the outer courtyard, through the muckle faulding yetts, and aneath the auld portcullis; and the whole front of the house was lighted, and there were pipes and fiddles, and as much dancing and deray within as used to be in Sir Robert's house at Pace and Yule, and such high seasons. They lap off, and my gudesire, as seemed to him, fastened his horse to the very ring he had tied him to that morning, when he gaed to wait on the young Sir John.

"God!" said my gudesire, "if Sir Robert's death be but a dream!"

He knocked at the ha' door just as he was wont, and his auld acquaintance, Dougal MacCallum, – just after his wont, too, – came to open the door, and said, "Piper Steenie, are ye there, lad? Sir Robert has been crying for you."

My gudesire was like a man in a dream – he looked for the stranger, but he was gane for the time. At last he just tried to say, "Ha! Dougal Driveower, are ye living? I thought ye had been dead."

"Never fash yoursell wi' me," said Dougal, "but look to yoursell; and see ye tak naething frae onybody here, neither meat, drink, or siller, except just the receipt that is your ain."

So saying, he led the way out through halls and trances that were weel kend to my gudesire, and into the auld oak parlour; and there was as much singing of profane sangs, and birling of red wine, and speaking blasphemy and sculduddry, as had ever been in Redgauntlet Castle when it was at the blithest.

But, Lord take us in keeping! what a set of ghastly revellers they were that sat round that table! – My gudesire kend mony that had long before gane to their place, for often had he piped to the most part in the hall of Redgauntlet. There was the fierce Middleton, and the dissolute Rothes, and the crafty Lauderdale; and Dalyell, with his bald head and a beard to his girdle; and Earlshall, with Cameron's blude on his hand; and wild Bonshaw, that tied blessed Mr Cargill's limbs till the blude sprang; and Dunbarton Douglas, the twice-turned traitor baith to country and king. There was the Bluidy Advocate MacKenyie, who, for his worldly wit and wisdom, had been to the rest as a god. And there was Claverhouse, as beautiful as when he lived, with his long, dark, curled locks, streaming down over his laced buff-coat, and his left hand always on his right spule-blade, to hide the wound that the silver bullet had made. He sat apart from them all, and looked at them with a melancholy, haughty countenance; while the rest hallooed, and sung, and laughed, that the room rang. But their smiles were fearfully contorted from time to time; and their laughter passed into such wild sounds, as made my gudesire's very nails grow blue, and chilled the marrow in his banes.

They that waited at the table were just the wicked serving-men and troopers, that had done their work and cruel bidding on earth. There was the Lang Lad of the Nethertown, that helped to take Argyle; and the Bishop's summoner, that they called the Deil's Rattle-bag; and the wicked guardsmen, in their laced coats; and the savage Highland Amorites, that shed blood like water; and many a proud serving-man, haughty of heart and bloody of hand, cringing to the rich, and making them wickeder than they would be; grinding the poor to powder, when the rich had broken them to fragments. And mony, mony mair were coming and ganging, a' as busy in their vocation as if they had been alive.

Sir Robert Redgauntlet, in the midst of a' this fearful riot, cried, wi' a voice like thunder, on Steenie Piper, to come to the board-head where he was sitting; his legs stretched out before him, and swathed up with flannel, with his holster pistols aside him, while the great broadsword rested against his chair, just as my gudesire had seen him the last time upon earth – the very cushion for the jackanape was close to him, but the creature itsell was not there – it wasna its hour, it's likely; for he heard them say as he came forward, "Is not the Major come yet?" And another answered, "The jackanape will be here betimes the morn." And when my gudesire came forward, Sir Robert, or his ghaist, or the deevil in his likeness, said, "Weel, piper, hae ye settled wi' my son for the year's rent?"

With much ado my father gat breath to say, that Sir John would not settle without his honour's receipt.

"Ye shall hae that for a tune of the pipes, Steenie," said the appearance of Sir Robert – "Play us up 'Weel hoddled, Luckie.'"

Now this was a tune my gudesire learned frae a warlock, that heard it when they were worshipping Satan at their meetings; and my gudesire had sometimes played it at the ranting suppers in Redgauntlet Castle, but never very willingly; and now he grew cauld at the very name of it, and said, for excuse, he hadna his pipes wi' him.

"MacCallum, ye limb of Beelzebub," said the fearfu' Sir Robert, "bring Steenie the pipes that I am keeping for him!"

MacCallum brought a pair of pipes might have served the piper of Donald of the Isles. But he gave my gudesire a nudge as he offered them; and looking secretly and closely, Steenie saw that the chanter was of steel, and heated to a white heat; so he had fair warning not to trust his fingers with it. So he excused himself again, and said, he was faint and frightened, and had not wind aneugh to fill the bag.

"Then ye maun eat and drink, Steenie," said the figure; "for we do little else here; and it's ill speaking between a fou man and a fasting."

Now these were the very words that the bloody Earl of Douglas said to keep the King's messenger in hand, while he cut the head off MacLellan of Bombie, at the Threave Castle; and that put Steenie mair and mair on his guard. So he spoke up like a man, and said he came neither to eat, or drink, or make minstrelsy; but simply for his ain – to ken what was come o' the money he had paid, and to get a discharge for it; and he was so stout-hearted by this time, that he charged Sir Robert for conscience-sake – (he had no power to say the holy name) – and as he hoped for peace and rest, to spread no snares for him, but just to give him his ain.

The appearance gnashed its teeth and laughed, but it took from a large pocket-book the receipt, and handed it to Steenie. "There is your receipt, ye pitiful cur; and for the money, my dog-whelp of a son may go look for it in the Cat's Cradle."

My gudesire uttered mony thanks, and was about to retire, when Sir Robert roared aloud, "Stop, though, thou sack-doudling son of a whore! I am not done with thee. Here we do nothing for nothing; and you must return on this very day twelvemonth, to pay your master the homage that you owe me for my protection."

My father's tongue was loosed of a suddenty, and he said aloud, "I refer mysell to God's pleasure, and not to yours."

He had no sooner uttered the word than all was dark around him; and he sunk on the earth with such a sudden shock, that he lost both breath and sense.

How lang Steenie lay there, he could not tell; but when he came to himsell, he was lying in the auld kirkyard of Redgauntlet parochine, just at the door of the family aisle, and the scutcheon of the auld knight, Sir Robert, hanging over his head. There was a deep morning fog on grass and gravestane around him, and his horse was feeding quietly beside the minister's twa cows. Steenie would have thought the whole was a dream, but he had the receipt in his hand, fairly written and signed by the auld Laird; only the last letters of his name were a little disorderly, written like one seized with sudden pain.

Sorely troubled in his mind, he left that dreary place, rode through the mist to Redgauntlet Castle, and with much ado he got speech of the Laird.

"Well, you dyvour bankrupt," was the first word, "have you brought me my rent?"

"No," answered my gudesire, "I have not; but I have brought your honour Sir Robert's receipt for it."

"How, sirrah? – Sir Robert's receipt! – You told me he had not given you one."

"Will your honour please to see if that bit line is right?"

Sir John looked at every line, and at every letter, with much attention; and at last, at the date, which my gudesire had not observed, – *"From my appointed place,"* he read, *"this twenty-fifth of November."* – "What! – That is yesterday! – Villain, thou must have gone to hell for this!"

"I got it from your honour's father – whether he be in heaven or hell, I know not," said Steenie.

"I will delate you for a warlock to the Privy Council!" said Sir John. "I will send you to your master, the devil, with the help of a tar-barrel and a torch!"

"I intend to delate mysell to the Presbytery," said Steenie, "and tell them all I have seen last night, whilk are things fitter for them to judge of than a borrel man like me."

Sir John paused, composed himsell, and desired to hear the full history; and my gudesire told it him from point to point, as I have told it you – word for word, neither more nor less.

Sir John was silent again for a long time, and at last he said, very composedly, "Steenie, this story of yours concerns the honour of many a noble family besides mine; and if it be a leasing-making, to keep yourself out of my danger, the least you can expect is to have a red-hot iron driven through your tongue, and that will be as bad as scaulding your fingers with a redhot chanter. But yet it may be true, Steenie; and if the money cast up, I shall not know what to think of it. – But where shall we find the Cat's Cradle? There are cats enough about the old house, but I think they kitten without the ceremony of bed or cradle."

"We were best ask Hutcheon," said my gudesire; "he kens a' the odd corners about as weel as – another serving-man that is now gane, and that I wad not like to name."

Aweel, Hutcheon, when he was asked, told them, that a ruinous turret, lang disused, next to the clock-house, only accessible by a ladder, for the opening was on the outside, and far above the battlements, was called of old the Cat's Cradle.

"There will I go immediately," said Sir John; and he took (with what purpose, Heaven kens) one of his father's pistols from the hall-table, where they had lain since the night he died, and hastened to the battlements.

It was a dangerous place to climb, for the ladder was auld and frail, and wanted ane or twa rounds. However, up got Sir John, and entered at the turret door, where his body stopped the only little light that was in the bit turret. Something flees at him wi' a vengeance, maist dang him back ower – bang gaed the knight's pistol, and Hutcheon, that held the ladder, and my gudesire that stood beside him, hears a loud skelloch. A minute after, Sir John flings the body of the jackanape down to them, and cries that the siller is fund, and that they should come up and help him. And there was the bag of siller sure aneugh, and many orra things besides, that had been missing for mony a day. And Sir John, when he had riped the turret weel, led my gudesire into the dining-parlour, and took him by the hand, and spoke kindly to him, and said he was sorry he should have doubted his word, and that he would hereafter be a good master to him, to make amends.

"And now, Steenie," said Sir John, "although this vision of yours tends, on the whole, to my father's credit, as an honest man, that he should, even after his death, desire to see justice done to a poor man like you, yet you are sensible that ill-dispositioned men might make bad constructions upon it, concerning his soul's health. So, I think, we had better lay the haill dirdum on that ill-deedie creature, Major Weir, and say naething about your dream in the wood of Pitmurkie. You had taken ower muckle brandy to be very certain about onything; and, Steenie, this receipt," (his hand shook while he held it out,) – "it's but a queer kind of document, and we will do best, I think, to put it quietly in the fire."

"Odd, but for as queer as it is, it's a' the voucher I have for my rent," said my gudesire, who was afraid, it may be, of losing the benefit of Sir Robert's discharge.

"I will bear the contents to your credit in the rental-book, and give you a discharge under my own hand," said Sir John, "and that on the spot. And, Steenie, if you can hold your tongue about this matter, you shall sit, from this term downward, at an easier rent."

"Mony thanks to your honour," said Steenie, who saw easily in what corner the wind was; "doubtless I will be conformable to all your honour's commands; only I would willingly speak wi' some powerful minister on the subject, for I do not like the sort of soumons of appointment whilk your honour's father—"

"Do not call the phantom my father!" said Sir John, interrupting him.

"Weel, then, the thing that was so like him," – said my gudesire; "he spoke of my coming back to him this time twelvemonth, and it's a weight on my conscience."

"Aweel, then," said Sir John, "if you be so much distressed in mind, you may speak to our minister of the parish; he is a douce man, regards the honour of our family, and the mair that he may look for some patronage from me."

Wi' that, my gudesire readily agreed that the receipt should be burnt, and the Laird threw it into the chimney with his ain hand. Burn it would not for them, though; but away it flew up the lum, wi' a lang train of sparks at its tail, and a hissing noise like a squib.

My gudesire gaed down to the manse, and the minister, when he had heard the story, said, it was his real opinion, that though my gudesire had gaen very far in tampering with dangerous matters, yet, as he had refused the devil's arles (for such was the offer of meat and drink), and had refused to do homage by piping at his bidding, he hoped, that if he held a circumspect walk hereafter, Satan could take little advantage by what was come and gane. And, indeed, my gudesire, of his ain accord, long forswore baith the pipes and the brandy – it was not even till the year was out, and the fatal day passed, that he would so much as take the fiddle, or drink usquebaugh or tippenny.

Sir John made up his story about the jackanape as he liked himsell; and some believe till this day there was no more in the matter than the filching nature of the brute. Indeed, ye'll no hinder some to threap, that it was nane o' the Auld Enemy that Dougal and my gudesire saw in the Laird's room, but only that wanchancy creature, the Major, capering on the coffin; and that, as to the blawing on the Laird's whistle that was heard after he was dead, the filthy brute could do that as weel as the Laird himsell, if no better. But Heaven kens the truth, whilk first came out by the minister's wife, after Sir John and her ain gudeman were baith in the moulds. And then my gudesire, wha was failed in his limbs, but not in his judgment or memory – at least nothing to speak of – was obliged to tell the real narrative to his freends, for the credit of his good name. He might else have been charged for a warlock.

Thrawn Janet

Robert Louis Stevenson

The Reverend Murdoch Soulis was long minister of the moorland parish of Balweary, in the vale of Dule. A severe, bleak-faced old man, dreadful to his hearers, he dwelt in the last years of his life, without relative or servant or any human company, in the small and lonely manse under the Hanging Shaw. In spite of the iron composure of his features, his eye was wild, scared, and uncertain; and when he dwelt, in private admonitions, on the future of the impenitent, it seemed as if his eye pierced through the storms of time to the terrors of eternity. Many young persons, coming to prepare themselves against the season of the Holy Communion, were dreadfully affected by his talk. He had a sermon on 1st Peter, v. and 8th, "The devil as a roaring lion," on the Sunday after every seventeenth of August, and he was accustomed to surpass himself upon that text both by the appalling nature of the matter and the terror of his bearing in the pulpit. The children were frightened into fits, and the old looked more than usually oracular, and were, all that day, full of those hints that Hamlet deprecated. The manse itself, where it stood by the water of Dule among some thick trees, with the Shaw overhanging it on the one side, and on the other many cold, moorish hill-tops rising toward the sky, had begun, at a very early period of Mr. Soulis's ministry, to be avoided in the dusk hours by all who valued themselves upon their prudence; and guidmen sitting at the clachan alehouse shook their heads together at the thought of passing late by that uncanny neighbourhood. There was one spot, to be more particular, which was regarded with especial awe. The manse stood between the highroad and the water of Dule with a gable to each; its back was toward the kirktown of Balweary, nearly half a mile away; in front of it, a bare garden, hedged with thorn, occupied the land between the river and the road. The house was two stories high, with two large rooms on each. It opened not directly on the garden, but on a causewayed path, or passage, giving on the road on the one hand, and closed on the other by the tall willows and elders that bordered on the stream. And it was this strip of causeway that enjoyed among the young parishioners of Balweary so infamous a reputation. The minister walked there often after dark, sometimes groaning aloud in the instancy of his unspoken prayers; and when he was from home, and the manse door was locked, the more daring schoolboys ventured, with beating hearts, to "follow my leader" across that legendary spot.

This atmosphere of terror, surrounding, as it did, a man of God of spotless character and orthodoxy, was a common cause of wonder and subject of inquiry among the few strangers who were led by chance or business into that unknown, outlying country. But many even of the people of the parish were ignorant of the strange events which had marked the first year of Mr. Soulis's ministrations; and among those who were better informed, some were naturally reticent, and others shy of that particular topic. Now and again, only, one of the older folk would warm into courage over his third tumbler, and recount the cause of the minister's strange and solitary life.

[Publisher's Note: from this point the story is written in Scots, as Stevenson intended. Translations can be found online if so desired.]

* * *

Fifty years syne, when Mr. Soulis cam' first into Ba'weary, he was still a young man – a callant, the folk said – fu' o' book learnin' and grand at the exposition, but, as was natural in sae young a man, wi' nae leevin' experience in religion. The younger sort were greatly taken wi' his gifts and his gab; but auld, concerned, serious men and women were moved even to prayer for the young man, whom they took to be a self-deceiver, and the parish that was like to be sae ill-supplied. It was before the days o' the moderates – weary fa' them; but ill things are like guid – they baith come bit by bit, a pickle at a time; and there were folk even then that said the Lord had left the college professors to their ain devices an' the lads that went to study wi' them wad hae done mair and better sittin' in a peat-bog, like their forbears of the persecution, wi' a Bible under their oxter and a speerit o' prayer in their heart. There was nae doubt, onyway, but that Mr. Soulis had been ower lang at the college. He was careful and troubled for many things besides the ae thing needful. He had a feck o' books wi' him – mair than had ever been seen before in a' that presbytery; and a sair wark the carrier had wi' them, for they were a' like to have smoored in the Deil's Hag between this and Kilmackerlie. They were books o' divinity, to be sure, or so they ca'd them; but the serious were o' opinion there was little service for sae mony, when the hail o' God's Word would gang in the neuk of a plaid. Then he wad sit half the day and half the nicht forbye, which was scant decent – writin' nae less; and first, they were feared he wad read his sermons; and syne it proved he was writin' a book himsel', which was surely no fittin' for ane of his years and sma' experience.

Onyway it behoved him to get an auld, decent wife to keep the manse for him an' see to his bit denners; and he was recommended to an auld limmer – Janet M'Clour, they ca'ed her – and sae far left to himsel' as to be ower persuaded. There was mony advised him to the contrar, for Janet was mair than suspeckit by the best folk in Ba'weary. Lang or that, she had had a wean to a dragoon; she hadnae come forrit for maybe thretty year; and bairns had seen her mumblin' to hersel' up on Key's Loan in the gloamin', whilk was an unco time an' place for a God-fearin' woman. Howsoever, it was the laird himsel' that had first tauld the minister o' Janet; and in thae days he wad have gane a far gate to pleesure the laird. When folk tauld him that Janet was sib to the deil, it was a' superstition by his way of it; an' when they cast up the Bible to him an' the witch of Endor, he wad threep it doun their thrapples that thir days were a' gane by, and the deil was mercifully restrained.

Weel, when it got about the clachan that Janet M'Clour was to be servant at the manse, the folk were fair mad wi' her an' him thegether; and some o' the guidwives had nae better to dae than get round her door cheeks and chairge her wi' a' that was ken't again her, frae the sodger's bairn to John Tamson's twa kye. She was nae great speaker; folk usually let her gang her ain gate, an' she let them gang theirs, wi' neither Fair-gui-deen nor Fair-guid-day; but when she buckled to, she had a tongue to deave the miller. Up she got, an' there wasnae an auld story in Ba'weary but she gart somebody lowp for it that day; they couldnae say ae thing but she could say twa to it; till, at the hinder end, the guidwives up and claught hand of her, and clawed the coats aff her back, and pu'd her doun the clachan to the water o' Dule, to see if she were a witch or no, soum or droun. The carline skirled till ye could hear her at the Hangin' Shaw, and she focht like ten; there was mony a guidwife bure the mark of her neist day an' mony a lang day after; and just in the hettest o' the collieshangie, wha suld come up (for his sins) but the new minister.

"Women," said he (and he had a grand voice), "I charge you in the Lord's name to let her go."

Janet ran to him – she was fair wud wi' terror – an' clang to him, an' prayed him, for Christ's sake, save her frae the cummers; an' they, for their part, tauld him a' that was ken't, and maybe mair.

"Woman," says he to Janet, "is this true?"

"As the Lord sees me," says she, "as the Lord made me, no a word o't. Forbye the bairn," says she, "I've been a decent woman a' my days."

"Will you," says Mr. Soulis, "in the name of God, and before me, His unworthy minister, renounce the devil and his works?"

Weel, it wad appear that when he askit that, she gave a girn that fairly frichtit them that saw her, an' they could hear her teeth play dirl thegether in her chafts; but there was naething for it but the ae way or the ither; an' Janet lifted up her hand and renounced the deil before them a'.

"And now," says Mr. Soulis to the guidwives, "home with ye, one and all, and pray to God for His forgiveness."

And he gied Janet his arm, though she had little on her but a sark, and took her up the clachan to her ain door like a leddy of the land; an' her scrieghin, and laughin' as was a scandal to be heard.

There were mony grave folk lang ower their prayers that nicht; but when the morn cam' there was sic a fear fell upon a' Ba'weary that the bairns hid theirsels, and even the men folk stood and keekit frae their doors. For there was Janet comin' doun the clachan – her or her likeness, nane could tell – wi' her neck thrawn, and her held on ae side, like a body that has been hangit, and a grin on her face like an unstreakit corp. By an' by they got used wi' it, and even speered at her to ken what was wrang; but frae that day forth she couldnae speak like a Christian woman, but slavered and played click wi' her teeth like a pair o' shears; and frae that day forth the name o' God cam' never on her lips. Whiles she wad try to say it, but it michtnae be. Them that kenned best said least; but they never gied that Thing the name o' Janet M'Clour; for the auld Janet, by their way o't, was in muckle hell that day. But the minister was neither to haud nor to bind; he preached about naething but the folk's cruelty that had gi'en her a stroke of the palsy; he skelpt the bairns that meddled her; and he had her up to the manse that same nicht, and dwalled there a' his lane wi' her under the Hangin' Shaw.

Weel, time gaed by: and the idler sort commenced to think mair lichtly o' that black business. The minister was weel thocht o'; he was aye late at the writing, folk wad see his can'le doon by the Dule water after twal' at e'en; and he seemed pleased wi' himsel' and upsitten as at first, though a' body could see that he was dwining. As for Janet she cam' an' she gaed; if she didnae speak muckle afore, it was reason she should speak less then; she meddled naebody; but she was an eldritch thing to see, an' nane wad hae mistrysted wi' her for Ba'weary glebe.

About the end o' July there cam' a spell o' weather, the like o't never was in that countryside; it was lown an' het an' heartless; the herds couldnae win up the Black Hill, the bairns were ower weariet to play; an' yet it was gousty too, wi' claps o' het wund that rummled in the glens, and bits o' shouers that slockened naething. We aye thocht it but to thun'er on the morn; but the morn cam', an' the morn's morning, and it was aye the same uncanny weather, sair on folks and bestial. Of a' that were the waur, nane suffered like Mr. Soulis; he could neither sleep nor eat, he tauld his elders; an' when he wasnae writin' at his weary book, he wad be stravaguin' ower a' the countryside like a man possessed, when a' body else was blythe to keep caller ben the house.

Abune Hangin' Shaw, in the bield o' the Black Hill, there's a bit enclosed grund wi' an iron yett; and it seems, in the auld days, that was the kirkyaird o' Ba'weary, and consecrated by the Papists before the blessed licht shone upon the kingdom. It was a great howff, o' Mr. Soulis's onyway; there he would sit an' consider his sermons; and inded it's a bieldy bit. Weel, as he cam' ower the wast end o' the Black Hill, ae day, he saw first twa, an' syne fower, an' syne seeven corbie craws fleein' round an' round abune the auld kirkyaird. They flew laigh and heavy, an' squawked to ither as they gaed; and it was clear to Mr. Soulis that something had put them frae their ordinar. He wasnae easy fleyed, an' gaed straucht up to the wa's; and what suld he find there but a man, or the appearance of a man, sittin' in the inside upon a grave. He was of a great stature, an' black as hell, and his e'en were singular to see. Mr. Soulis had heard tell o' black men mony's the time; but there was something unco about this black man that daunted him. Het as he was, he took a kind o' cauld grue in the marrow o' his banes; but up he spak for a' that; an' says he: "My friend, are you a stranger in this place?" The black man answered never a word; he got upon his feet, an' begude to hirsle to the wa' on the far side; but he aye lookit at the minister; an' the minister stood an' lookit back; till a' in a meenute the black man was ower the wa' an' runnin' for the bield o' the trees. Mr. Soulis, he hardly kenned why, ran after him; but he was sair forjaskit wi' his walk an' the het, unhalsome weather; and rin as he likit, he got nae mair than a glisk o' the black man amang the birks, till he won doun to the foot o' the hillside, an' there he saw him ance mair, gaun, hap, step, an' lowp, ower Dule water to the manse.

Mr. Soulis wasnae weel pleased that this fearsome gangrel suld mak' sae free wi' Ba'weary manse; an' he ran the harder, an' wet shoon, ower the burn, an' up the walk; but the deil a black man was there to see. He stepped out upon the road, but there was naebody there; he gaed a' ower the gairden, but na, nae black man. At the binder end, and a bit feared as was but natural, he lifted the hasp and into the manse; and there was Janet M'Clour before his een, wi' her thrawn craig, and nane sae pleased to see him. And he aye minded sinsyne, when first he set his een upon her, he had the same cauld and deidly grue.

"Janet," says he, "have you seen a black man?"

"A black man!" quo' she. "Save us a'! Ye're no wise, minister. There's nae black man in a' Ba'weary."

But she didnae speak plain, ye maun understand; but yam-yammered, like a powny wi' the bit in its moo.

"Weel," says he, "Janet, if there was nae black man, I have spoken with the Accuser of the Brethren."

And he sat doun like ane wi' a fever, an' his teeth chittered in his heid.

"Hoots," says she, "think shame to yoursel', minister"; and gied him a drap brandy that she keept aye by her.

Syne Mr. Soulis gaed into his study amang a' his books. It's a lang, laigh, mirk chalmer, perishin' cauld in winter, an' no very dry even in the top o' the simmer, for the manse stands near the burn. Sae doun he sat, and thocht of a' that had come an' gane since he was in Ba'weary, an' his hame, an' the days when he was a bairn an' ran daffin' on the braes; and that black man aye ran in his held like the owercome of a sang. Aye the mair he thocht, the mair he thocht o' the black man. He tried the prayer, an' the words wouldnae come to him; an' he tried, they say, to write at his book, but he couldnae mak' nae mair o' that. There was whiles he thocht the black man was at his oxter, an' the swat stood upon him cauld as well-water; and there was other whiles, when he cam' to himsel' like a christened bairn and minded naething.

The upshot was that he gaed to the window an' stood glowrin' at Dule water. The trees are unco thick, an' the water lies deep an' black under the manse; and there was Janet washin' the cla'es wi' her coats kilted. She had her back to the minister, an' he, for his pairt, hardly kenned what he was lookin' at. Syne she turned round, an' shawed her face: Mr. Soulis had the same cauld grue as twice that day afore, an' it was borne in upon him what folk said, that Janet was deid lang syne, an' this was a bogle in her clay-cauld flesh. He drew back a pickle and he scanned her narrowly. She was tramp-trampin' in the cla'es, croonin' to hersel'; and eh! Gude guide us, but it was a fearsome face. Whiles she sang louder, but there was nae man born o' woman that could tell the words o' her sang; an' whiles she lookit side-lang doun, but there was naething there for her to look at. There gaed a scunner through the flesh upon his banes; and that was Heeven's advertisement. But Mr. Soulis just blamed himsel', he said, to think sae ill of a puir, auld afflicted wife that hadnae a freend forbye himsel'; an' he put up a bit prayer for him an' her, an' drank a little caller water – for his heart rose again the meat – an' gaed up to his naked bed in the gloaming.

That was a nicht that has never been forgotten in Ba'weary, the nicht o' the seeventeenth of August, seventeen hun'er' an' twal'. It had been het afore, as I hae said, but that nicht it was better than ever. The sun gaed doun amang unco-lookin' clouds; it fell as mirk as the pit; no a star, no a breath o' wund; ye couldnae see your han' afore your face, and even the auld folk cuist the covers frae their beds and lay pechin' for their breath. Wi' a' that he had upon his mind, it was gey and unlikely Mr. Soulis wad get muckle sleep. He lay an' he tummled; the gude, caller bed that he got into brunt his very banes; whiles he slept, and whiles he waukened; whiles he heard the time o' nicht, and whiles a tyke yowlin' up the muir, as if somebody was deid; whiles he thocht he heard bogles claverin' in his lug, an' whiles he saw spunkies in the room. He behoved, he judged, to be sick; an' sick he was – little he jaloosed the sickness.

At the hinder end, he got a clearness in his mind, sat up in his sark on the bed-side, and fell thinkin' ance mair o' the black man an' Janet. He couldnae weel tell how – maybe it was the cauld to his feet – but it cam' in up upon him wi' a spate that there was some connection between thir twa, an' that either or baith o' them were bogles. And just at that moment, in Janet's room, which was neist to his, there cam' a stramp o' feet as if men were wars'lin', an' then a loud bang; an' then a wund gaed reishling round the fower quarters of the house; an' then a' was ance mair as seelent as the grave.

Mr. Soulis was feared for neither man nor deevil. He got his tinder-box, an' lit a can'le. He made three steps o't ower to Janet's door. It was on the hasp, an' he pushed it open, an' keeked bauldly in. It was a big room, as big as the minister's ain, a' plenished wi' grand, auld, solid gear, for he had nathing else. There was a fower-posted bed wi' auld tapestry; and a braw cabinet of aik, that was fu' o' the minister's divinity books, an' put there to be out o' the gate; an' a wheen duds o' Janet's lying here and there about the floor. But nae Janet could Mr. Soulis see; nor ony sign of a contention. In he gaed (an' there's few that wad ha'e followed him) an' lookit a' round, an' listened. But there was naethin' to be heard, neither inside the manse nor in a' Ba'weary parish, an' naethin' to be seen but the muckle shadows turnin' round the can'le. An' then, a' at ance, the minister's heart played dunt an' stood stock-still; an' a cauld wund blew amang the hairs o' his heid. Whaten a weary sicht was that for the puir man's een! For there was Janet hangin' frae a nail beside the auld aik cabinet: her heid aye lay on her shouther, her een were steeked, the tongue projeckit frae her mouth, and her heels were twa feet clear abune the floor.

"God forgive us all!" thocht Mr. Soulis, "poor Janet's dead."

He cam' a step nearer to the corp; an' then his heart fair whammled in his inside. For by what cantrip it wad ill-beseem a man to judge, she was hingin' frae a single nail an' by a single wursted thread for darnin' hose.

It's a awfu' thing to be your lane at nicht wi' siccan prodigies o' darkness; but Mr. Soulis was strong in the Lord. He turned an' gaed his ways oot o' that room, and lockit the door ahint him; and step by step, doon the stairs, as heavy as leed; and set doon the can'le on the table at the stairfoot. He couldnae pray, he couldnae think, he was dreepin' wi' caul' swat, an' naething could he hear but the dunt-dunt-duntin' o' his ain heart. He micht maybe have stood there an hour, or maybe twa, he minded sae little; when a' o' a sudden, he heard a laigh, uncanny steer up-stairs; a foot gaed to an' fro in the chalmer whaur the corp was hingin'; syne the door was opened, though he minded weel that he had lockit it; an' syne there was a step upon the landin', an' it seemed to him as if the corp was lookin' ower the rail and doun upon him whaur he stood.

He took up the can'le again (for he couldnae want the licht), and as saftly as ever he could, gaed straucht out o' the manse an' to the far end o' the causeway. It was aye pit-mirk; the flame o' th can'le, when he set it on the grund, brunt steedy an clear as in a room; naething moved, but the Dule water seepin' and sabbin' doon the glen, an' yon unhaly footstep that cam' ploddin' doun the stairs inside the manse. He kenned the foot ower weel, for it was Janet's; and at ilka step that cam' a wee thing nearer, the cauld got deeper in his vitals. He commended his soul to Him that made an' keepit him; "and O Lord," said he, "give me strength this night to war against the powers of evil."

By this time the foot was comin' through the passage for the door; he could hear a hand skirt alang the wa', as if the fearsome thing was feelin' for its way. The saughs tossed an' maned thegether, a long sigh cam' ower the hills, the flame o' the can'le was blawn aboot; an' there stood the corp of Thrawn Janet, wi' her grogram goun an' her black mutch, wi' the heid upon the shouther, an' the grin still upon the face o't – leevin', ye wad he said – deid, as Mr. Soulis weel kenned – upon the threshold o' the manse.

It's a strange thing that the saul of man should be that thirled into his perishable body; but the minister saw that, an' his heart didnae break.

She didnae stand there lang; she began to move again an' cam' slowly towards Mr. Soulis whaur he stood under the saughs. A' the life o' his body, a' the strength o' his speerit, were glowerin' frae his een. It seemed she was gaun to speak, but wanted words, an' made a sign wi' the left hand. There cam' a clap o' wund, like a cat's fuff; oot gaed the can'le, the saughs skrieghed like folk; an' Mr. Soulis keened that, live or die, this was the end o't.

"Witch, beldame, devil!" he cried, "I charge you, by the power of God, begone – if you be dead, to the grave – if you be damned, to hell."

An' at that moment the Lord's ain hand out o' the Heevens struck the Horror whaur it stood; the auld, deid, desecrated corp o' the witch-wife, sae lang keepit frae the grave and hirsled round by deils, lowed up like a brunstane spunk and fell in ashes to the grund; the thunder followed, peal on dirling peal, the rairing rain upon the back o' that; and Mr. Soulis lowped through the garden hedge, and ran, wi' skelloch upon skelloch, for the clachan.

That same mornin', John Christie saw the Black Man pass the Muckle Cairn as it was chappin' six; before eicht, he gaed by the change-house at Knockdow; an' no lang after, Sandy M'Lellan saw him gaun linkin' doun the braes frae Kilmackerlie. There's little doubt but it was him that dwalled se lang in Janet's body; but he was awa' at last; and sinsyne the deil has never fashed us in Ba'weary.

But it was a sair dispensation for the minister; lang, lang he lay ravin' in his bed; and frae that hour to this, he was the man ye ken the day.

The Laird o' Coul's Ghost

J. Maxwell Wood

Upon the third day of February, 1722, at seven o'clock at night, after I had parted with Thurston [his name Cant], and was coming up the Burial Road, one came riding up after me: upon hearing the noise of his horse's feet, I took it to be Thurston, but upon looking back, and seeing the horse of a greyish colour, I called "Who is there?" The answer was, "The Laird of Coul [his name Maxwell], be not afraid." Then looking to him by the help of the dark light which the moon afforded, I took him to be Collector Castellow designing to put a trick upon me, and immediately I struck at him with all my force with my cane, thinking I should leave upon him a mark, to make him remember his presumption; but being sensible, I aimed as well as ever I did in my life, yet my cane finding no resistance, but flying out of my hand the distance of about 60 feet, and observing it by its white head, I dismounted and took it up, and had some difficulty in mounting again, what by the ramping of my horse and what by reason of a certain kind of trembling throughout my whole joints, something likewise of anger had its share in the confusion; for, as I thought, he laughed when my staff flew away. Coming up with him again, who halted all the time I sought my staff, I asked once more

"Who he was?" He answered, "The Laird of Coul." I enquired, "If he was the Laird of Coul, what brought him hither?" and "What was his business with me?"

Coul – The reason of my waiting on you is that I know you are disposed to do for me a thing which none of your brethren in Nithsdale will so much as attempt, though it serve to ever so good purposes. I told him I would never refuse to do a thing to serve a good purpose, if I thought I was obliged to do it as my duty. He answered, since I had undertaken what he found few in Nithsdale would, for he had tried some upon that subject, who were more obliged to him than ever I was, or to any person living: I drew my horse, and halted in surprise, asking what I had undertaken?

Ogilvie – Pray, Coul, who informed you that I talked at that rate?

Coul – You must know that we are acquainted with many things that the living know nothing about. These things you did say, and much more to that purpose; and all that I want is that you fulfil your promise and deliver my commissions to my loving wife.

Ogilvie – 'Tis a pity, Coul, that you who know so many things, should not know the difference between an absolute and a conditional promise.

But did I ever say that if you would come to Innerwick and employ me that I would go all the way to Dumfries upon that errand? That is what never so much as once entered into my thought.

Coul – What was in your thought I do not pretend to know, but I can depend upon my information that these were your words; but I see you are in some disorder; I will wait on you again, when you have more presence of mind.

By the time we were got to James Dickson's inclosure below the churchyard, and while I was collecting in my mind whether ever I had spoken these words he alleged, he broke from me through the churchyard with greater violence than ever any man on horseback is capable of, and with such a singing and buzzing noise as put me in greater disorder than I was all the time I was with him. I came to my house, and my wife observed something more than ordinary paleness in my countenance, and would allege that something ailed me. I called for a dram and told her I was a little uneasy. After I found myself a little eased and refreshed, I retired to my closet to meditate on this the most astonishing adventure of my whole life.

The Second Conference

Upon the 5th of March, 1722. Being at Blarehead baptising the shepherd's child, I came off at sunsetting, or a very little after. Near Will. White's march the Laird of Coul came up with me on horseback as formerly, and, after his first salutation, bid me not be afraid, for he would do me no harm. I told him I was not in the least afraid, in the name of God and of Christ my Saviour, that he would do the least harm to me; for I knew that He in whom I trusted was stronger than all them put together, and if any of them should attempt even to do the horse I rode upon harm, as you have done to Dr Menzies' man, if it be true that is said, and generally believed about Dumfries, I have free access to complain to my Lord and Master, to the lash of whose resentment you are as much liable now as before.

Coul – You need not multiply words upon that head, for you are as safe with me and safer, if safer can be, than when I was alive.

I said – Well then, Coul, let me have a peaceable and easy conversation with you for the time we ride together, and give me some information about the affairs of the other world, for no man inclines to lose his time in conversing with the dead without having a prospect of hearing and learning something that may be useful.

Coul – Well, sir, I will satisfy you as far as I think it proper and convenient. Let me know what information you want from me.

Ogilvie – Well, then, what sort of body is it that you appear in, and what sort of a horse is it that you ride on that appears so full of mettle?

Coul – You may depend upon it 'tis not the same body that I was witness to your marriage in, nor in which I died, for that is in the grave rotting; but it is such a body as answers me in a moment, for I can fly as fast as my soul can do without it, so that I can go to Dumfries and return again before you ride twice the length of your horse: nay, if I incline to go to London, or to Jerusalem, or to the moon, if you please, I can perform all these journeys equally soon, for it costs me nothing but a thought or wish; for this body you see is as fleet as your thought, for in the same moment of time that you carry your thoughts to Rome I can go there in person. And for my horse, he is much like myself, for 'tis Andrew Johnstoun, who was seven years my tenant, and he died 48 hours before me.

Ogilvie – So it seems when Andrew Johnstoun inclines to ride you must serve him for a horse, as he now does you?

The Third Conference

Upon the 9th of April, 1722, as I was returning from Old Hamstocks, Coul struck up with me upon the back, at the foot of the ruinous inclosure before we come to Dodds. I told him his last conversation had proven so acceptable to me that I was well pleased to see him again, and that there was a vast number of things which I wanted to inform myself further of, if he would be so good as to satisfy me.

Coul – Last time we met I refused you nothing that you asked, and now I expect you will refuse me nothing that I ask.

Ogilvie – Nothing, sir, that is in my power, or that I can with safety to my reputation and character. What then are your demands upon me?

Coul – All I desire is that, as you promised that Sabbath day, you will go to my wife, who now possesses all my effects, and tell her the following particulars, and desire her in my name to rectify these matters. First, that I was justly owing to Provost Crosby £500 Scots, and three years' interest; but upon hearing of his death, my good-brother (the laird of Chapel) and I did forge a discharge narrating the date of the bond, the sum, and other particulars, with this onerous clause that at that time it was fallen by and could not be found, with an obligation on the Provost's part to deliver up the bond as soon as he could hit upon it, and this discharge was dated three months before the Provost's death; and when his only son and successor, Andrew Crosby, wrote to me concerning this bond, I came to him and showed him that discharge, which silenced him, so that I got my bond without more ado. And when I heard of Robert Kennedy's death, with the same help of Chapel, I got a bill upon him for £190 sterling, which I got full and compleat payment of, and Chapel got the half. When I was in Dumfries the day Thomas Greer died, to whom I was owing an account of £36 sterling, Chapel, my good-brother, at that time was at London, and not being able of myself, being but a bad writer, to get a discharge of the account, which I wanted exceedingly, I met accidentally with Robert Boyd, a poor writer lad in Dumfries. I took him to Mrs Carrick's, gave him a bottle of wine and told him that I had paid Thomas Greer's account, but wanted a discharge, and if he would help me to it I would reward him. He flew away from me in great passion, saying he would rather be hanged, but if I had a mind for these things I had best wait till Chapel came home. This gave me great trouble, fearing that what he and I had formerly done was no secret. I followed Boyd to the street, made an apology that I was jesting, commended him for his honesty, and took him solemnly engaged that he should not repeat what had passed. I sent for my cousin Barnhourie, your good-brother, who with no difficulty, for one guinea and a half undertook and performed all that I wanted, and for one guinea more made me up a discharge for £200 Scots, which I was owing to your father-in-law and his friend Mr Morehead, which discharge I gave in to John Ewart when he required the money, and he, at my desire, produced it to you, which you sustained. A great many of the like instances were told, of which I cannot remember the persons' names and sums. But, added he, what vexes me more than all these is the injustice I did to Homer Maxwell, tenant to Lord Nithsdale, for whom I was factor. I had borrowed 2000 merks from him, 500 of which he borrowed from another hand, and I gave him my bond. For reasons I contrived, I obliged him to secrecy. He died within the year. He had nine children, and his wife had died a month before himself. I came to seal up his papers for my lord's security. His eldest daughter entreated me to look through them all, and to give her an account what was their stock and what was their debt. I very willingly undertook it, and in going through his papers I put my own bond in my pocket. His circumstances proved bad, and the nine children are now starving. These things I desire you to represent to my wife; take her brother with you, and let them be immediately rectified, for she has sufficient fund to do it upon, and, if that were done, I think I would be easy and happy. Therefore I hope you will make no delay.

Ogilvie – After a short pause I answered – 'Tis a good errand, Coul, that you are sending me to do justice to the oppressed and injured; but notwithstanding that I see myself among the rest that come in for £200 Scots, yet I beg a little time to consider on the matter.

The Fourth Conference

Upon the 10th of April, 1722, coming from Old Camus, upon the post road I met with Coul, as formerly, upon the head of the path called the *Pease*. He asked me if I had considered the matter he had recommended? I told him I had, and was in the same opinion that I was of when we parted: that I could not possibly undertake his commission unless he would give it in writing under his hand. I wanted nothing but reason to determine me, not only in that, but all other affairs of my life. I added that the list of his grievances was so long that I could not possibly remember them without being in writing.

I know, said he, that this is a mere evasion; but tell me if your neighbour, the laird of Thurston, will do it? I would gladly wait upon him.

Ogilvie – I am sure, said I, he will not, and if he inclined so I would do what I could to hinder him, for I think he has as little concern in these matters as I. But tell me, Coul, is it not as easy for you to write your story as it is to tell it, or to ride on – what-is-it-you-call-him? for I have forgotten your horse's name.

Coul – No, sir, 'tis not, and perhaps I may convince you of it afterwards.

Ogilvie – I would be glad to hear a reason that is solid for your not speaking to your wife yourself. But, however, any rational creature may see what a fool I would make of myself if I should go to Dumfries and tell your wife that you had appeared to me and told me of so many forgeries and villainies which you had committed, and that she behoved to make reparation. The event might, perhaps, be that she would scold me; for as 'tis very probable, she will be loth to part with any money she possesses, and therefore tell me I was mad, or possibly might pursue me for calumny. How could I vindicate myself? how should I prove that ever you had spoken with me? Mr Paton and the rest of my brethren would tell me that it was a devil who had appeared to me, and why should I repeat these things as truth, which he that was a liar from the beginning had told me? Chapel and Barnhourie would be upon my top and pursue me before the Commissary, and everybody will look upon me as brainsick or mad. Therefore, I entreat you, do not insist upon sending me an April errand. The reasonableness of my demand I leave to your consideration, as you did your former to mine, for I think what I ask is very just. But dropping these matters till our next interview, give me leave to enter upon some more diverting subject; and I do not know, Coul, but through the information given to me, you may do as much service to mankind as the redress of all the wrongs you have mentioned would amount to, etc.

Biographies
& Sources

John Buchan

A Journey of Little Profit

(Originally published in *The Yellow Book 9*, 1896, then in *Grey Weather*, 1899)

John Buchan (1875–1940) was a novelist, historian and politician, most famous for his spy-thriller *The Thirty-Nine Steps*. Growing up in Fife, Scotland, Buchan developed a strong passion for the region's natural landscape and wildlife, elements which would later feature prominently in his writing. Upon the outbreak of the First World War, he wrote for the British War Propaganda Bureau and worked for *The Times* as a correspondent in France. He was also an editor of the *Spectator*. In addition to his writing career, Buchan worked in diplomacy, serving as the private secretary of Alfred Milner.

Allan Cunningham

The Haunted Ships

(Originally published in *The London Magazine*, 1821)

Allan Cunningham (1784–1842) was a poet, song writer and author, born in Keir, Dumfriesshire. After working as a stonemason's apprentice, Cunningham began his writing career by collecting old Scottish ballads and contributing his own works to Robert Hartley Cromek's *Remains of Nithsdale and Galloway Song* (1810). He went on to publish numerous poems, songs and novels. Between 1810 and 1814 he also worked as a parliamentary reporter in London.

James Hogg

Mary Burnet

(Originally published in *The Shepherd's Calendar: Tales Illustrative of Pastoral Occupations, Country Life, and Superstitions*, 1828)

James Hogg (1770–1835) was a novelist, poet and essayist. Hogg was primarily self-educated and worked as a shepherd and farmhand in his early life. He wrote in both English and Scots, publishing such works as *The Private Memoirs and Confessions of a Justified Sinner* (1824) and *The Pilgrims of the Sun* (1815). Known as the 'Ettrick Shepherd', Hogg was sometimes published under this name. Part of a circle of great writers of the time, he was friends with Sir Walter Scott, among others.

W.T. Linskill

The Screaming Skull of Greyfriars

(Originally published in *St Andrews Ghost Stories*, 1921)

W.T. Linskill was the author of *St Andrew's Ghost Stories,* published in 1921. Holding a strong fascination with spirits and the occult, Linskill collected numerous accounts of supernatural occurrences in and around St Andrews, Scotland, from various first-hand witnesses. With numerous medieval structures, the seaside town of St Andrews is known for its many tales of ghostly encounters.

George MacDonald

The Old Nurse's Story

(Originally published in *The Haunters & the Haunted: Ghost Stories and Tales of the Supernatural*, 1921)

George MacDonald (1824–1905) was born in Aberdeenshire, Scotland. As an author and poet, MacDonald helped to pioneer modern fantasy literature, and he became a prominent figure in the genre. He published numerous fairy tales and works of supernatural fantasy, as well as pieces on Christian theology. He was a mentor to the author Lewis Carroll, and his works greatly influenced numerous well-known authors including W.H. Auden and Mark Twain.

Fiona Macleod

The Sin-Eater

(Originally published in *The Sin-Eater and Other Tales*, 1895)

Fiona Macleod (1855–1905) was the pen-name of William Sharp. Born in Paisley, Scotland, Sharp wrote fiction, poetry and literary biography. He was also an editor of the poetry of several authors including Sir Walter Scott and Algernon Charles Swinburne. After being introduced to the English poet Dante Gabriel Rossetti, Sharp joined the Rosetti literary group and began writing full-time in 1891. A member of the secret society known as the Hermetic Order of the Golden Dawn, Macleod's fascination with the supernatural and the occult was often reflected in his writing.

Elliott O'Donnell

The Ghost of the Hindu Child, or the Hauntings of the White Dove Hotel, and *Glamis Castle*

(Originally published in *Scottish Ghost Stories*, 1911)

Elliott O'Donnell (1872–1965) was an author primarily of supernatural fiction. Inspired by his claim that he saw a ghost at the age of five, his best-known works involve ghosts and other supernatural occurrences. Born in Bristol, England, O'Donnell later travelled to the United States, where he worked on an Oregon cattle ranch and then became a police officer during the 1894 Chicago rail strike. Returning to England, he became a schoolmaster and trained for theatre in London before becoming a full-time writer. His most popular works include *The Sorcery Club* (1912) and *Scottish Ghost Stories* (1911).

Margaret Oliphant

The Open Door

(Originally published in *Two Stories of the Seen and Unseen*, 1885)

Margaret Oliphant (1828–97) was born in Wallyford, Scotland. A novelist and historical writer, Oliphant wrote within the genres of supernatural, domestic realism and historical fiction. Beginning to write in childhood, her first novel, *Passages in the Life of Mrs. Margaret Maitland*, was published in 1849. She went on to publish novels, short stories and historical works at a prolific rate, and she contributed numerous articles to *Blackwood's Magazine*. Her best-known books include *Miss Marjoribanks* (1866) and *The Wizard's Son* (1884).

Sir Walter Scott

Wandering Willie's Tale

(Originally published in *Redgauntlet: A Tale of the Eighteenth Century*, 1824)

Sir Walter Scott (1771–1832) was a Scottish novelist, playwright, poet and historian. Born in Edinburgh, Scott wrote in his spare time while working as a judge and legal administrator. He was an active member of the Highland Society and served as president of the Royal Society of Edinburgh. Having a massive impact on literature in both Europe and the United States, many of his works have come to be considered classics in the literary canon, including *Ivanhoe* (1819) and *The Bride of Lammermoor* (1819). His writing helped establish the historical novel genre, and many became touchstones of European Romanticism.

Robert Louis Stevenson

Thrawn Janet

(Originally published in *The Merry Men and Other Tales and Fables*, 1887)

Robert Louis Stevenson (1850–94) was born in Edinburgh, Scotland. An author of novels, essays, poetry and travel writing, Stevenson is known for his classic works *Strange Case of Dr Jekyll and Mr Hyde* (1886) and *Treasure Island* (1883). Stevenson wrote and travelled extensively despite having poor health for much of his life. Moving to Samoa in 1890, his writing shifted from romantic adventure fiction towards darker realism upon witnessing the negative effects of American and European interference in the South Sea islands. Since his death in 1894 he has become one of the best-known authors of the nineteenth century.

J. Maxwell Wood

The Laird o' Coul's Ghost

(Originally published in *Witchcraft and Superstitious Record in the South-Western District of Scotland*, 1911)

J. Maxwell Wood, M.B., is the author of *Witchcraft and Superstitious Record in the South-Western District of Scotland*, published in 1911. In addition to ghost stories, Wood collected scores of tales involving fairies, brownies, bogles and wraiths, among other beings that populate the supernatural lore of Scotland.

A Selection of Fantastic Reads

A range of Gothic novels, horror, crime,
mystery, fantasy, adventure, dystopia,
utopia, science fiction and more: available
and forthcoming from Flame Tree 451

Categories: Bio = Biographical, BL = Black Literature, C = Crime,
F = Fantasy, FL = Feminist Literature, G = Gothic, H = Horror, L = Literary,
M = Mystery, MF = Myth & Folklore, P = Political, SF = Science Fiction,
TH = Thriller. Organized by year of first publication.

1764	*The Castle of Otranto*, Horace Walpole	G
1786	*The History of the Caliph Vathek*, William Beckford	G
1768	*Barford Abbey*, Susannah Minifie Gunning	G
1783	*The Recess Or, a Tale of Other Times*, Sophia Lee	G
1791	*Tancred: A Tale of Ancient Times*, Joseph Fox	G
1872	*In a Glass Darkly*, Sheridan Le Fanu	C, M
1794	*Caleb Williams*, William Godwin	C, M
1794	*The Banished Man*, Charlotte Smith	G
1794	*The Mysteries of Udolpho*, Ann Radcliffe	G
1795	*The Abbey of Clugny*, Mary Meeke	G
1796	*The Monk*, Matthew Lewis	G
1798	*Wieland*, Charles Brockden Brown	G
1799	*St. Leon*, William Godwin	H, M
1799	*Ormond, or The Secret Witness*, Charles Brockden Brown	H, M
1801	*The Magus,* Francis Barrett	H, M
1807	*The Demon of Sicily*, Edward Montague	G
1811	*Undine*, Friedrich de la Motte Fouqué	G
1814	*Sintram and His Companions*, Friedrich de la Motte Fouqué	G
1818	*Northanger Abbey*, Jane Austen	G
1818	*Frankenstein*, Mary Shelley	H, G
1820	*Melmoth the Wanderer*, Charles Maturin	G
1826	*The Last Man*, Mary Shelley	SF
1828	*Pelham*, Edward Bulwer-Lytton	C, M
1831	*Short Stories & Poetry*, Edgar Allan Poe (to 1949)	C, M
1838	*The Amber Witch*, Wilhelm Meinhold	H, M

1842	*Zanoni*, Edward Bulwer-Lytton	H, M
1845	*Varney the Vampyre*, Thomas Preskett Prest	H, M
1846	*Wagner, the Wehr-wolf*, George W.M. Reynolds	H, M
1847	*Wuthering Heights*, Emily Brontë	G
1850	*The Scarlet Letter*, Nathaniel Hawthorne	H, M
1851	*The House of the Seven Gables*, Nathaniel Hawthorne	H, M
1852	*Bleak House*, Charles Dickens	C, M
1859	*The Woman in White*, Wilkie Collins	C, M
1859	*Blake, or the Huts of America*, Martin R. Delany	BL
1860	*The Marble Faun*, Nathaniel Hawthorne	H, M
1861	*East Lynne*, Ellen Wood	C, M
1861	*Elsie Venner*, Oliver Wendell Holmes	H, M
1862	*A Strange Story*, Edward Bulwer-Lytton	H, M
1862	*Lady Audley's Secret*, Mary Elizabeth Braddon	C, M
1864	*Journey to the Centre of the Earth*, Jules Verne	SF
1868	*The Huge Hunter*, Edward Sylvester Ellis	SF
1868	*The Moonstone*, Wilkie Collins	C, M
1870	*Twenty Thousand Leagues Under the Sea*, Jules Verne	SF
1872	*Erewhon*, Samuel Butler	SF
1874	*The Temptation of St. Anthony*, Gustave Flaubert	H, M
1874	*The Expressman and the Detective*, Allan Pinkerton	C, M
1876	*The Man-Wolf and Other Tales*, Erckmann-Chatrian	H, M
1878	*The Haunted Hotel*, Wilkie Collins	C, M
1878	*The Leavenworth Case*, Anna Katharine Green	C, M
1886	*The Mystery of a Hansom Cab*, Fergus Hume	C, M
1886	*Robur the Conqueror*, Jules Verne	SF
1886	*The Strange Case of Dr Jekyll & Mr Hyde*, R.L. Stevenson	SF
1887	*She*, H. Rider Haggard	F
1887	*A Study in Scarlet*, Arthur Conan Doyle	C, M

1890	*The Sign of Four*, Arthur Conan Doyle	C, M
1891	*The Picture of Dorian Gray*, Oscar Wilde	G
1892	*The Big Bow Mystery*, Israel Zangwill	C, M
1894	*Martin Hewitt, Investigator*, Arthur Morrison	C, M
1895	*The Time Machine*, H.G. Wells	SF
1895	*The Three Imposters*, Arthur Machen	H, M
1897	*The Beetle*, Richard Marsh	G
1897	*The Invisible Man*, H.G. Wells	SF
1897	*Dracula*, Bram Stoker	H
1898	*The War of the Worlds*, H.G. Wells	SF
1898	*The Turn of the Screw*, Henry James	H, M
1899	*Imperium in Imperio*, Sutton E. Griggs	BL, SF
1899	*The Awakening*, Kate Chopin	FL
1902	*The Hound of the Baskervilles*, Arthur Conan Doyle	C, M
1902	*Of One Blood: Or, The Hidden Self*, Pauline Hopkins	FL, BL
1903	*The Jewel of Seven Stars*, Bram Stoker	H, M
1904	*Master of the World*, Jules Verne	SF
1905	*A Thief in the Night*, E.W. Hornung	C, M
1906	*The Empty House & Other Ghost Stories*, Algernon Blackwood	G
1906	*The House of Souls*, Arthur Machen	H, M
1907	*Lord of the World*, R.H. Benson	SF
1907	*The Red Thumb Mark*, R. Austin Freeman	C, M
1907	*The Boats of the 'Glen Carrig'*, William Hope Hodgson	H, M
1907	*The Exploits of Arsène Lupin*, Maurice Leblanc	C, M
1907	*The Mystery of the Yellow Room*, Gaston Leroux	C, M
1908	*The Mystery of the Four Fingers*, Fred M. White	SF
1908	*The Ghost Kings*, H. Rider Haggard	F
1908	*The Circular Staircase*, Mary Roberts Rinehart	C, M
1908	*The House on the Borderland*, William Hope Hodgson	H, M

1909	*The Ghost Pirates*, William Hope Hodgson	H, M
1909	*Jimbo: A Fantasy*, Algernon Blackwood	G
1909	*The Necromancers*, R.H. Benson	SF
1909	*Black Magic*, Marjorie Bowen	H, M
1910	*The Return*, Walter de la Mare	H, M
1911	*The Lair of the White Worm*, Bram Stoker	H
1911	*The Innocence of Father Brown*, G.K. Chesterton	C, M
1911	*The Centaur*, Algernon Blackwood	G
1912	*Tarzan of the Apes*, Edgar Rice Burroughs	F
1912	*The Lost World*, Arthur Conan Doyle	SF
1913	*The Return of Tarzan*, Edgar Rice Burroughs	F
1913	*Trent's Last Case*, E.C. Bentley	C, M
1913	*The Poison Belt*, Arthur Conan Doyle	SF
1915	*The Valley of Fear*, Arthur Conan Doyle	C, M
1915	*Herland*, Charlotte Perkins Gilman	SF, FL
1915	*The Thirty-Nine Steps*, John Buchan	TH
1917	*John Carter: A Princess of Mars*, Edgar Rice Burroughs	F
1917	*The Terror*, Arthur Machen	H, M
1917	*The Job*, Sinclair Lewis	L
1918	*Brood of the Witch-Queen*, Sax Rohmer	H, M
1918	*The Land That Time Forgot*, Edgar Rice Burroughs	F
1918	*The Citadel of Fear*, Gertrude Barrows Bennett (as. Francis Stevens)	FL, TH
1919	*John Carter: A Warlord of Mars*, Edgar Rice Burroughs	F
1919	*The Door of the Unreal*, Gerald Biss	H
1919	*The Moon Pool*, Abraham Merritt	SF
1919	*The Three Eyes*, Maurice Leblanc	SF
1920	*A Voyage to Arcturus*, David Lindsay	SF
1920	*The Metal Monster*, Abraham Merritt	SF
1920	*Darkwater*, W.E.B. Du Bois	BL

1922	*The Undying Monster*, Jessie Douglas Kerruish	H
1925	*The Avenger*, Edgar Wallace	C
1925	*The Red Hawk*, Edgar Rice Burroughs	SF
1926	*The Moon Maid*, Edgar Rice Burroughs	SF
1927	*Witch Wood,* John Buchan	H, M
1927	*The Colour Out of Space*, H.P. Lovecraft	SF
1927	*The Dark Chamber*, Leonard Lanson Cline	H, M
1928	*When the World Screamed*, Arthur Conan Doyle	F
1928	*The Skylark of Space*, E.E. Smith	SF
1930	*Last and First Men*, Olaf Stapledon	SF
1930	*Belshazzar*, H. Rider Haggard	F
1934	*The Murder Monster*, Brant House (Emile C. Tepperman)	H
1934	*The People of the Black Circle*, Robert E. Howard	F
1935	*Odd John*, Olaf Stapledon	SF
1935	*The Hour of the Dragon*, Robert E. Howard	F
1935	*Short Stories Selection 1*, Robert E. Howard	F
1935	*Short Stories Selection 2*, Robert E. Howard	F
1936	*The War-Makers*, Nick Carter	C, M
1937	*Star Maker*, Olaf Stapledon	SF
1936	*Red Nails*, Robert E. Howard	F
1936	*The Shadow Out of Time*, H.P. Lovecraft	SF
1936	*At the Mountains of Madness*, H.P. Lovecraft	SF
1938	*Power*, C.K.M. Scanlon writing in *G-Men*	C, M
1939	*Almuric*, Robert E. Howard	SF
1940	*The Ghost Strikes Back*, George Chance	SF
1937	*The Road to Wigan Pier*, George Orwell	P, Bio
1938	*Homage to Catalonia*, George Orwell	P, Bio,
1945	*Animal Farm*, George Orwell	P, F
1949	*Nineteen Eighty-Four*, George Orwell	P, F

| 1953 | *The Black Star Passes*, John W. Campbell | SF |
| 1959 | *The Galaxy Primes*, E.E. Smith | SF |

New Collections of Ancient Myths, Early Modern and Contemporary Stories

2014	*Celtic Myths*, J.K. Jackson (ed.)	MF
2014	*Greek & Roman Myths*, J.K. Jackson (ed.)	MF
2014	*Native American Myths*, J.K. Jackson (ed.)	MF
2014	*Norse Myths*, J.K. Jackson (ed.)	MF
2018	*Chinese Myths*, J.K. Jackson (ed.)	MF
2018	*Egyptian Myths*, J.K. Jackson (ed.)	MF
2018	*Indian Myths*, J.K. Jackson (ed.)	MF
2018	*Myths of Babylon*, J.K. Jackson (ed.)	MF
2019	*African Myths*, J.K. Jackson (ed.)	MF
2019	*Aztec Myths*, J.K. Jackson (ed.)	MF
2019	*Japanese Myths*, J.K. Jackson (ed.)	MF
2020	*Arthurian Myths*, J.K. Jackson (ed.)	MF
2020	*Irish Fairy Tales*, J.K. Jackson (ed.)	MF
2020	*Polynesian Myths*, J.K. Jackson (ed.)	MF
2020	*Scottish Myths*, J.K. Jackson (ed.)	MF
2021	*Viking Folktales*, J.K. Jackson (ed.)	MF
2021	*West African Folktales*, J.K. Jackson (ed.)	MF
2022	*East African Folktales*, J.K. Jackson (ed.)	MF
2022	*Persian Myths*, J.K. Jackson (ed.)	MF
2022	*The Tale of Beowulf*, J.K. Jackson (ed.)	MF
2022	*The Four Branches of the Mabinogi*, J.K. Jackson (ed.)	MF
2022	*American Ghost Stories*, Brett Riley (Intro.)	H, G
2022	*Irish Ghost Stories*, Maura McHugh (Intro.)	H, G
2022	*Scottish Ghost Stories*, Helen McClory (Intro.)	H, G
2022	*Victorian Ghost Stories*, Reggie Oliver (Intro.)	H, G

A TASTE FOR THE FANTASTIC

FLAME TREE offers several series with stories from the distant past to the far future, covering the entire range of imaginative literature and great works that shaped our world.

From the fireside tradition of oral storytelling, early written versions of mythology (such as Norse, African, Egyptian and Aztec) emerge in the majestic works of literature of the Middle Ages (Dante, Chaucer, Boccaccio), the Early Modern period (Shakespeare, Milton, Cervantes) and the classic speculative tales by way of Shelley, Stoker, Lovecraft and H.G. Wells.

You'll find too, early Feminist adventure fiction, and the foundations of Black proto-science fiction literature from the 1900s.

Our short story collections also gather new tales by modern writers to bring together the sensibilities of humankind from the past, the present and the future.

Find us in all good bookshops, and at *flametreepublishing.com*